SALEM

FALLEN RAVENS MC

CRYSTAL DANIELS

SANDY ALVAREZ

FALLEN RAVENS MC

SALEM

CRYSTAL DANIELS

SANDY ALVAREZ

1

SALEM

I smoke my cigarette and watch the beads of sweat roll down the man's left temple as Mystic hands over a manila envelope, then proceeds to count the money in the bag. I open the envelope. Inside is a picture of our target, and I place the image on top of the table. Our nervous client's eyes dart around the dimly lit room, the vein in his neck pulsating with the rapid beating of his heart. The flickering of candle flames casts dancing shadows across the stone walls surrounding us, as if Lucifer himself is lurking in the darkened corners of the room. I take a deep breath, breathing in the nicotine along with the earthy smell of oak moss as a cold October draft creeps in. What can I say? I like to set the mood when a man asks me to kill someone. I exhale the smoke from my lungs.

I'm a killer for hire. An angel of death. In the end, we all meet the same fate—the sharp edge of the reaper's scythe. For a price, I will take the life of a sinner, and I'll be a soul taker—their debt collector.

"It's all there, brother." Mystic zips the bag closed then passes it to Laredo.

"So, we have a deal?" The man's voice cracks and he swallows hard.

"Killin' someone makin' you nervous?" I flick ashes against the surface of the table.

The disheveled man straightens his back, sitting a bit taller in his seat. "I'm not killing anyone."

"Oh, but you are." I take another pull of nicotine into my lungs, feeling the burn, then slowly breathe it out, my nostrils flaring as the smoke exits my body. "You are not without sin, Mr. Holland." His eyes widen at the use of his name. "This man's death is your cross to bear."

"I'm paying you to do it."

"Yes, but it is you who decides this man's fate tonight, Mr. Holland. You prepared to live with yourself? To know a man's death is because of you?"

His eyes narrow to slits, and his expression hardens. He becomes a different man before my eyes, and the shift in his behavior draws me in like a moth to a flame. "He tortured and murdered my daughter. The bastard deserves to die."

And there it is. The reasoning behind his sin. An eye for an eye.

Maybe I should ask him why not do it himself. I study him for a second. No; the man isn't a killer. One who has lost everything, but that's it. The man across from me is nothing more than an empty vessel. His entire life savings is probably in that bag he brought here tonight. None of which is my concern.

There's a half-empty liquor bottle with a black scorpion resting at the bottom, sitting beside two empty glasses at the center of the table. I reach across and grip the bottle. "Have a drink." I pour two ounces into each tumbler then push his drink in front of him. Before me, the President of Fallen Ravens permanently sealed a contract with a shot of Mezcal, and like everything else, I intend to keep with tradition.

He lifts the glass to his lips. "Last chance to take your money and walk," I say. The man downs his tequila then stands. I look at Mystic and nod, then my brother walks our client out the door.

I lean back in my chair and down the shot. Slamming the empty glass down on the table, I lift the image of the soon-to-be-dead man. It's a mugshot, probably pulled from the internet. His head is shaved and covered in satanic tattoos. My lip twitches. Perfect. "Harlem." I lift the 4x6 image in the air. "Find his location."

My brother steps forward.

"You got it."

A short time later, just before midnight, my men and I bring our rides to a rolling stop near the end of an unmarked dirt road just outside of town. The man we're hunting lives in the ramshackle of a house barely visible in the distance. "I'm going to enjoy this one." Juneau dismounts his bike, and the rest of us follow. Our target tonight has a rap sheet a mile long. Eddie Hollister goes by the street name Skunk. He's a stain on humanity itself. Like Juneau, I'm going to enjoy extinguishing this piece-of-shit waste of space.

Most clients want things done in a swift, professional manner. One bullet and the person is dead. This time, a little extra cash was tossed our way to make him suffer, and that's what we plan to do.

The sky darkens as large storm clouds move in, blotting out the moon. Rumbles of thunder sound off in the distance. A heaviness looms as we trek the rest of the way. Death walks alongside my men and me.

It's eerily quiet. A little too much for my liking. I point to Laredo, Harlem, and Juneau and motion for them to circle around back. Mystic and Baja and I draw our weapons and step onto the rickety porch. Baja tries the door. To our surprise, it's not locked.

Dumb bastard. We stroll right in. The place reeks of booze and ammonia. "Meth house," Mystic whispers. The rotten egg stench is so pungent I take a bandana from my back pocket to cover my mouth, and my men do the same. "I think they cook it down in the basement," Mystic says as we move through the kitchen, then on to the living room, where we find three men passed out on the couches. Beer cans and used needles litter the coffee table. I take a good look at each man, none being our target.

"What do you want to do with them?" Baja asks.

"We're not here for them. If they stay in the condition they're in, they live another day."

The sound of a floorboard creaking instantly has me aiming my gun down the hallway to our right. Harlem steps out of the shadows. Behind him are Laredo and Juneau, with a bound and gagged Eddie Hollister leading the way. His bloodshot eyes lock on my face. He's scared. Good. "Outside. We don't want to wake Eddie's friends here." Eddie struggles against the forward movement, so Harlem places the barrel end of his gun to his head for a bit of persuasion.

Outside, we walk our guest toward the once-fruitful cornfield at the back of the house, which is now nothing more than a wasteland of clumped dry earth. A pole where an old, tattered scarecrow once stood in the fields still stands. I walk up to the wooden stake in the ground, giving it a shake to test the stability. It will do. I turn to my men. "Tie him to it." Juneau removes the pack he's carrying on his back and drops it to the ground while Harlem and Laredo hold Eddie in place. Juneau produces nylon rope from the backpack and binds our guy to the pole. Eddie moans, his muffled voice asking "What do you want?"

Juneau has a pair of pliers in his grasp. He looks at me, and I nod before he steps closer to Eddie. Juneau lifts Eddie's hands, bound at the wrists, grips one of his nails with the tool's metal tip, then pulls. His thumbnail comes off with ease, and the bastard screams. Juneau repeats the process several more times until every fingernail lies on the ground at Eddie's feet.

Snot runs down over Eddie's lips, and drool drips off his chin as he coughs around the gag stuffed in his mouth. His screams eventually turn to heavy breathing. Juneau backs away, and I step in front of Eddie and rip the gag from his mouth. He takes a deep breath.

"Who the fuck?" Eddie sputters but doesn't get the chance to finish what he was trying to say before my fist connects with his face. His teeth crack against my bare knuckles. I pull the picture of the young woman he killed from my pocket, and his eyes double in size as I hold it in front of his face. "I see you recognize her."

"Fuck you. I don't know the bitch." Eddie spits, and his blood spatters across my cut.

My lip twitches. "You took this girl's life."

His focus grows distant while staring at the young woman's image. A slight smile forms on his face, and I can tell he's reliving the moment. "Killing her gave me such a rush." Eddie snickers. "Ending her life was far better than any needle high." I raise my weapon and aim it at his head. He breathes heavily, his cold eyes locking with mine. Blood dribbles from his busted lip. "You're no better than me."

"Maybe not, but I'll still be breathin' tomorrow while the crows eat at your corpse." I put a bullet in his head, then a stillness settles around us as Eddie's body slumps against the wooden pole.

Thunder breaks the silence and a bolt of lightning streaks across the sky. I turn to Baja. "Take the picture." Baja pulls a camera from Juneau's bag, snaps a picture of the lifeless body, then tosses the camera into the backpack. "Let's get the fuck out of here."

. . .

An hour later, we're back at the clubhouse, throwing a few drinks back. I push myself from the table, the chair scraping against the floor, and stand. "You know where to find me." I walk up the stone steps leading out of the dank cellar and step into the bitter cold of a Salem night in Massachusetts.

Dry leaves crunch beneath my boots as I stride across the property. We're isolated out here where Fallen Ravens' compound is located. I stop in front of an old mausoleum, partially collapsed from years of neglect, and sit upon the weathered pieces of rubble I'd like to call my throne. I pull out my drug of choice from the inside of my cut—marijuana. I strike a match, stoke the tip, and hold the first toke for several seconds. After the fourth hit, I feel the tingling effect and feel the tension in my body release.

I look out across the property—a cemetery, to be specific. Roughly two dozen headstones mark the graves of the dead, all long forgotten out here in the middle of nowhere. In the distance is an old stone church, surrounded by ancient oak trees. The wind blows, causing the naked branches to creak. The church doubles as Fallen Ravens' clubhouse—our sanctuary. I chuckle to myself at the irony—us, a bunch of sinners residing in a sacred place where men should come to find absolution.

I take another toke.

A twig snaps, and my attention shifts to the edge of the dark forest near the property line several yards away. A stray cat emerges from the tree line, heading in my direction. In no time, the black cat rubs up against my pant leg. "How's it goin', Nimbus?" I reach down and scratch the cat's head. Nimbus lifts it, his green eye reflecting the light of the moon, and meows.

Along with his one eye missing, he also has no tail. I don't know the cat's story. All I know is he showed up one day and hasn't left since. The men don't seem bothered by his roaming about the place, and neither do I. As far as I'm concerned, he fits right in with the rest of us.

The sound of wings flapping catches Nimbus' attention, and he watches a raven perch atop a headstone in the shape of a cross. My thoughts drift to Chicago, our former President and founder of the club. He died a few years back, murdered by the Demon Jokers, a rival MC. He chose the raven as the club's icon because of its ominous association with evil and death.

I wouldn't be here today if it weren't for my former President.

To understand the present, one would first need to understand my past and where it all began. I breathe in the last hit from the joint between my fingers. Feeling relaxed, I open the veil to my past. My thoughts take me back to when I was young—back to the beginning of all my jaded memories.

He's beating her again. Probably because he came home to her doped up on pills again. I think she does it to escape reality. Who could blame her? For as long as I can remember, my life has been this way. I don't know any other truth but the one I drown in daily. My mother's pleas go unheard as he smacks her across the face one more time. It's a typical night in the Crawford household, and because I can't bear to see her cry, I always try to help. "Stop!" I run into the living room and place myself between my parents.

"Ash, please. Go to your room," my mom pleads, but I stand my ground.

My entire body shakes with fear. I know what's coming to me, but I stand there anyway and lock eyes with my monster. My father. I brace myself. He buries his fist in my stomach, knocking the breath from my lungs, and I double over. "You step to me like a man; I'll treat you like one, you little shit!" I force myself to stand once more and look him in the eyes once more.

"One day, I will kill you."

. . .

The fog lifts, and I'm back in the present. I shake off the residual effects of the memory. I was twelve at the time I said those fateful words. It wasn't long after that day I began staying away from home. The streets of Salem became my playground. I found my solace with friends like Mystic. He was an outcast himself, thrown to the side by society because his father was a member of the Fallen Ravens. Unlike me, he was born into this life. But I was born for it. The more I hung around with Mystic, the more I got to see the life an MC brotherhood had to offer. Unlike my family, they protected those they called their own.

I wanted to be a part of Fallen Ravens, and I wanted what I'd never had—a family.

My mind drifts again, to when I was sixteen, taking me back to the night that changed the course of my life irrevocably.

"Listen, my old man said you could crash on the couch as long as you like." I sit in the passenger seat of Mystic's midnight blue Chevy Chevelle his father gave him for his birthday last week and stare at my house. My father's truck is parked in the driveway.

"I need some extra clothes and to make sure she's still alive." I grab the handle and open the car door. "Mind waitin'?"

"Sure." Mystic jerks his chin.

I get out of the car and cross the lawn. The closer I get to the house, the tighter my gut gets, twisting into a thick knot. An uneasy feeling settles over me when I walk through the front door. Something is burning. I follow the scent into the kitchen and find spaghetti sauce has bubbled over the edge of the pot sitting on the stove, the bottom scorched black. I reach out and turn off the burner. Dry pasta noodles are scattered about the kitchen floor, along with cooking utensils. On the table sits an empty bottle of my father's favorite whiskey. My heart races, thudding hard against my ribcage as I move toward the back of the house, in the direction of my parents' bedroom. The door is cracked, so I press my palm against it, opening it further. I hear water running in the bathroom.

"You whore!" my father shouts.

In the bathroom, I find him hunched over the tub, water spilling over the edge onto the tiled floor, with his hands wrapped around my mother's neck. Her eyes are open beneath the surface of the water, but there is no life in them. She's dead.

My father releases his hold and spins around to see me standing behind him. He stands because I let him. My hands fist at my sides, and he takes notice.

"You want a go at me, boy?" His drunk ass sways, almost losing his footing on the slick floor. He charges, slamming all his weight into me, pressing my back against the wall. His hands go for my neck, but before he succeeds, I bring my knee up into his balls. He grunts in pain and stumbles backward. He comes at me again. I lift the ceramic tank cover off the back of the toilet and swing. I hear his skull crack as I bring it down across his head. Blood streams down the front of his face. He teeters, his eyes glazing over before he falls, hitting knees-first on the bathroom floor. I drop the tank cover. It clatters, shattering in half once it hits the tile. Reaching down, I grab my father by the collar of his shirt and drag him to the tub where my dead mother lies. With a fist full of hair, I wrench his head back. I want him to look at me one final time. His breathing is heavy as his eyes lock with mine.

"I told you one day I would kill you."

"You ungrateful piece of shit. She never loved you, and I never loved you. No one will ever love you. I win." He uses his final moment alive to drive a verbal stake in my heart. It's the moment I learn to flip the switch, and I let the darkness take over.

"Wrong motherfucker. I win." I shove his face into the bathwater and hold him under until his arms stop flailing, and his body goes limp.

I look at the scene in front of me one final time. I'd just taken my first life and feel no remorse.

. . .

"Salem." I hear Mystic calling my name, and it drags me from the pits of my own personal hell.

I clear my throat. "Yeah?"

"You alright?"

"I'm good, brother." I stand. Mystic stares at me for a beat. He's my best friend and, by the look on his face, knows where my head has been. "Needed a breather." I walk in the direction of the clubhouse, and Mystic keeps pace beside me.

"Come on, let's get you home."

I drape my arm onto Mystic's shoulder. "Brother, I am home."

2
SAGE

Pretending the broom handle is a microphone, I sing along to the music blaring through my phone. I'm just about to belt out the second line of the main chorus when Juniper comes through the door with a sour look on her face. Setting the broom down, I walk over to the table my phone is sitting on and turn the music off. "What happened?"

"There was a mix-up with the paint we ordered, and the guy down at the hardware store says it will be at least another week before it arrives."

"You're kidding me?" My good mood deflates.

I prop the broom against the wall and look back at my best friend. "The salon opens in ten days."

"Tell me something I don't know," Juniper huffs as she plops down on the sofa that is situated just inside the entrance door. Last week when Juniper and I were out shopping for décor for the salon, we happened upon an antique shop a couple of blocks from here. The sofa was sitting in the back of the store underneath a pile of boxes, but the second I spied the treasure, I fell in love with it. At first, the old woman who owns the shop was hesitant to sell us the piece of furniture because of its state. Still, under the broken legs and grime covering the cushions, I saw its potential. Juniper and I spent two days screwing on new legs and giving it a good scrub with some upholstery cleaner, making it new again. The Victorian-style sofa is a deep purple and made of velvet. Juniper and I are heavy into anything Victorian and grunge. In fact, our salon will be inspired by the look. That is, if our paint order is on time. Apparently, the local hardware store only carries basic white interior paint.

"Look, the guy assured me it would be here," Juniper adds. "It will be cutting it close, but we'll just have to bust our asses to make sure we open as scheduled."

I think for a second, then look at my friend and nod. "You're right. We got this."

Juniper jumps from the sofa. "Damn right we do."

We didn't come this far to have something as stupid as paint stand in our way. Dyed 2 Perfection is our baby. Our dream. Has been since we were kids.

Juniper and I grew up together in a small town in Nebraska. My mom and her mom teach at the college in our hometown. My mom teaches math, whereas Juniper's mom teaches English. Even our names sound perfect together. Sage and Juniper. Sage was my dad's idea. Mom said by the time I was born, they still hadn't picked out a name for me. Dad said they didn't need to, that he would know when he saw me. And he did. Mom said as soon as the doctor put me in my dad's arms, he looked into my eyes and said he could tell I had an old soul. That I would grow up to be wise. So, he named me Sage.

I think Juniper and I were destined to be best friends, just like our parents. They are tight and have been since Juniper and I were in third grade. My mom had just gotten a new teaching position at the local college, so we packed up and moved from Ohio to Nebraska. Unfortunately, the school was already halfway through the year, making me the dreaded new kid in class. I already had problems in Ohio making friends and knew it would be no different at my new school. Or so I thought.

During my first day at the new school was when I met my new best friend. I was minding my own business playing on the swing when a group of girls came over and started messing with me. Calling me fat, laughing at the fact I wore glasses, and that bitch Lynn Perkins started pointing and telling everyone I was so fat I would break the swing. That, in turn, had all her little minion sheep joining in. You know how every school has that one group of girls that make it their life mission to bully kids who look like me? That was Lynn Perkins. And though I was used to kids like her, it still didn't hurt any less when they spewed their hate. Then out of nowhere came a tall skinny girl with curly blonde hair.

"Lynn, why don't you shut your ugly pug face up," the blonde girl spat.

Lynn took her focus off me and turned toward the girl who had come to my defense. "Why don't you mind your own business."

My blonde savior rolled her eyes. "God, you're so lame." Then she marched past Lynn and her minions, and she grabbed my hand and pulled me away from the swing. "Come on, let's get away from here before we catch a case of ugly from pug face here." She cut her eyes to Lynn, who was red-faced from embarrassment.

Keeping my hand in hers, the girl led me over to the other side of the playground. "I'm Juniper, by the way."

"I'm Sage."

From that day forward, Juniper and I have been inseparable. After school that day, I went home and told my mom what had happened. She then contacted Juniper's mom to thank her for raising the kind of kid who stands up to bullies. Turned out

Juniper's mom was a teacher at the same college as my mom, and they became instant friends as well.

Juniper and I stayed best friends all through school while putting up with Lynn and her minions because some things never change. We both knew what it was like to be bullied. Me for being chubby and Juniper for her name. Which I always thought was crazy because I love it. Although by the time we hit high school, it became apparent why Lynn hated Juniper so much. My best friend blossomed in a way that drove all the boys crazy, including Lynn's boyfriend. I learned jealousy is the only reason a girl like Lynn puts other girls down. In high school, I became comfortable in my own skin. I no longer saw my curves as a curse. I had wide hips, a big ass, and luscious boobs. With the help of my best friend and my mother hyping me up, telling me how beautiful I was, I soon started seeing myself as they did. Turns out, there were a lot of boys who liked girls like me too. I will never forget the day Lynn caught her boyfriend hitting on me in the hallway after Spanish class our tenth-grade year. Karma is a bitch, and the dishes she serves are gloriously delicious.

After graduation, Juniper and I went to cosmetology school together. We both worked at the local hair salon in our town for five years while saving every penny we made to make our dreams of having our own salon a reality. As for why we chose Salem, I can't really say. Juniper and I both knew we wanted to leave Nebraska, and we both wanted to live on the East coast. Mostly, we both wanted to be adventurous. At first, we started looking at realtor listings in the Boston area, but this place came up in the search. Not only was the size, space, and location perfect, but there was also a tiny two-bedroom, one-bathroom apartment upstairs that came with it. Not only did Juniper and I fall in love with the building and its location, but the solution to the problem of finding a place to live fell right into our laps.

From what we have seen so far, the town is excellent too.

Salem is a far cry from Nebraska. And if you haven't heard the history behind this town, you've been living under a rock. I have to say my favorite thing about Salem is its architecture. It's a mixture of Victorian, Gothic, Queen Anne, Greek, and Colonial.

"Look!" Juniper points to the window at the front of the salon, to the small figure wrapped in a wool coat with a green scarf hanging around her neck, walking on the sidewalk across the street. She looks to be around our age, and she unlocks the store's front door across the way from us and slips inside.

A moment later, she flips the closed sign around to open.

"Let's go over there," I say, already snagging my jacket off the coat rack and slipping it on. Ever since we moved to town two weeks ago, Juniper and I have been curious about the cute little shop across the street with the sign above the door that reads BELLADONNA'S. We had started to wonder if the place was closed permanently, but after asking around, we found out the store was not out of business. Those same people were also quick to inform us that the young woman who owned the place was a bit of an outcast. Some of the older residents even went as far as to warn us away but wouldn't really say why. All they said was that the woman is nothing but trouble. That, of course, made Juniper and I want to meet her even more. My parents didn't raise me to judge another person based on gossip or what others think. My dad says opinions are like assholes, everyone has one, and they all usually stink. And I always listen to my dad. I'm a daddy's girl, what can I say.

When I step outside onto the cobblestone sidewalk, a gust of wind kicks up, making my hair whip around my face and the leaves whirl around my feet. I look up and down the street, waiting for cars to pass before stepping off the curb. With Juniper at my side, we make our way up to Belladonna's. The bell over the door alerts her of our arrival, and the same woman we saw moments ago startles from her perch on a stool behind the front counter. She stares at Juniper and me for a beat, her big green eyes blinking and a hand holding a muffin, paused at her lips.

I offer a huge smile. "Hi!"

"Hey," Juniper chirps from beside me.

That seems to knock the woman out of her stupor. She quickly sets her muffin down and wipes her hands down the front of her blouse. "Hello. Can I help you, ladies?"

"My name is Sage, and this is Juniper." I hook a thumb over my shoulder toward my best friend. "We just moved to Salem, and we're getting ready to open a hair salon across the street."

"Oh...really?" The woman seems hesitant to engage in conversation, but when I offer another warm smile, she continues, "I'm Sukie. I own Belladonna's."

"It's nice to meet you, Sukie."

"Yeah," Juniper jumps in. "We've been wanting to come to say 'hi' for over a week, but you've been closed."

"Oh...a...yeah. I was feeling a little under the weather. And I don't get many people coming in here. At least not the locals. They don't..." Sukie says but then stops.

"Well, do you mind if we have a look around?" I ask, already spying some products I'd love to check out.

"S-Sure. If you have any questions, feel free to ask."

I watch as Juniper picks up a lavender bottle, twists the top off, and places it to her nose. "Oh my god, Sage. You have to smell this shampoo." She holds out the bottle.

Taking it from her, I inhale the scent of lavender and vanilla. "Oh wow. That is nice."

"Look." Juniper holds up another bottle. "The conditioner smells just as divine. And look, there's also a hair mask."

I turn back to Sukie, standing close by. She watches us, and a small smile plays on her lips.

"Do you make all this yourself? It says so on the bottle, and I see it also says it's organic."

"Yes. Everything in here I make myself, and, yes, it's all organic. I grow the flowers and herbs myself, and I even use my own products." Sukie tucks a lock of her long, thick brown hair behind her ear. Her hair, though it has no style and looks like it's never been colored or highlighted, is lush, shiny, and healthy-looking.

"Your hair is to die for, girl," Juniper says, taking the words right out of my mouth. "What I wouldn't give to have my hands in it. You ever looking for a change, you come to see us and we'll hook you up."

Sukie runs her fingers through her thick strands of hair while smiling shyly. "Thank you. I'll be sure to keep that in mind."

"Just telling it like it is." Juniper winks before heading off to do more shopping.

"Well, you guys take your time, and if you need anything else, I'll be right over there." Sukie points to the front of the shop where she was sitting when we first came in.

"Will do, Sukie. Thanks."

Thirty minutes later, Juniper and I make our way up to the register, arms loaded with hair care products, bubble bath, lotions, and face scrub. We even found some candles.

"Oh my. You guys want all of this?" Sukie's eyes go round when we dump our findings onto the counter. "I think you got one of everything." She giggles.

"And I can't wait to take it home and try it. If this stuff does as great as I think it will, would you be willing to supply enough stock for our salon? We're always on the hunt for new products, especially organic."

"Really?" Sukie asks, her mouth gaped open.

"Yeah, girl," Juniper cuts in.

"That would be great." Sukie's face lights up.

"It's settled then. Juniper and I will try this stuff and then let you know what we need for the salon."

"Okay. That works for me." Sukie rings up our purchase. "I'm going to toss in some incense sticks. They're new, and I'd like some opinions on them." She reaches under the register and tosses a few little packages in our bags.

"Right on. We'll let you know." I hand over some cash.

"I'm thrilled you guys decided to stop in." Sukie hands me my change.

"Us too." I smile.

"Yeah. It was good meeting you, Sukie," Juniper adds.

Before heading out of the store, I look back over my shoulder and give Sukie one last wave. And just as Juniper goes to open the door, the thunderous sound of several motorcycles roaring down the street causes the windows to rattle and the ground beneath my feet to vibrate.

"Damn," Juniper breathes as I'm sure she's taking in the same sight as me.

"Who are they?" I mutter to myself, but Sukie, who has come up behind us, answers anyway.

"Fallen Ravens."

"Who?" I cock my head in her direction.

"Fallen Ravens. They are Salem's local MC," she supplies.

"MC?" This coming from Juniper.

Sukie looks away from where the last motorcycle turned the corner, disappearing out of sight, and regards both mine and Juniper's confused expressions.

"Motorcycle Club."

"Really?" I ask.

Sukie's lips thin as she nods. "Really."

"What's their deal?"

Sukie shrugs. "It's not my place to say. Most of what you'll hear will be rumors, since nobody actually has the guts to associate with any of the Ravens. At least not anyone I know. Then again, I don't have many friends. But what I will say is; rumors are just that. Take what you may or may not hear with a grain of salt. When it comes to the MC, it could be true, or it could be total malarky."

"Interesting." Juniper raises a brow.

"Yeah. You two will find Salem is all kinds of interesting."

For some reason, I get the feeling Sukie's remark was meant as a warning rather than a tidbit of information.

Later that night, after sampling Sukie's products, drinking wine, and eating enough pizza to put me in a perpetual food coma, I can't help but let my mind wander back to the bikers. I'd be lying if I said I wasn't curious about this so-called motorcycle club or the men I saw riding down the street. Their faces were concealed, and I didn't miss the air of authority that rolled off of each man.

"Sage." Juniper calls my name, pulling me out of my biker fog.

"What?" I groan as I rub my full belly.

"I called your name three times. Here." She tosses my phone at me, hitting me in the boob.

Lifting my head, I glare down at my best friend, who is perched at the opposite end of the sofa as me. "Bitch." I rub my boob while putting the phone to my ear and ignore her cackling.

"Hello."

"Hey, Shortcake."

I smile at my dad's voice. "Hi, Dad."

"What's that no-good friend of yours up to?" he asks, and I can hear the teasing in his voice. My dad adores Juniper so I know he's joking.

"She's being a pain in my butt as usual," I tell him, while nudging her with my foot.

"Don't believe her Mr. Briggs! It's all lies!" Juniper shouts, making my dad laugh.

"How are you girls settling in?"

"We're getting there. The chairs for the salon were delivered yesterday, and the mirrors should arrive this weekend. Juniper and I will look for some furniture for the apartment tomorrow. The heifer is a bed hog, and I don't think I'll make another week sharing with her." It's Juniper's turn to glare at me, and I stick my tongue out at her. Yes, I'm aware we are grown women who act like we're five, but if you can't be a goof around your best friend, then who can you be a goof around?

"How's Mom?" I ask.

"She's good. Missing you."

"Tell her I miss her too, and I'll video chat with her this weekend, and show her how far we've gotten in the salon."

My dad's voice goes soft. "She'll like that."

"I miss you, Dad."

"I miss you too, baby girl. Your mom and I will make plans to come out in a few weeks."

"I'd like that."

"Talk to you tomorrow. Love you, Sage."

"Love you too, Dad."

3
SALEM

I snap my eyes open, waking to the sounds of waves crashing against the rocky shoreline yards from my bedroom window. Along with them, a salty breeze floats through the partially opened window and across the top of the black satin sheet draped across my body. I stare at the shadows across the ceiling and take a deep breath. I roll onto my side. My past sometimes bleeds into the present in the form of dreams, and the one I woke from visits often.

Knowing I won't fall back asleep, I cast the sheets to the empty side of the bed and swing my legs over the edge of the mattress. The cold hardwood floor connects with the soles of my bare feet, further awakening my senses. Thirsty, I reach over to the bedside table and lift what's left of last night's drink to my parched lips, the whiskey slightly chilled from the cold temperature of the room. Warmth and spices coat my tongue and heat my throat on the way down. Not the ideal way to start my day, but fuck it. I place the glass back on the table, then stand and stride across the bedroom. The old floors creak under me on my way out of the bedroom and across the narrow hallway to the bathroom. I don't bother with turning the lights on. The little bit of moonlight provides enough illumination through the large window.

The entire bathroom is designed to bring the outside in. Dark gray honeycomb-shaped tile covers the walls and floors, and a seamless piece of glass separates the shower area from the rest of the bathroom, because I wanted nothing obstructing the view. Reaching into the shower, I turn on the water and step beneath the stream before it warms. The cold water is a shock to the system but welcomed. It only takes a few seconds for the water to heat, and my shoulders slump as all the muscles in my upper body relax. I tilt my head back, hot water flowing over my face as I run my fingers through my hair.

I still can't shake the feeling of a storm heading our way. I can hear the last words Chicago spoke before his death. His voice is faint but unmistakable. *It's not over. It's only just begun.*

I snatch shampoo from the corner shelf and wash my hair before moving on to the rest of my body. I rinse off, then turn off the cold water, leaving nothing but the hot running. I press my forearms against the windowpane and stare out over the sea as the sun begins to rise over the harbor. Warm hues of orange and red set the horizon on fire.

My home, an old lighthouse attached to a simple one-story cottage, is the second-largest purchase I ever made. The old man whose family owned this property for generations died a few years back. His only living relative, a sleazy nephew from out west, put it up for sale. Turns out, he was in neck-deep debt with loan sharks and in desperate need of money, and his life depended on it.

The place isn't fancy; it needs many repairs, and I'm still renovating a few aspects of the historic home, but it's mine.

The hot water finally runs cold, so I turn it off, snag the towel hanging on a hook just outside the shower stall, and step out. I dry myself before walking naked across the hall, back into my bedroom, and pull a pair of jeans from the dresser drawer. After stepping into them, I make my way to the front of the house where the kitchen is located and make myself some coffee. With my mug that reads *Fuck You* in hand, I head toward the spiral staircase leading to the best spot in the house. Once at the top of the lighthouse tower, I walk around the light beacon, then open and step through the narrow door onto the observation deck that wraps around the tower.

I take a sip of coffee and lean my hip against the railing. Best way to start the day. I breathe in the crisp morning air and the briny scent of the harbor. Several yards away on a cluster of rocks, I watch seagulls arguing over a fish carcass. For years, I lived in town in the strip club's third-floor loft. Living in downtown Salem is a different vibe than being on the water. Living here is an escape from everyday life—a peace I can't find anywhere else but from the sea.

I stay outside several more minutes, listening to the waves break against the shoreline, before heading inside. I'm setting my mug in the kitchen sink when my phone rings. I move in the direction of my bedroom, see Mystic's name lighting up the screen, and answer. "What's up?"

"My blood pressure. The damn liquor shipment that was supposed to be here yesterday has been delayed another day."

My day just keeps getting better. "I'll swing by Bishop's on the way in. Just shoot me a text of what we need to get through another night, and I'll take care of it."

Mystic sighs. "Thanks, brother. By the way, we have three auditions in the next two hours. You gonna be here?"

Newbies. I scrub my chin and grin. Hopefully, they're good and not wasting my time. The club could use a fresh face or two. "Wouldn't miss it." I pick up my black wrist watch lying on top of the dresser and look at the time. "I'll see you in an hour," I say, then end the call.

. . .

A short time later, I'm shrugging on my cut and heading out the door. A chilled wind causes fallen leaves to dance around my feet while strolling toward my car. I open the door to my midnight blue 1969 Dodge Daytona Charger and sit behind the wheel. Chicago said if I could fix her, I could have her. I busted my ass for a solid summer to get this car running. I was eighteen at the time, and the prospect of having my own wheels meant a lot. I also wanted to prove my worth to Chicago and the club. I stood at a fork in the road that summer. One path had uncertainty— the possibility of new beginnings. The other was cloaked in darkness and painted in red. The shadow of death walked that long road, but I didn't fear him, for he was an old friend. The opportunities and decisions I made that year charted the course of my life.

After placing my key in the ignition, I shrug off my memories, put the car in drive, and head toward town. Salem, Massachusetts. I pass by historical landmarks on my way to the liquor store, like The Witch House, which is connected to the witch trials of 1692. If you like dark history, Salem's roots run deep in it. We are also a popular tourist destination, especially during the fall season. The town's history is haunting, which appeals to visitors. To me, it's simply home.

I pull into the parking lot just as Bishop is climbing out of his truck. He waves in my direction as I park the car then climb out. "Ash." Bishop extends his hand and I shake it. "How's it goin'?"

I've known Bishop Graves for years. He and his wife own and operate Graves Wine and Spirits here in Salem. He is also Chicago, our former President's brother. He is not a Fallen Raven. Though he respects all aspects of the life and will do anything for us, he never wanted club life, and his brother appreciated that. "I can't complain," I grunt.

Bishop scratches beneath his long gray beard. The resemblance between him and his dead brother is so close you'd think they were twins, but Bishop is the oldest. "I'm assuming this isn't a wellness visit?" He lifts his brow.

"I need some whiskey to get the club through the night. The shipment we've been expecting for two weeks now is delayed again."

Bishop nods. "Alright." With a jerk of his chin, he turns toward the building. "You get what you need." He unlocks the door, steps inside, and waits for me to follow before locking the door again.

"Appreciate it." I clap him on the back. "How's your old lady?" I ask on my way toward the stock room. Ellie, his wife, is battling dementia. A few months ago, during a club-organized benefit for the town's youth center, she didn't recognize me—not until hours later. I've known Ellie and Bishop since Chicago took me in. They are family, and it is hard to watch dementia steal so much away from them both.

Bishop shuffles his feet on the wood floor behind me, then strides over to a pile of boxes stacked against the wall. "She has her good days and bad." He pauses and stares at his feet and grins. "Yesterday was a good day." Bishop clears his throat and passes me a box. "I'm actually glad you stopped by."

I set the full box down on the floor, and Bishop passes me another empty container. "Yeah?" I continue to fill another box.

"Dale had a bunch of men roll into his bar a few nights back, and he thinks they might be up to no good."

I give him my full attention. Dale is Bishop and Ellie's only son, who lives a couple of towns over. "They givin' him problems?"

"No, but one of Dale's waitresses informed him she overheard one say Fallen Ravens, and another specifically asked her if she knew anyone by the name Ash Crawford?"

Heat rises in my gut, and my fingers flex against the sides of the box I'm holding. Strangers are poking around and askin' about my club and me; not wise considering we can make a man disappear—permanently.

Nothing more is said about the subject. A short time later, I have what I need loaded in the trunk of my car. I turn to Bishop. "Thanks again." I clasp his shoulder, and he does the same to mine.

"Anytime."

"Give Ellie my best."

"You got it." Bishop nods then begins walking back toward the entrance to the store. I wait for him to disappear inside before getting into my car and heading for the other end of town.

The Fallen, our gentlemen's club, comes into view. I pull around back to unload the boxes and find Laredo seated on his Harley, with a set of legs wrapped around his waist and arms draped over his shoulders. I cut the engine, step out of my ride, and lean against the front fender. Laredo pries his mouth off the woman he is entangled with and helps her climb off him and his bike. My brother swings his leg over and stands. After whispering something in the woman's ear, he slaps her on the ass. The tall brunette looks in my direction, gives a smile, then turns and walks toward an old faded-yellow Volkswagen bug parked on the other side of the dumpster. Laredo strides to where I am. "Mornin'," he says with a grin.

"You crashed here again last night?"

"Yeah, brother." He pulls a pack of cigarettes from the inside of his cut and lights it. "The contractors should have my power restored this afternoon." Laredo tilts his head back and blows the smoke from his lungs. "I may have bitten off more than I can chew restoring that old Clayton estate."

"It'll be worth it in the end, brother." I push off from the car. "Help me unload this whiskey." I head for the back end of the vehicle, and Laredo follows. I open the trunk.

"Bishop saves our asses again." He lets the cigarette dangle between his lips and snags a box. I stack another case in his arms, then grab a load in mine as well, and we head for the back entrance of the club, where the door is partially open already.

We set the boxes on the bar top, and Alder, our bartender, strolls toward us from the opposite end of the bar. He tosses the bar rag in his hand over his shoulder and begins unboxing the liquor. Mystic appears. "Girls are in the back getting ready for their auditions."

I nod, then lead the way across the room. Mystic, Laredo, and I each take a seat at a table in front of the center of the dance stage. Astrid, our top dancer, approaches the table with a smile. "Men." The front door to the club swings open, letting the morning sun filter into the dimly lit building, and in strides Baja and Juneau.

I stand to greet my brothers. "How's it going?"

"We heard there's new skin auditioning." Juneau grins. "Figured we'd get a sneak peek before we head into town and open shop for the day." He and Baja pull another two chairs to the table and join the rest of us. Laredo, the southern gentleman he is, stands, gives his seat to Astrid, and drags another nearby for himself.

Music begins playing, and Astrid smiles as a tall blonde saunters onto the stage. Astrid is the house mom to all the girls we employ, and having her around when newbies come in looking for a job has been a part of the hiring process for a couple of years now. She has good intuition about the women who walk in here looking for employment. "Her name is Harlow." The young woman moves effortlessly to the music. "She's not the strongest on pole work, but her stage presence is outstanding."

The men and I watch Harlow complete her performance. "Not

bad," I say in a neutral tone. A new song filters through the speakers, and for a few minutes the men and I watch the second dancer do her best to wow us. Unfortunately, the young woman's nerves get the better of her, and it affects her performance.

"Her name is Bellamy. She's a sweet girl. I knew she wouldn't make the cut, but I wanted to give her the opportunity anyway, because she really needs a job." Astrid shrugs. "Honestly, I don't think this line of work, dancing anyway, is for her."

"Call Lo. I heard she's looking to fill a waitress position," Baja states.

Astrid smiles at him. "I'll let her know." Music plays again. "I saved the best for last fellas." The stage lights strobe to the beat of the music. "Her name is Arabella, but she goes by the stage name Honey Holiday."

Baja shifts forward in his seat, becoming captivated by Arabella's performance. She starts out doing a bit of sultry burlesque, then moves into a more sensual, what you would expect from a strip routine. "Wait for it." Astrid's face lights up. "I could learn a few things from her."

Arabella begins her pole routine. "Damn," Laredo mutters at the way the dancer's erotic acrobatic moves wow us all.

"Right?" Astrid agrees with Laredo. "She'll become a favorite for sure."

The music stops, and Arabella exits the stage. Baja's head turns, following her movement toward the back.

I drum my fingertips against the surface of the table. "Mystic will get Harlow and Arabella on the payroll." Then I eye Astrid, who already has her attention set on me. "Have Delaney give them both medical check-ups."

Astrid frowns. "What about Bellamy?"

"Take Baja's advice and send her to Lo's. I'll call and give her a heads up."

Astrid jumps from the chair. "Perfect. I'll catch you, men, later," she says, then takes her leave.

"Well, I guess I should get my ass to work. I have a client coming in for the outline of the back piece he's getting, and it will take most of the day to complete," Juneau says and goes to push away from the table.

"Hold up," I announce. "It may be nothin', but I need to fill you in on a scratch of information Bishop threw my way this morning." My words get all my men's full attention. "Dale had a group of men hanging around the bar askin' questions about the club."

Laredo leans forward, placing his elbows on the table. "Dale happen to catch any names or where they were traveling from?"

I shake my head. "No."

"You thinkin' it's somethin' to concern ourselves with?" Juneau asks.

"Don't know. Bishop said one of the men mentioned me specifically." I run my hand through my hair, pushing it out of my face. "For now, keep your eyes open and have some of our contacts around town to do the same."

4
SAGE

"Are you ready?" I stand at the salon door and look at Juniper, who is just as giddy as I am.

"Let's do it." She claps her hands.

Turning around, I flip the lock on the door then turn the closed sign over, making Dyed 2 Perfection officially open. The two women who have been waiting outside on the sidewalk for the past ten minutes walk inside.

"Hello, ladies," I greet them with a huge smile. "How are you today?"

Both women look to be in their forties. One has dirty blonde hair and the other a dark brown.

"We're doing great, but I'm in a pickle," the one with the blonde hair says. "But we will be even better if you could work with us this morning. My daughter is getting married this evening, and the whole bridal party requires styling, and a few of us will need a cut and color. There are eight of us in total. We normally go to the salon in the next town, but everyone there came down with food poisoning. Then we remembered hearing something about this place opening today. Please, please tell me you can help," the woman pleads, and I can hear the desperation in her voice.

Juniper and I share a look then I look back to the two women with worry etched all over their faces. "Call everyone. Juniper and I would love to help you."

Relief and joy roll off the woman in waves as she lets out a huge exhale, letting her shoulders sag. "Oh my god. Angels. The both of you. I'm going to call my daughter now." The woman turns but stops short and turns back. "By the way. I'm Libby, and this is Carla." She offers her hand. "Excuse my bad manners."

I laugh. "No problem. It's nice to meet you, Libby. I'm Sage, and this is Juniper." I nod to my left.

While Libby calls her daughter to get the bridal party in, Juniper and I consult with Carla about their needs today. She informs us that two bridesmaids and the bride need highlights and all eight women need styling.

"We have a makeup artist already; would it be a problem if she comes here and does the girl's makeup in between them getting their hair done?" the mother of the bride asks while holding the phone to her ear.

"I think we can make that work. We have an empty station at the end where she can set up at." I gesture to the empty chair beside Juniper.

"Perfect! Thank you, thank you," Libby says before turning back to her conversation while Juniper and I head into the back for extra supplies.

"Can you believe our luck?" Juniper says as she grabs a few extra smocks off the hook next to the color station.

"I know. I think we might have bit off more than we can chew, but I'm not about to pass up this opportunity."

Juniper shakes her head. "Hell, no. We got this."

I smile. "Yeah, we do."

The two of us are quiet for a minute, and I know my best friend is thinking the same thing as me.

"We did it, Juju, I whisper." I watch as Juniper blinks away tears, and I do the same.

Juniper grabs my hand. "We did it."

A moment later, I collect myself. "No more crying until we can crack open a bottle of wine. Right now, we have a shit ton of work to do."

After a quick nod, Juniper wipes her face, and we get ready to greet the women we just heard walk through the door of the salon.

Eight long hours later, I'm waving goodbye to the ladies as they exit the salon. "Bye, ladies. Libby, I'll see you next week," I call out. Today turned out better than expected. Libby ended up making an appointment to come in next week. Her daughter loved the caramel highlights Juniper gave her and decided to revisit our salon. And, Carmen, Julia's maid of honor and best friend who is also getting married, booked us for her bridal party six months from now.

Libby told us about several salons in town, but they are older women and don't have much experience geared toward younger clients. I completely understood what she meant. The salon we worked in back home catered more toward its elderly clients. I tried a few times to get the owner to let us offer more in coloring, but Mrs. Connie, though sweet as pie, was stuck in her ways. She didn't believe in today's new fashion colors. The woman almost had a heart attack when I showed up to work with purple streaks in my hair.

"Can you believe we finished in time?" Juniper asks after locking the door behind Libby.

"Right? Thank goodness it's going to be a late ceremony." Juniper and I spent the day listening to the bride retell the story of how she and her fiancé met and how they will be saying I do at ten thirty-seven tonight, exactly one year to the minute they shared their first kiss. At first, I thought it was kind of crazy having a late wedding, but seeing how the bride adored her soon-to-be husband, I decided the whole concept was pretty romantic.

"You know, I thought I'd feel beat after a day like today, but I'm actually kind of pumped." I spin in my chair, facing Juniper. "I know the plan was to pick up a bottle of wine and order takeout, but what do you say we go out and celebrate?"

Juniper grins. "What do you have in mind? There's a bar over on Brinkley Street. Want to check it out?"

I think for a minute. "What about a club? I feel like dancing."

"Seriously?" Juniper quirks a brow. "Have you seen any clubs in this town?"

I shrug. "I don't know, and we can ask our Uber driver if they know of a place." Juniper mulls over my plans. "Come on, Juju. Let's live a little."

"Fine." Juniper rolls her eyes. "But if whatever place we end up in is skeevy, we are leaving and going back to our original plan."

"Deal. Now, come on. Let's lock up and go get ready."

Going to a club was not something I would have considered back home. Not that our small town had one, but even so, I don't think I would have gone. I'm not a dancer, but being here, on my own, I find myself wanting to spread my wings and broaden my horizons.

For tonight's look, I choose a red, ruffled, halter dress with a plunging neckline that makes the girls look great. The hem is short, hitting a few inches above my knees. I top it off with a gold belt, cinched around my waist, showing off my hourglass figure. Tonight, I opted to leave my long hair down, only adding a few loose curls, and went light on the makeup but added a pop of color by wearing my favorite red lipstick.

"Holy shit, Sage." Juniper gasps when I walk into the living room.

"Right?" I do a full twirl, showing off just how killer this dress is. "And I could say the same for you." I admire the black dress my best friend is wearing.

A car honking draws both our attention, and I look toward the window. "Our ride is here." I walk over to the small table beside the front door, grab my keys, and toss them in my small handbag along with my cash and ID.

A minute later, Juniper and I are settling into the backseat of the Uber. Behind the wheel is a guy that looks to be in his early twenties, and I watch as his eyes widen and land on my chest.

"Eyes up, buddy." Juniper snaps her fingers, drawing the guy's attention from my boobs to her face. He at least has the decency to look sheepish.

"Sorry," he mumbles. "Where are you two headed?"

"Is there a club around here you can take us to?" I ask.

"A club?" The guy scrunches his brow.

"Yeah. A club," Juniper repeats. "You know, a place where people go dancing and drinking," she adds sarcastically.

I nudge her shoulder and give her a look that says be nice. She rolls her eyes in return.

"Uhh, yeah. I know a place, but I don't think..."

"Great," Juniper cuts the driver off.

"Okaaay," the guy draws out as he faces forward and shifts the car into drive.

Once we're on the road, I shift toward Juniper. "Did you have to be so rude?"

"Please," she huffs. "The guy was drooling over your tits like he's never seen a pair before. He started his service with bad manners, and you know I can't stand that shit."

Oh, I know all too well my best friend's stance on men who treat women like shiny objects that are only here to serve and esthetically please their wandering eyes. Fifteen minutes later, the car stops, and I stare out the window in awe of the place. The

Fallen is a three-story brick cathedral-style structure with large blacked-out windows lining each story. Aside from the name on the front of the building and the few people milling around outside, you wouldn't know the place is a club. Not what I'd imagine a club to look like anyway. "Are you sure this is a club?" I ask.

"Yep." The driver smiles.

I give him a skeptical look but ultimately slide out of the car with Juniper behind me. A large, bearded man covered in tattoos stands a few feet beyond the door when we enter the club. He looks at Juniper and eyes her with apparent interest but otherwise leaves us alone. He greets us with a chin lift, which is a good sign.

The moment we step inside, I stop in my tracks and stare at my surroundings. "Is this a...?"

"That little shithead Uber driver brought us to a strip club," Juniper gasps with disbelief.

I try to fight back a giggle but fail.

"This shit is not funny, Sage."

"It's a little funny." I smirk. "Come on. We're here, we may as well have a drink. I didn't get all dressed up for nothing."

"Fine," Juniper huffs as we make our way further inside where we are assaulted by the thumping bass of the music. "There are a couple of empty seats at the bar," Juniper shouts. I follow her line of sight and nod.

"What can I get you, ladies?" the female bartender asks when we sidle up to the bar.

"I'll have a Martini—dirty."

"I'll take the same," Juniper adds.

"You got it." The woman taps the top of the bar, and I watch as she sashays to the other end of the bar in her skin-tight leather pants, where she begins mixing our drinks. She returns less than two minutes later.

"Thanks." I smile.

"No problem. Holler when you're ready for a refill."

Lifting the glass, I put the rim to my lips and turn in my stool to finally get a good look at the club. For starters, I run my palm across the back of the black leather upholstered stool I'm sitting on, noting how comfortable it is for a barstool.

There are two levels. The floor above us is a large loft space, accented by slatted walls with neon purple backlighting. But the top floor doesn't appear to be open to customers. Here on ground level, the bar, where I'm sitting, takes up the entire right side, along the wall of the massive open floor plan. In the center of the room is a square dance floor with two stripper poles. Plush purple velvet smoker's chairs surround the perimeter of the stage. Numerous tables with chairs are scattered in the space between the bar and where the dancers perform. Private booths are located on the other side of the room, and one other private area is tucked away in the back corner. All the black and magenta lighting over-head makes the deep blue walls glow, reminding me of the way water reflects light from the moon.

By the time my eyes settle back on the stage, the music cuts off, and the room goes quiet. Strobes of neon lights splatter colors across the dance floor and You Give Love A Bad Name by Bon Jovi begins to play through the speakers. A woman with long shiny red hair, creamy, pale skin, and wearing a lavender bra with matching thong and garters walks out on stage with her mile-long legs leading the way. Her presence demands the attention of every person in the room the second her six-inch heels hit the floor. When she starts seductively swaying her hips, I can't help but keep my eyes glued to her every move. She knows how to use her body and how she seduces the pole is mesmerizing. When the woman finishes her number, I turn to see Juniper fanning herself. We share a look. "That was hot. I wish I could move like that."

"Oh, honey. With that body, I'm sure you could," the

bartender cuts in as her eyes give me a once over. "What's your name?"

"Sage," I breathe. I may not swing that way, but I won't lie and say this beautiful woman in front of me doesn't affect me.

"Pretty name, Sage. I'm Aspen."

"Nice to meet you, Aspen." I hold out my hand.

Aspen takes my hand in hers. "You too, beautiful."

My best friend giggles. I've lost the ability to form words and can feel my face heat at the bartender's attention.

I tuck a strand of hair behind my ear. "Thank you."

She winks. "How about a refill?"

"Yes, please."

While Aspen fixes my drink, I swivel toward Juniper, who's grinning from ear to ear. "Shut up."

Juniper holds her hand up. "I didn't say anything."

"No, but I know whatever you're about to say is on the tip of your tongue."

My best friend grins and rolls her eyes.

"It's the dress," I jest.

"It's not the dress. It's you. You're a damn knockout, Sage. I've been telling you that since we were fifteen."

It's my turn to roll my eyes. "Please. I'm five feet tall on a good day. You're the one with the killer legs and the best head of hair I've ever had my hands on."

"Yeah, but you have tits and ass. Tits and ass make up for long legs any day of the week."

I sigh.

"You've never been good at taking compliments. But take it from me, getting hit on by that woman—" Juniper gestures toward Aspen "—has got to be the best compliment in the world. Cause that woman..." She leaves her sentence hanging. And I know what she's getting at. Aspen is not only gorgeous but has an air of confidence that says she could get any man or woman she wanted and knows it.

"Watch my drink. I need to go to the lady's room." I nudge Juniper then hop down off the stool. On my way toward the back of the club, I weave around tables and end up in the direct path of a group of men heading in my direction. My steps falter when I catch sight of the leather vests they're wearing and try to think where I've seen them before. The three men look to be on a mission, their facial expressions like stone. They aren't paying attention, because they nearly run me over when passing. I stumble while stepping to the right to avoid the collision. The men don't even spare me a glance. Rude. Looking over my shoulder, I catch a glimpse of their retreating backs, and it suddenly hits me where I've seen them. Those are the bikers I saw that day outside Belladonna's. Fallen Ravens Motorcycle Club.

One of the men senses eyes on him and turns his head, looking straight at me. Sukie warned us to mind our own business when it comes to the Ravens, so that's what I intend to do.

A few minutes later, I return to the bar, finding Juniper in conversation with a cute twenty-something man with dirty blond hair. The guy is wearing gray suit pants and a black button-down shirt with the sleeves rolled up.

"Come on, just one drink," I hear the guy say.

"Thanks, but I'm here to celebrate with my friend. Maybe some other time." Juniper turns him down politely though her tone says she's not interested in the guy.

"It's just one drink. I'm sure your friend won't mind," he tries again.

I shake my head—way wrong answer. Juniper and I have a code: we never ditch the other. No matter how cute the guy is.

"She may not, but I do." Juniper's tone changes. "Now, I'd appreciate it if you'd let me get back to the company I was enjoying before you came over here and so rudely made the assumption I'd prefer your company and what is sure to be a boring conversation to that of my best friend." On the last note, Juniper turns in her seat, giving her back to the guy hitting on her.

The guy looks pissed and embarrassed, and for a second, I think he's going to do the typical asshole thing by making a scene or calling Juniper a few choice names. Luckily, he chooses to walk away. I can't stand when men strike out with a woman, and just because it bruises their fragile little egos, they resort to putting the woman down. Suddenly we're bitches. All because we don't give them what they're after. Gone are the days when women give in to the pressure of men and their expectations.

"I love you, Juju." I grin at my best friend.

"I love you too, heifer." Juniper drapes her arm around my neck and smacks a kiss on my cheek, making me laugh.

"Oh, look." She points to the stage. "Another dancer is coming out."

I turn my attention to the woman on stage, but something else pulls me in—a man at a booth in the left corner beside the stage. The spot is a bit secluded but not so much that I can't see the lap dance he's getting. The man is wearing the same leather vest as the men I saw on my way to the bathroom with the Fallen Ravens emblem etched on the back. He's wearing a black Henley with the sleeves rolled up, showing off his ink-covered arms beneath the vest. The biker senses he's being watched. I witness the moment he is aware of my gaze and, for the life of me, I can't look away. He's beautiful. My breath catches in my throat when his eyes lock on mine, holding me captive. All while the woman dances over him. She sits on his lap with her back to his front, grinding her ass against his crotch. I bite my bottom lip the same time my pussy tingles as I imagine it's me dancing for him.

5
SALEM

Currently, at the back of the club, I'm tucked away in one of our private booths. Juneau brought some of our new product in for sampling not too long ago, so, between that and a couple of whiskeys, I have zero fucks to give. Leaning back, I clasp my hands behind my head and feel the music vibrating through my body while Astrid gives me some attention.

"Looks like you have an admirer," Mystic notes from beside me. I don't have to follow his line of sight. Mystic clears his throat. "I have some fun of my own waiting by the bar. I'll catch you later, brother." Mystic jerks his chin and walks away. My eyes haven't left their current target since noticing the curvaceous woman wearing a sexy red dress. She keeps stealing glances our way. She also looks a bit out of her element, too innocent and pure to be in my establishment.

Fuck, I'm turned on, and it has nothing to do with the way Astrid's ass is grinding against my dick. Instead, it has everything to do with the doe-eyed angel watching me from across the room. The curvy goddess has my full attention. Her long midnight-black hair, with streaks of purple, flows over her bare shoulders. My eyes fall to her red-painted lips, and I instantly wonder what they would feel like wrapped around my cock. She has a shapely figure, with curves in all the right places. She's built for pleasure—to be pleasured by a man with a ferocious appetite. A man like me. My eyes roam upward, back to her face, where our eyes meet once more. She holds me captive with her piercing blue eyes. The way she looks at me like she's reaching into the very depths of my soul is unnerving, yet I cannot break our connection.

Astrid continues to dance in front of me, dropping to the floor at my feet, settling between my knees. I keep my attention on my mystery woman. Her red lips part ever so slightly, and my insides turn over while her eyes fall, watching Astrid drag her hand down my chest and over my swollen cock.

This woman is the best kind of temptation.

She could quickly become an obsession.

Let's see how far my little voyeur will go.

I keep my eyes on the woman in red when I speak. "Take it out," I tell Astrid. Will my blue-eyed temptress continue to watch, or will she break the spell she has over me and look away? Adrenaline rushes through my body. The need for this little show to keep going outweighs the fact that we're surrounded by people.

Astrid undoes my jeans and begins freeing my cock.

And just like that, my mystery woman tears her eyes away, shattering the connection between us. I wait for her to turn back, wanting to feel the sting of her stare again.

Astrid grips my cock in her hand, giving it a firm squeeze, just how I like it. I hiss as the head of my dick is engulfed by the warmth of her mouth and close my eyes. All I see are my mystery woman's icy blues staring back at me, and suddenly she's the one on her knees. It's her red lips wrapped around my cock, sliding up and down my shaft. It's her tongue flicking against the sensitive spot just beneath the head of my dick, rubbing against the piercing I have there. In a building full of people and music playing, it's my mystery woman I fantasize about as the tension builds. The woman in red haunts my thoughts while chasing my release.

I tuck my cock back inside my jeans. The high I had before is gone. Astrid looks at me, smiles then leans in and kisses my cheek. "Want to see me later?" she asks.

"Not tonight," I grunt. The truth is, I still have the woman in red on my mind, and she's already become a distraction.

"You should go find her." I look at Astrid while she pushes to her feet. "I'm always aware of my surroundings, Salem, and I know all about the buxom woman in the killer red dress." I say nothing. "If you change your mind, you know where to find me." Astrid takes her leave. And that's why Astrid and I get along. Sex between us is casual—no strings attached. She likes it that way, and so do I.

I lean forward and snatch the pack of cigarettes off the table, place one between my lips, then strike a stick from a book of matches. I stare into the flame on the end of the matchstick. Again, I'm consumed with thoughts of my mystery woman. Who is she? I light my cigarette, drop the matchstick into the ashtray on the table, and then pull a lungful of smoke and nicotine. I hold it in until my lungs burn, trying to focus on anything else but her. I let out a long exhale and run my fingers through my hair. "What the fuck, Ash? Either go find her and fuck her or get the woman out of your head." I press my back against the leather sofa, glance out over the crowd, and attempt to clear my head.

As I'm scanning the room, a flash of red catches my attention. My little voyeur is still sitting at the end of the bar, talking with a tall blonde. My focus shifts to the guy sitting on the other side of her. His body language is sketchy as fuck. I watch him look around a few times before he reaches out and hovers his hand over a glass nearby.

I'm on my feet and moving across the room. Along the way, I

catch Laredo's eye where he's standing at the entrance to the club. One look is all my brother needs, and he's moving through the crowd, following my direction. Aspen, our female bartender who works the bar alongside Alder, also spots me and realizes something is wrong. She taps Alder on the shoulder, alerting him.

I get to my target just as his victim, my mystery woman, grabs the glass the bastard spiked. My right-hand shoots out, gripping the unsuspecting piece of shit by the hair on the back of his head and slamming his face into the bar top while simultaneously placing my left hand over the top of the drink my woman has her fingers wrapped around.

"What the hell?" I hear two separate female voices exclaim. The dickhead beneath my grip squirms as I keep him pinned down. Mere inches from her body brushing against mine, I tower over my woman in red. She whips around, and for a second time tonight, those blue eyes pierce mine, then fall to the man struggling to break free of my hold on him.

"Get your fucking hands off of me, asshole!" the man yells. I lift his head and slam it onto the bar again while not breaking eye contact with her.

"I was going to drink that," the woman in red sasses, trying to pull her drink from beneath my grip.

"Never leave your drink unattended," I growl.

My mystery woman raises her brow. "Did you just growl at me?" She turns to the tall blonde who has moved in to stand beside her. "Did he just growl at me?"

The blonde thinks she looks concerned with the situation and also tries hiding a smile back. "I think so, babe."

"Look, I don't know what the deal is between you men, but..."

I interrupt the dark-haired spitfire of a woman. "This piece of shit here," I lift the guy's head from the bar, "slipped something in your drink."

"How do you...you saw him do that from way over there?" She

pulls her hand from the glass. Aspen walks over, and I hand her the drink.

"Shit." Aspen looks at me with a sorrowful look, then to my mystery woman. "I'm sorry, Sage. It's part of my job to keep an eye out for assholes like him."

So Sage is her name.

"You can't prove shit," the man spits, sneering at Sage. "Someone would have to drug me to stick my dick in this fat bitch."

Rage fills my body at the word vomit he spews. I spin the motherfucker around to face me. I want him to get a good look at my face before I beat the sin out of him. "The only way a man like you gets laid is by druggin' unsuspecting women. There's a special place in hell for pussies like you." I ram my fist into his face, feeling his nose break against my knuckles.

"You motherfucker." He cups his face in the palms of his hands, blood instantly flowing between his fingers. "You broke my goddamn nose."

Then out of nowhere, a single gunshot rings out, causing panic in the club and people to flee toward the exit. As the building empties, three men approach the bar. "Hey," one of the men shouts. "If you know what's good for you, you'll take your hands off my brother."

I signal to Alder. "You and Aspen take the women up to my office."

"Hey," the blonde says as Alder rounds the end of the bar. "We didn't do shit." I cut my eyes at the blonde. She grabs her friend by the hand. Sage hesitates to look away as Alder urgently moves them toward the stairs leading to my office.

Once Alder leads the women away, I turn toward Laredo. "Y'all done fucked up now," he says as I shove the rapist heap of garbage toward him. My brother twists the asshole's arms behind his back.

The man with the gun takes aim at me. "Looks like you're the one who fucked up." They step a bit closer, and that's when I get a good look at the cuts the men are wearing. Fucking Demon Jokers.

"You look like you've seen a ghost." The gun-wielding biker smirks. I glance at the name on the front of his vest, Choke, but he has no title. "Now, let my brother go."

"Or what?"

"Or I put a bullet in your head, but not before I allow my brother to have his way with your bitch." Choke snickers.

I look to Laredo and nod for him to release the bastard. My brother gives the man a shove toward his keeper, who isn't wearing any colors. And just as he's within a couple feet of Choke, I reach to my side, pull my weapon, take aim at the back of the piece of shit's head and put a bullet in it. I quickly take aim at Choke, who took a second too long to react, and I pull the trigger again, placing a bullet in the motherfucker's chest.

"I hear we have ourselves a party," Mystic says from behind the two men left standing. There beside Mystic with their guns ready are Baja, Juneau, and Harlem.

"No one comes into my house, into my town, and threatens my club. Now, I don't know who has resurrected Demon Jokers." I stride forward and press the barrel end of my gun between the eyes of one of the other bikers. I look at his name patch. "Spider." My jaw clenches, and my fingers flex against the handle of my weapon. "You and your brother get your trash out of my club and tell your president, whoever he may be, this is his only warning."

"You heard the man," Harlem says. "Pick up your dead and get the fuck out of our town." Along with Baja and Juneau, they escort the bikers out of the club. I turn to Laredo.

"I have another situation to handle. You and Mystic wrap shit up."

"You got it, brother," Laredo gives me a chin lift, and I head for the stairs leading up to the loft.

I find Alder standing guard while Aspen is sitting with Sage and her friend on the black leather sofa at the back of my office. "What's going on?" Sage asks in a shaky voice.

"Let's go." I know my tone is stern and don't attempt to soften it.

"We aren't going anywhere with you. There are men with guns down there. We aren't moving until we get an answer, and the police arrive." She crosses her arms beneath her breast, further pushing them out. My eyes fall to the hearty amount of cleavage on display.

"Excuse me." Her friend stands and places her hand on her hip. "Stop gawking at my friend's tits and answer her."

"What's happenin' downstairs with those men is none of your fuckin' business. And there will be no cops. Now, let's go. I'm taking you two home."

Aspen looks at Sage. "You can trust him." Sage looks from Aspen to me then at her friend before standing. She uses her palms to smooth down the front of her red dress.

I face Alder. "Let my brothers know." When he nods, I turn back toward Sage and her friend. Knowing I don't want them to see the mess left behind downstairs, I decide to take them down the fire escape stairs. I walk over to the tall window and lift the window pane, then step out onto the metal balcony with a set of stairs leading down to the ground. The blonde steps out first. When it's Sage's turn, her heel gets stuck in the balcony grate. It causes her to lose her balance, and I reach out, stopping her fall. Sage gasps. "I'm so sorry." She immediately pushes off me and begins trying to pry her shoe-free. I reach down and slip her heel off her tiny foot, then proceed to pull it loose. Sage removes her other shoe and stands barefoot. "Here." I hand her the other shoe.

"Um, thanks," she murmurs.

"You gettin' shy on me, Sage?" Her name rolls off my lips with ease. "Cause earlier, you weren't so reserved." My words cause her face to flush and her pupils dilate. I'm having as much of an effect on her as she is on me. My cock swells thinking about earlier. I wait for her to respond. Instead, she turns her back to me and follows her friend down the stairs.

Once on the ground, I guide them down to my parked car and open the back door. They both hesitate. "I'm not gonna do nothin' but take you home." They share a look, then slide into the back-seat together, and I close the door. I walk around to the driver's side, get behind the wheel, and start the car. "Where's home, ladies?"

"Dyed 2 Perfection," the blonde says.

I know the place but don't say so. Instead, I put the car in drive and pull away from the club. On the drive through town, I steal glances at Sage through the rearview mirror. Tonight, we found out about the rebirth of Demon Jokers MC. There is no denying after sending back their dead, trouble will follow. Getting involved with a woman isn't a distraction I need right now. That's what I tell myself. Then again, maybe one night with her in my bed would quench the thirst I have. One taste. That's all I need to feed the hunger building inside.

Sage locks eyes with me in the mirror, and her heated stare says it all. I would destroy her.

Deep down, I have a feeling she would destroy me.

I roll the car to a slow stop outside the salon and say nothing, waiting for the women to climb out. "Thank you..." Sage pauses a beat.

My grip tightens on the steering wheel as my insides begin fighting against the words I'm about to say. "You and your friend are to never step foot in my club again. Understand?" My tone is cold and detached—all necessary to keep Sage as far away from me as possible. The only sound that follows my warning is the slamming of the car door. I wait to see them disappear into the building. Sage never looks back, and I drive away.

6

SAGE

The clock on my bedroom wall struck 2:00 am five minutes ago, and sleep is still avoiding me. I haven't been able to get my mind off what happened just a few hours before. I don't know what's plaguing me more: the whole bar scene where an asshole slipped drugs into my drink, the bar fight which included gun violence, or the man who caught my attention the moment I entered the club.

It didn't take me long to realize the man with hypnotic hazel eyes was a member of Fallen Ravens MC. He had to be at least six feet, five inches tall, making his hulking body tower over my five-foot frame. He also had tattoos covering both arms and colorful ink peeking out from beneath the collar of his shirt. The leather vest he was wearing caught my attention just as quickly as his eyes. Salem was the name I saw etched across the front of his vest. The second I saw it, alarm bells started going off inside my head, and I thought back to the conversation Juniper and I'd had with Sukie outside her shop. Every instinct warned me the biker was dangerous and to look away, so why couldn't I? A magnetic force drew me to him. He gave me a look saying, *I dare you to look away.*

I'm not a thrill-seeker, and I am not the kind of girl drawn to bad boys. In fact, I'm the complete opposite. I play everything in my life safe. Sure, I like to have fun, but I don't purposely chase after the unknown. The most daring thing I've ever done was move away from home to Salem with Juniper. Since I was a kid, my dad had instilled *have fun but be safe*. Those are words I live by. My father also didn't sugarcoat how cruel the world can sometimes be. He didn't shelter me from all the bad that can happen to young women unaware of the evils lurking in the shadows, or how being naive and ignoring the little voice inside your head can get you hurt.

For the first time in my life, I went against everything he'd taught me. All it took was a handsome biker with hazel eyes.

We should've never stepped foot inside that club. Sukie was right; those men are dangerous, and I need to stay far away.

To make matters worse, I left my clutch behind at the club. Even though it's my favorite bag, I would consider leaving it, but my ID is in it. The thought of having to go back after we were ordered to never come back makes my insides twist.

"Hey."

I startle and turn to find Juniper standing inside the doorway to my bedroom. "I've been calling your name." She looks at me with worry.

I sigh and shake my thoughts away. "Sorry. What's up?" I rub my tired eyes with the heels of my palms. "How come you're still up?"

Juniper leans against the door jam. "Probably the same reason as you. What happened tonight was pretty fucking wild."

I nod. "It's one for the books; that's for sure."

"Are you going to be okay?" Juniper asks.

"Yeah, I'm good."

Juniper smiles. "There's some hot tea on the stove. I got it from Sukie. It's supposed to help you sleep. I don't know what's in it, but I can already feel it working. That woman makes magic potions, I think."

"Really?" I give a sleepy half-smile. "In that case, I'll take a cup."

"Want me to stay up with you?" Juniper steps away from the door as I pass through.

I shake my head. "No. Go on and get some sleep. I won't be far behind you after I drink some of Sukie's herbal tea concoction."

Juniper makes her way down the hall to her bedroom, then stops and turns back. "I vote we stay in with a bottle of wine and takeout the next time we have something to celebrate."

My lip twitches. "Deal."

"Goodnight, Sage."

"Night, Juju."

Well, it's safe to say that Sukie is most definitely the creator of the magic sleep potion. Thanks to her tea, I was able to get a few hours of sleep and feel surprisingly refreshed. I make a mental note to stop by Belladonna's later today for more.

"Sage, are you coming? It's ten to nine!" Juniper shouts from the front of our apartment. We have clients coming in at nine-fifteen and two more at eleven. Apparently, word travels fast around town. After I got up an hour ago, I decided to check the salon messages, and I was giddy when greeted with a slew of appointment requests. Juniper and I have four clients each today, three on Monday, and several already scheduled for later in the week.

"One minute!" I yell back as I finish tying my hair up in a high ponytail. I quickly swipe a coat of mascara on my lashes. Once I'm done, I sit on the edge of my bed and pull on a pair of brown wedge boots to go with my jeans and green sweater.

By the time I walk into the living room, Juniper is standing at the front door holding two travel mugs of coffee. She thrusts one toward me. "Here."

I take the cup. "You're the best."

"I know. Now let's go."

Juniper and I walk down the stairs from our apartment to the salon. I go about flipping all the lights on while she unlocks the entrance door.

Five minutes later, our first two clients walk in. "You must be Emmy and Dina?" I ask. Both women smile. The blonde looks in her mid-twenties and the girl with darker hair looks no older than fifteen or sixteen. The blonde is the first to speak. "We are. I'm Dina, and this is my sister Emmy, but everyone calls her Em."

"It's nice to meet you. My name is Sage, and this is Juniper." I nod toward my friend.

"Wow, is that really your name?" Em looks at Juniper with wide eyes.

"It sure is."

"I love it! It's such a cool name," The young girl gushes.

"Thank you, lovely. I like your name too." Juniper smiles.

The girl rolls her eyes like most teens do these days. "My name is so lame."

"Hey." Her sister lightly punches her arm. "Better than being stuck with Dina."

I decide right away I like this sister duo. Their banter reminds me a lot of how Juniper and I are with each other. "So, ladies, what are we doing today?" I ask.

"Can I have hair like yours?" Em looks back and forth between her big sister and me. "The purple is so pretty."

Dina eyes her sister while chewing her bottom lip.

I'm quick to jump in when I see her hesitation. "How about a few pieces sprinkled throughout or maybe just framing her face," I suggest. "We don't have to go really heavy like mine. We can ease into it and see how you like it, and always add more later."

Dina thinks for a moment but cannot resist the puppy dog eyes her sister is giving her. "Okay, fine."

"Yes!" Em throws herself in my chair, giving me the indication she's ready to rock and roll with the purple.

"Will you need to get permission from your parents before we do this?" I ask, running my fingers through Emmy's long hair. "I don't want to send your mom and dad into a tailspin when you return home with purple hair," I say jokingly, but immediately regret my words when Emmy goes quiet.

"It's just Em and me," Dina says.

My face falls, and Dina doesn't need to explain that their parents aren't in the picture. "I'm sorry, and I shouldn't have..."

Dina cuts me off. "Seriously, it's fine. You couldn't have known."

I know there is a story there, but I don't ask, and luckily Juniper saves the moment by cutting in.

"What about you, Dina? What are we doing with that luscious head of yours today? How about pink?"

Juniper's suggestion earns us a giggle from Emmy.

"What?" Dina turns to her little sister. "You don't think I could rock the pink?"

"Heck no. You're not cool enough." Emmy full-on laughs.

"I take offense to that." Dina turns away from us and sits in Juniper's chair. "Since my brat sister has rudely informed me I can't have pink hair, I guess I'll just go with a tone and a cut."

Two hours later, I remove the cape from around Emmy and watch as her face literally brightens right before my eyes the moment she gets a glimpse at her new look in the mirror.

"You like?" I ask with a matching smile.

"Oh my god, Sage! I love it. Thank you, thank you." Emmy immediately pulls her phone from her pocket and begins snapping selfies of herself. "Wait until Liz sees me. She's going to die."

Emmy walks over to the sofa by the door and sits with her face buried in her phone.

"Don't be surprised if every girl in the school shows up here to get their hair done now." Dina shakes her head.

"You won't hear us complaining." I sit in the chair Emmy just vacated.

Dina grins then looks at me warmly. "Thanks for convincing me to let you do her hair like that. I wasn't too sure at first about the purple, but it really is pretty. And I haven't seen her smile like that in a long time."

By the time closing rolls around, Juniper and I are dead on our feet but thrilled for the fact that not only have we gained several new clients but people who we now consider friends.

"Hey." Juniper appears from the back of the shop where she was folding towels.

"What's up?" I ask.

"I thought I'd make some stir-fry for dinner but need to go to the store. Want to ride with me?"

I look down at my watch. "I would, but I need to go by the hardware store and pick up some brackets to hang up the last two mirrors over there." I jerk my head toward the two gold-framed mirrors leaning against the back wall of the salon. "And they're closing in an hour."

"No problem." Juniper grabs her purse and keys. "Is there anything you want me to pick up while I'm there?"

"I'd love you forever if you brought some ice cream home." I grin.

"I suppose I can do that. Any special requests?"

I shake my head. "Surprise me."

"You got it." Juniper gives me a little finger wave over her shoulder then she's out the door.

Knowing I need to be doing the same, I grab my keys and toss my phone into my pocket before slipping my coat and scarf on. And since the hardware store is only two blocks away, I decide to walk. After locking up the shop and setting the alarm, I set off down the sidewalk. To my right, I catch a glimpse of Sukie through her storefront window and wave when our eyes meet.

By the time I reach the hardware store, I'm cursing myself for not driving because it feels like my hands and nose have gone numb from the cold. Thankfully, when I pull open the door to Billy's, a burst of warm air blankets me.

"Sage, back so soon?" Billy, the older gentleman who owns the store, greets me from behind the counter. Juniper and I have been in here almost every day since moving to Salem, and Billy has been a godsend.

"Hi, Billy. How are you doing today?" I ask, stepping farther inside.

"Doing good, sweetheart. What brings you by?"

"I need something for hanging mirrors."

"No problem. I'll get my nephew, Brandon, to help you. You haven't met him yet since he's been out of town. He sometimes takes long weekends up at his cabin. He's an avid hiker. I swear I can't tear that boy away from his hikin' and fishin'." He chuckles.

I smile at Billy just as a man appears from behind a display shelf.

"Did somebody say my name?"

"Indeed, I did." Billy smiles. "Would you mind helping Sage find some brackets, Brandon?"

Brandon turns toward me. He offers a megawatt smile without missing a beat, showing off his perfectly straight white teeth and the cute dimple in his left cheek. Brandon stands around six feet tall and sports the classic boy-next-door look, right down to his blue eyes, mop of blonde hair, and faded jeans, along with a blue flannel shirt. Brandon is a handsome man.

Judging by the confident way he carries himself, he knows it. Typically, Brandon would be the type of man I'd go for. As soon as that thought drifts into my mind, it's quickly replaced by hazel eyes, dark hair, and tattoos. *Sage, stop thinking about that man.*

Once I finish chastising myself, I notice Brandon staring at me expectantly. I blink away the biker fog from my brain. "Did you say something?"

Brandon chuckles. "I asked what kind of brackets you were looking for."

"Oh, I'm not sure. I need something for hanging a large mirror."

With a nod, Brandon gestures for me to follow him. "So, are you the lady who just opened up the hair salon a few blocks over?"

"That's me. Actually, it's my best friend and me," I tell him. "Feel free to spread the word."

"I'll be sure to tell a buddy of mine. His girlfriend, Hazel, is a teacher at the elementary school, so I'm sure she'd be happy to get the word out as well."

"Oh wow, that would be great." I beam.

"It's not a problem." Brandon shows off his dimple again. "Us small businesses have to stick together, right?" He turns back toward the display shelf and swipes a box of brackets. "Here you go."

I take the box from him. "Thanks."

"You're welcome. If you ever need any help down at the salon with heavy lifting or hanging those mirrors, let me or my uncle know, and I can come down and help out," Brandon offers.

"You know what, I just might take you up on that offer some time," I say as we make our way up to the register. "And tell Hazel to come by the shop anytime. I look forward to meeting her," I add.

Brandon rings me up and hands the bag over with my purchase in it. "Sure thing. Have a good night, Sage."

"You too, Brandon." I wave over my shoulder then call out to Billy, who is stocking a shelf. "Night, Billy."

"Until next time, sweetheart."

On the walk home, my cell rings, so I pull it from my coat pocket. A picture of my dad lights up the screen, and I instantly warm up inside. "Hey, Dad."

"Baby girl. Did I catch you at a good time?"

"Anytime you call is a good time, Dad."

"You know how to make an old man feel special."

"That's because you are special. How's Mom?"

"Your mother is good. She said to tell you hi."

"Tell Mom I said hi back and that I love her."

"Will do, baby girl. Now, tell me about your day? How's Juniper?"

"Juju is good, and things with the salon are great. We're booked solid for the next two weeks."

"Oh really? That's great news. I never doubted you two for a minute."

"I'll admit I was nervous, but I have a good feeling about Salem, Dad. And the people here are kind and welcoming." My memory briefly flashes back to what happened at the club last night, but there is no way I'm going to mention anything about it to my father. If I did, he would drive down here tonight and insist I come home. Besides, everything I just said is the truth. I like Salem and the people. I'm just going to stick to my plan and forget about my biker. Shit. There I go again, referring to him as my biker, and I have to stop thinking about him.

"Earth to Sage, are you there?" Dad chuckles.

"Sorry, Daddy. I'm here."

"What has you so distracted?"

"Oh, nothing really," I lie.

"You forget who you're talking to? I know you, Sage. When you zone out, it's because you have something weighing on that mind of yours."

Damnit, he's right. "It's nothing bad. I'm just thinking about the shop, and all the stuff that still needs to be done. In fact, I'm on my way home from the hardware store now, and I picked up some brackets to hang mirrors."

"Are you walking?" he asks.

"Yeah. It's only a couple blocks from my apartment."

"Do you have your pepper spray? What about your taser?"

"Yes, Dad. I have both," I lie. My taser is in the bag I left at the club. "Stop worrying."

"That's an impossible task for any father."

"I suppose you're right but still, I'm covered."

"Listen, your mom and I will be there in a few weeks, so if you want, you can leave some of that stuff for me to do when we get there."

"You do know you're the one who taught me how to use tools, Dad. I think I can hang a couple of mirrors." I giggle.

"I know you can, but your old man is going to miss taking care of his little girl."

My heart swells at my dad's confession. "Don't worry, Dad, the apartment needs a new hot water heater soon, so I'll save that task for you instead of having to pay someone to install the new one."

"I look forward to it, Shortcake."

"Me too, Dad. I'll talk to you tomorrow. Love you."

"Love you too."

7
SALEM

It's nearly noon, and I'm sitting in an empty pew in the church's sanctuary, which also doubles as our shared space. Across the room is the bar area. The rest of the room is filled with a couple of pool tables, leather sofas, a flatscreen TV, and a stripper pole where the altar podium once stood. I sit alone with a cigarette in one hand and a partially filled bottle of whiskey in the other. I, along with Harlem, crashed here last night after cleaning up the aftermath of violence at the strip club. I lift the liquor bottle to my lips and take another drink. I feel restless with a gamut of thoughts racing through my head. I take a pull of the cigarette, hold the nicotine in for a beat, then expel the smoke from my body with a heavy sigh. I should focus on the club's current issue of the resurrection of Demon Jokers. As it stands, we have no idea of the club's numbers or who their new President is. We also have the Salem Police Department's attention after last night's incident. Someone had called the authorities reporting shots fired, and a rookie officer who needed to flex his power was waiting for me when I returned from dropping Sage and her friend off at their apartment. With the weight of all this trouble on my shoulders, all I can think about is her. She has a hold on me, and I don't fucking like it. I can't think straight. One minute I'm sorting out what the hell to do about the fucking Demon Jokers and the sheriff breathing down my back; the next, my headspace is consumed by thoughts of my woman in red—Sage.

I flick the half-smoked cigarette to the floor at my feet and snuff it out, grinding it beneath the toe of my black leather boot. Frustration courses through my veins, and I fall back against the pew, scrubbing my palm down my face. "Get her out of your fuckin' head," I mutter.

I hear footsteps falling against the wood floor behind me and instinctively reach to my side, gripping my weapon. "It's just me, Prez," Harlem says in a relaxed tone. He sits beside me in the pew. "Get who out of your head, brother?" He questions what he over-heard me grumble.

I pass him the bottle, and he takes it from my hand. "Every-fuckinthing." I'm silent for a beat, and Harlem sits with me. He takes a drink from the bottle then sets it on the floor. "You hear anything from Laredo and Baja?"

Harlem presses his back against the old oak pew. "Not yet." Laredo and Baja hit the road at first light this morning, headed toward the Demon Jokers last known location to put eyes on our current threat. "Think we're dealin' with somethin' serious here?"

"My gut says our troubles with those sons of bitches have only begun." The rumble of bikes outside alerts Harlem and me to company. I stand, as does Harlem, and we walk outside. The after-noon sun is blinding after sitting in the dark church. Juneau and Mystic roll their bikes to a stop beside Harlem's and mine, then dismount.

Mystic walks to where I stand. "You look like shit."

I huff. "Thanks."

"How's Lorelei?" I ask, knowing she's been sick with a cold.

Mystic smiles, as he always does when the conversation is about his little girl. "Fever broke a few hours ago."

I nod. "Good to hear."

Mystic shifts, crossing his arms over his chest. "I hate to piss in your Cheerios, but..." he says, and I look from him to Juneau. A pulsating pain begins thudding at my temples.

"Lay it on me." I rub my temples, trying to relieve the pressure building.

"Got a call from Huxley an hour ago. He'll be stoppin' by the club to pay you a visit this evening before the doors open.". Great. The last thing we need is the sheriff breathing down our necks while we do our own brand of taking care of business. I pinch the bridge of my nose. At least the old man gave us a heads up.

The sound of bikes draws our attention toward the tree-lined dirt road leading to the clubhouse. It's Laredo and Baja. They pull in beside the rest of the bikes and cut their engines. "Everyone's asses to church," I proclaim, and lead the way inside our compound sanctuary, where we gather in a large dark room where there is no sunlight. "Tell us what you know." I take my seat.

Laredo glances around the table as he speaks. "The new members of Demon Jokers are holed up on the same property. We couldn't see what was going on inside of the two-story building because most of the windows were boarded up."

"Got some numbers for us?" I ask.

"Without getting too close and risking being seen, we counted six milling around outside," Baja says.

"They're not messin' around with security, either. The entire compound is surrounded with electrified ten foot fencing, and the members we had eyes on were each carrying an M16." Laredo pauses a beat and reaches into his cut, pulling out his phone. He taps the screen then slides it across the table toward me. I pick it up and flip through the photos he took of the compound and the men. I haven't laid eyes on the property since we coated Demon Jokers clubhouse in their own blood after the death of Chicago and several other Fallen Ravens members.

That day is a dark shadow walking with us daily. A stern reminder of the path we walk and the dangers that lurk. Demon Jokers and Fallen Ravens had a bitter rivalry for years. Chicago's and Mayhem's—the dead President of Demon Jokers—hatred for one another ran deep. The Demon Jokers had zero respect for others. The Fallen Ravens aren't and have never been saints. We sin, and we break man's laws. But Demon Jokers decided they wanted what wasn't theirs. They wanted Salem.

One fall night, Demon Jokers hit several Fallen Ravens members' homes. They murdered Mystic's dad, along with four other members. Mayhem died that night as well, executed in his sleep.

In one night, we lost our President and several other club officers. We lost our brothers—our family. Those of us untouched, including Mystic, straddled our iron horses and rode into battle, straight through the gates of hell, guns blazing. I glance across the table at Mystic, and the hardened look on his face tells me he's reliving the same memory as I.

We spilled a lot of blood that night and watched as the President of Demon Jokers took his final breath.

I clear the fog of that night from my head and focus. "Ghost doesn't live far from Demon Jokers' compound. I'll give him a call, see if he's willin' to do a little investigating for us." Ghost, who is retired special ops, prefers living a life of solitude. When needed, he'll do shit for the club from time to time. Chicago knew him, so that's how I know him, but to this day, I don't know his real name —none of us do.

"What's the game plan while we wait for more intel?" Mystic asks with tension in his voice.

I glance at the table, making sure to examine each of my

brothers. "This club, our family, and business are top priority. We stay vigilant. If they come lookin' for a fight, we'll give them one."

The sun is starting to dip low in the sky as Mystic and I mount our bikes outside Mystic Cannabis, our ten thousand-square-foot marijuana cultivation facility. The warehouse is located several blocks from the strip club. It wasn't long after they legalized marijuana here that the club decided to cash in on the industry. Mystic had already been growing products and bringing in money for the club for years. Now, he does it as a legit tax-paying corporation.

"What are your thoughts on opening our own dispensary?" Mystic throws a leg over his bike seat. "That building across the street from the tattoo shop still has a for-lease sign in the window."

I straddle my Harley. The potential for more money is appealing, but the timing of his proposed adventure isn't ideal. Then again, life can't be put on hold because of uncertainties. The last thing we should be doing is giving off any impression that Demon Jokers' newfound presence is threatening our day-to-day operations and living.

"Well?" Mystic waits for a response.

"Looks like we're getting into the dispensary business."

Mystic grins. It's the first time since all this bullshit with the Demon Jokers he hasn't had a hardened scowl on his face, which is way out of character. However, I don't blame him for the dark mood, and I feel the same. "I'll swing by and see Darby in the morning about the building lease."

My phone chimes, and I pull it from my pocket. Swiping the screen, I read a text from Laredo.

Laredo: Sheriff is here waiting on you.

Me: Be there in ten.

I look at Mystic. "Huxley is sittin' at the club. Let's ride."

The drive is short. Harlem, Laredo, Juneau, and Baja's Harleys are parked side by side up close to the building, and we back our rides alongside theirs. Sheriff Huxley's patrol vehicle is parked a few spaces away near the front entrance to the club, without him in it. Mystic and I walk inside and find our brothers sitting at a table with Huxley, who has a beer sitting in front of him.

"Drinkin' on the job?" I stop beside him, clasping his shoulder.

He lifts the bottle and takes a drink. "I was off the clock over an hour ago." He eyes me as I drag a chair from the nearby table and sit directly across from him. Mystic grabs a chair and joins us.

"Not here on official police business?" I raise my brow. Lifting my hand, I signal for Aspen at the bar to bring me a drink.

"I'm here to make sure whatever happened last night isn't an indicator for things to come. I don't want chaos in our town any more than you do," Huxley says. Aspen sets a bottle of bourbon on the table with a tumbler then walks away. Music begins filtering through the speakers, and Ariel, one of our girls, takes the stage, warming up before we open for the evening. The sheriff's eye wanders as he clearly admires the way the dancer's body moves before saying anything.

I pour the whiskey into the glass then rest my back against the chair. "I've told your officer all he needed to know."

The sheriff folds his arms across his chest. Another one of the girls walks by with a duffle bag slung over her shoulder, and Huxley makes eye contact with her.

"Hi Wes." She gives the sheriff a megawatt-smile.

Harlem chuckles, looking at Huxley. "Sunny, huh?"

Huxley cuts his eyes over to Harlem. "There are some things a man keeps to himself: How much money he makes, the women he beds, and his next move." On his last words, the sheriff shifts his attention back to me. "I'm sure we can all agree."

I down another shot of whiskey, enjoying the sting. Huxley looks like Sam Elliot and carries himself with confidence in who he is and what he does. He's the embodiment of walking tall in this town. It helps that he has an understanding of the club and me. We stay out of his affairs, and he stays out of ours. At the end of the day, we're both in the business of cleaning up the streets. I just go about it a different way. "Well said, Huxley." We all sit silently for a beat before I ask, "You happen to hear any chatter about Demon Jokers lately?" Curious to know if he has any knowledge.

Huxley strokes his mustache. "Can't say that I have. It's been a long time since that organization has been mentioned in my presence." He looks around the table at all my men, then back at me. "That question linked to the incident last night?" Huxley pries.

I don't lie. He should have enough information to keep him alerted to the uprising. "Demon Jokers are making a rebirth."

Huxley sucks in a breath then blows it out. "Alright." He pushes away from the table. "I won't take any more of your time." He eyes each of us again. "Whatever you do, keep the trash from stinkin' up my town."

"We don't shit where we eat, Huxley. You keep doin' what you do, my club will do what we do, and we'll both stay out of one another's path." My words carry a sharp edge. Huxley's poker face gives nothing away, and I expect no less from him. Saying nothing, he turns on his heels and casually strolls across the room and out of the club.

"You get in touch with Ghost?" Laredo asks.

"I put the call in, but no response yet. He'll be in touch." I pour another shot of whiskey into my glass.

"Ghost is a different breed of man. He's probably out in the middle of nowhere, hunting down his dinner and cuttin' down trees with an ax," Baja says.

While I'm enjoying the taste of whiskey I just downed, the entrance door to the club slowly opens, and before the person on the other side fully appears, I shout, "We're not open for another hour."

"Uh, Prez." Harlem grabs my attention, and I cut my eyes across the table at my brother. He lifts his chin. "You might wanna take care of that."

I turn my head in the direction he's looking and see my blue-eyed temptress from last night making her way toward the bar. "The fuck?" I push away from the table and shoot out of the chair. My feet move quickly across the floor. I'm furious the woman ignored my warning to stay away. "What the fuck are you doin' here?" I growl once within a few feet of her. Sage's steps falter, but she gives me a glare and keeps moving, not stopping until she's reached her destination.

Ignoring me entirely, she looks and speaks directly to Aspen. "Hi." She smiles. "I left my purse here last night—black leather clutch with a gold chain."

Aspen eyeballs me and reads the energy I'm radiating. "Let me look in the lost and found box at the other end of the bar." Aspen gives Sage a friendly smile. "Be right back."

"We seem to have a lack of understanding." My jaw ticks.

"You made yourself perfectly clear last night..." She turns her head, lifting her eyes to mine. Fuck if her smoldering stare doesn't make me hard all over again. "But I need my belongings, and they just so happen to be here at your lovely establishment," Sage says dryly then turns her body forward-facing, parallel with mine, and I can't help letting my eyes roam her curves. She's wearing a Mötley Crüe band tee that pulls taut across her breasts. My eyes continue downward to her ripped jeans and leopard print boots. I bring my attention back to her flawless, makeup-free face, framed by pieces of purple highlighted hair. She's a goddamn knockout. And she smells so good, like a field of flowers and fresh-baked vanilla cake.

Aspen makes her way back from the other end of the bar,

holding the black bag in question. I intercept the passing over of property before Sage has the chance to snatch it and run. "Excuse me!" She scrunches her face. "That's mine."

Ignoring her, I open the bag, and come across her ID. Sage Briggs from Nebraska. Twenty-five years old. *Fuck, she's only twenty-five.* "Midwestern girl, huh?" Sage quickly snatches the driver's license from my fingers.

"Do you always rummage through things that aren't yours, Mr.... I believe someone mentioned your name last night as Salem," she says with a huff of frustration.

My club name feels all wrong as it passes her lips. "Call me Ash." I hand over her bag. I also ignore the stunned look on Aspen's face when I give Sage my name.

"Ash," Sage murmurs, testing my name on her lips, and I can't deny how much I like hearing it.

I continue. "I make it a point to know everyone in town." Sage eyes me for a second, her lips pursed together.

"Well, now that I have my things, you don't have to worry about seeing me again." She goes to step away, but I reach out, grabbing her hand, stopping her from leaving. A zap of electricity shoots up my arm when I touch her. By the look on Sage's face, she felt it too.

"My warning last night is only about your safety—nothing personal."

Sage pulls her eyes off where my hand is still touching hers and locks eyes with me. "I'd say protecting me against a potential sexual assault and hauling me away from danger like I belonged to you last night, instead of allowing my friend and I to leave like the rest of the club-goers—" Sage takes a controlled breath, composing herself. "I'd say you made it personal." She's calling me out, and I can't deny any of it. "On top of all that, I can't help but worry about backlash. He and his friends didn't seem like the type who let shit go." My hand falls from hers.

I tug her close, making sure she listens to what I'm about to say. Sage tilts her head back to keep her eyes locked with mine. Her pupils dilate, and her breathing changes. I feel my nostrils flare, noticing the hunger reflecting in her eyes. It's taking all my control not to kiss her. "Those assholes have been dealt with." I lift my hand and brush the wisps of hair from her face. "I would never let anything happen to you."

Sage shakes her head. "You don't know me, and I don't know you. We're two strangers who met briefly under awful circumstances, and we owe each other nothing."

Her statement doesn't sit well with me. I find myself wanting to know more about the woman before me. Instead of acting on impulse, I say, "You're right." My tone is flat.

Sage reacts to my cold response by taking a step back, wanting to put space between us, and I give it to her. "I should get going." She clutches her bag to her chest.

"I'll walk you out."

"Don't bother."

I ignore her tone. Once outside, I walk with Sage to her ride, a blue sedan. I open the driver's door, and she sinks onto the seat. "It's for the best, you know; me...you, keeping our distance," Sage says, trying to convince us both.

"What if I told you I want to see you again?" I pose the question the instant it forms in my head, catching us both off guard. I can't take it back now. Sage stares at me, wide-eyed, parting her lips, then pressing them together. *What the fuck is wrong with me? Don't go there. I want her but I'm not good enough for her.* A battle ensues inside my head.

A phone rings, and Sage reaches for her cell, looking at the screen then at me while answering the call. "Hey." She's soft-spoken with the person on the other end of the line. "I'm heading your way now," she says, keeping her blue eyes on me. "Okay, bye." Sage lowers her hand and tosses the phone in the passenger seat. "I got to run."

"I'll see ya around." I close the door to her car, back away from the vehicle, and watch her drive away before heading back inside the club. Several sets of curious eyes follow my movement across the room as I head for the stairs leading up to my office.

"She gettin' under your skin, Prez?" Juneau chuckles as I walk by.

I huff. "She's feisty as hell. That woman is trouble with a capital T."

"The kind of trouble a man falls head over heels for," Baja mutters under his breath.

I keep on walking, taking the steps two at a time. The last thing I need right now is my brothers giving me shit over a woman. Even if the things they say are true.

8
SAGE

It's Sunday, the only day of the week the salon is closed, and also the day I get caught up on my neglected laundry. This is why I'm at the grocery store at seven o'clock in the morning buying laundry detergent. But there is something off with people this morning. The early morning shoppers like myself seem to be in a mood, and the vibe around me is somber and almost suffocating at the same time. Two elderly couples huddle together in a tense conversation over the produce, and there is low chatter amongst the cashiers at the front of the store.

"What's going on?" I ask the woman at the register as I unload my cart.

She looks at me with big eyes. "You didn't hear?"

My brow scrunches, and I shake my head. "Hear what?"

The cashier leans in close over the conveyor belt. "Someone killed Lucy Donaldson," she whispers.

I flinch, taken aback by her statement. "What?"

The woman nods. "It's true. Cory Perkins was out walking his dog in the park last night and found her body."

"Oh my god, that's terrible," I gasp. "I just moved to town a few weeks ago, and I don't know hardly anybody from around here, but..." I let my sentence hang as the terrible news seeps in.

"Oh, well, Lucy was a sweet girl. Her family owns the car dealership over on Sunchase, and she's been working there with her dad and two brothers while taking classes at the community college." She shakes her head. "Her parents must be devastated. Cory Perkins and his wife run the local pharmacy. Such a terrible experience: him having to see something like that."

A moment of silence hangs between us for a minute, and I now understand the somber mood I felt before.

"You're the lady who just opened up that hair salon, aren't you?" she asks. "What's it called?" She looks thoughtful then snaps her fingers. "Dyed 2 Perfection."

"Yes. Me and my best friend, Juniper, own the salon."

The woman gives me a small smile. "I'm Betty."

"Nice to meet you. I'm Sage."

As Betty rings up my purchase, I can't help but think about the young victim of such a senseless tragedy. That poor girl had her whole life ahead of her, and it makes me wonder who could do something like that.

The person who killed her could have just been someone drifting through Salem, but it very well could have been a resident. A chill runs down my spine at the thought of this person living here and walking the streets amongst us.

Movement from the corner of my eye pulls me from my wandering thoughts, and I catch sight of a familiar face walking through the door of the store. Sukie notices me and gives a little wave before her eyes dart around, and she effectively draws back into herself and the huge, oversized coat she has on. I have noticed about Sukie that she goes out of her way to go unnoticed.

"I see you know Sukie," Betty surmises.

"Yeah. Her shop is across the street from my salon. She's

sweet, and her products are some of the best I've ever used," I say, suddenly feeling a bit protective of my new friend.

Betty doesn't miss the bite to my tone and smiles. "Sukie is a sweet girl, and it's such a shame the way folks around here treat her and her momma."

"What do you mean?" I ask.

"Well, I don't know all the ins and outs, just that some years ago when Sukie was still in high school, her momma killed her step-dad. Mom claimed self-defense, but she still ended up getting a ten-year sentence. She got out in six years, though."

"That's terrible," I whisper.

"Sure is. The problem is her momma was married to the sheriff's son. Brock Huxley was following in his daddy's footsteps and a well-respected deputy. The people of Salem liked him and had a lot of respect for him. People around here didn't believe for a second she shot her husband in self-defense. When her momma went to jail, Sukie had to stay with her aunt, but the moment she turned eighteen, she came back to Salem. Now she spends her days running her store and taking care of her momma." Betty pauses what she's doing and looks at me. "You'll probably notice people around her treating her differently. Don't pay no mind to them. You keep on being nice to that sweet girl."

"I will. I'm not one to care what people think."

Returning home, I find Juniper sitting on the sofa with a cup of coffee in hand and her attention on the TV.

The body of nineteen-year-old Lucy Donaldson was discovered in a wooded area near Laurel Park early this morning. Authorities are working diligently to catch the person or persons involved, and there are no eyewitnesses or known suspects. The sheriff is asking if anyone has information, please come forward. The Donaldson family is asking for privacy so that they can mourn the loss of their daughter as they begin preparations for her funeral.

As the reporter speaks, a picture of the young woman is displayed. She was beautiful. In the photo, she has long dark hair, big blue eyes, and a massive smile on her face as she stands in between two boys that look slightly older, and I will assume are her brothers.

"Hey," Juniper says, knocking me out of my fog. "Can you believe this?" She turns back toward the TV.

"I heard about it from the lady down at the grocery store. She said a guy walking his dog found her."

I drop the bags in my hand off on the kitchen island, make myself a coffee, then sit beside Juniper on the sofa.

"Do you think it was someone local?" she asks, and I know she's referring to the killer.

"I don't know." I shiver as the words spill from my mouth.

"God, I hope not," Juniper adds. "We should send her family some flowers or something. I know we didn't know her, and we are new to Salem, but I still feel like we should do something."

"I think flowers would be nice," I agree.

"Your dad is going to flip when he hears the news. I mean, my parents are protective, but your dad..." Juniper doesn't get to finish her statement.

"I'm not telling him," I nearly shout. "He'll insist I come home. Hell, he already calls every day to make sure I have my pepper spray and taser whenever I leave the house. News of this girl will send him over the edge."

"You have to admit this is pretty damn scary, Sage."

"I know, but my dad will only worry, and he doesn't need the added stress. Especially after his heart attack last summer."

One day last summer, I came home from work on my lunch

break because I had spilled coffee all down the front of my blouse. Anyway, when I walked into the house, I found my father lying on the kitchen floor. I didn't know what was wrong with him, so I called 911 then followed the ambulance to the hospital. Turns out he had a heart attack. I also had to call my mom, who was at the school, and tell her what had happened. She was a complete mess by the time she arrived at the emergency room. She told me Dad had said he wasn't feeling too well that morning and would wait to go to the garage that afternoon. Mom beat herself up for weeks for not noticing any signs that he would have a heart attack, even though the doctors assured her there is sometimes no way to know. My dad is the glue that holds the three of us together. I couldn't bear it if something were to happen to him. And news of what happened to this young woman would no doubt send him into a tailspin.

"You're right. But it still feels wrong not to say something. And this means I can't tell my parents because they'd tell yours." Juniper sighs.

"Let's wait a few days at least. Either they'll catch who did this, or it was just some random person passing through town. In the meantime, I say we stick together when we go out," I suggest.

Later that night, I'm just getting off the phone with my parents when Juniper walks out into the living room with her wet hair up in a towel. "I heard something interesting from Betty this morning," I tell her.

Juniper plops down on the opposite end of the couch from me and arches a brow. "Betty?"

"She's the cashier down at the grocery store," I say. Juniper nods, so I continue. "Anyway, Sukie came in while I was there, and Betty went on to tell me some stuff about her, which I kind of think was shitty. If Sukie wanted people to know her business, she would tell them."

"What did this Betty woman tell you?" Juniper asks.

"She said that Sukie's mom killed her step-dad and claimed self-defense, but she still went to prison. She said people around here still don't believe her because her husband was supposedly this great guy everyone loved, and he was also the sheriff's son."

Juniper's eyes go big with this newfound information. "Is her mom still in prison?"

I shake my head. "No, all this happened when Sukie was in high school, and her momma only served six years. Betty said Sukie had to go live with her aunt but came back to Salem when she was eighteen. Now she has her shop and takes care of her mom. Betty also said I should ignore the way people around here treat Sukie. I get the feeling she meant people are assholes toward her."

"Fuck that shit!" Juniper practically yells. "Let me catch someone messing with her."

I smile because this is precisely how I knew Juniper would react. If there's one thing she can't stand, it's a bully.

"It feels wrong that we know such personal information about her, and it came from the lady who works at the grocery store." I pick up the glass of wine sitting on the table in front of me and take a sip.

"We don't have to say anything," Juniper hedges. "She'd probably get upset. I say we keep being her friend, and then one day she might be able to trust us enough to tell us herself."

"I agree. I like Sukie and don't give a shit what people around here have to say."

"I'll drink to that." Juniper holds up her glass.

. . .

It's the middle of the night and I find myself unable to sleep. Juniper crashed hours ago, but I can't stop thinking about two things. One being Salem, and the other being that girl who was killed. My mind briefly wanders to the thought of those bikers doing something. I quickly squash the idea of them being connected, though. Sure, Salem and the other men in his club come off as dangerous, and he's also an asshole, but something tells me they wouldn't harm an innocent young girl. I'd like to say, hanging around my dad, I have become a pretty good judge of character. My dad can size up a man in two seconds and tell you right away if he's someone with good intentions or someone to stay away from. And Salem doesn't give me a bad vibe. The only vibe he gives me has me wanting to punch him in the balls.

Shaking my head, I lean across the bed to turn off the lamp sitting on the nightstand when I hear what sounds like glass shattering. I'm frozen in place for about two seconds, then there is another crash. It sounds like it's coming from outside, and I don't waste any time jumping to my feet and making my way over to the bedroom window. Who the hell would be out there making such noise at one o'clock in the morning?

Peeling back the curtains, I look down at the darkened street. That's when I see two figures standing in front of Sukie's shop. There is glass on the sidewalk and a hole through the front window. I dash out of my bedroom and head straight for the door without thinking. I grab my pepper spray from my purse sitting on the kitchen island on the way out. My anger intensifies with every step my bare feet take on the stairs. How dare these assholes destroy Sukie's shop window like that? When I reach the exit behind my apartment, I take off at a run through the short alley until I come around the corner, ignoring the cold gravel digging into my bare feet or the fact that I'm in my silk pajama shorts and matching cami. The freezing wind blows straight through what little material is covering my body, but I could care less, because I only care about giving those sons of bitches a taste of their own medicine.

The moment I hit the street, one of the guys standing in front of the shop raises his arm. In his hand is what looks like a brick. "Hey, asshole!" I call out.

The second guy sees me, and I watch as his eyes get big. It's also then I realize these are not men but teenagers.

"Fuck, man. We have to get out of here," he tells his accomplice just before taking off. The other shithead, unfortunately, is not as quick as his friend. When he realizes what's happening, I launch myself at him.

"What the fuck." The guy grunts when we land in a heap on the cold concrete.

With his front pressed to the ground, I straddle his back, then proceed to put both hands on the back of his head and smash his face into the ground. "Take that, you little punk," I spit.

"Jesus Christ, lady." The guy starts thrashing around. "Get off me."

"I'm going to kick your ass, then I'm calling the cops."

The second the words are out of my mouth, a powerful arm is wrapped around my waist, and I'm hauled off the kid. Thinking his friend came back and now has me in his clutches, I shove my elbow back into his solid gut, making him grunt, then I throw my head around and connect with his face, this time making the guy curse.

"Fuck."

As soon as the word spills from his mouth, I recognize the voice and stop fighting.

"Don't think about goin' any fuckin' where," Salem grinds out.

"I'm not," I snap back. "That's kind of hard to do with you holding me."

"Not you." His breath fans out across the side of my face, making me shiver.

After a long moment, my feet find the ground when Salem sets me down. Only he keeps his arm wrapped around my chest.

"Stand your ass up." Salem has his hardened gaze on the punk I was wrestling with.

I don't dare look up at him, but from the corner of my eye, I can see he's pissed.

"Look, man, I'm sorry, okay. Please just let me go," the punk kid pleads with Salem and looks seconds away from peeing his pants.

"Shut the fuck up and go sit your ass down on the curb. I'll deal with you in a minute."

Surprisingly the guy does what he's told.

"Now you." Salem drags me across the street back toward my apartment.

"Will you slow down? The gravel is digging into my feet." I try jerking my arm out of his grasp, but at my plea, Salem comes to a complete halt, looks down at my bare feet, then rakes his eyes up and down my body as if he's noticing for the first time what I'm wearing, or should I say the lack thereof. He then proceeds to shuck off his own jacket and wrap it around my shoulders. The leather is warm and heavy, and I can smell a hint of his cologne mixed with something that smells an awful lot like weed.

Once he has me wrapped in his jacket, he startles me by picking me up and carrying me bridal style.

"I can freaking walk. I only said for you to slow down." I try to wiggle out of his arms, which only makes him squeeze me tighter.

"Stop," he growls.

"God, you're such a jerk."

"If you weren't runnin' around actin' reckless all the Goddamn time, we wouldn't be in this fuckin' situation."

Finally, we reach the back entry that leads up to my apartment, and Salem sets me down.

"Well, if you'd mind your own damn business..." I say, but

snap my mouth shut when Salem's body invades my space, and he brings his face an inch from mine.

"Salem is my town. And when naive young women put their noses where they don't belong, it becomes my business."

I narrow my eyes and go to open my mouth, but before I can, Salem cuts me off again.

"Zip it."

I let out an annoyed huff and cross my arms over my chest but keep my mouth closed.

"Have you any idea the kind of danger you put yourself in tonight?"

"I'm not about to stand by and watch some punk kids destroy Sukie's shop like that. And I don't care whose town this is; I'd do it again. Those little assholes don't deserve to get away with what they did. Other people in your town might be okay with the way Sukie is treated, but she's my friend, and I'm not okay with it." I make sure to emphasize the way I said your town.

"What you did was stupid and reckless, babe."

"I can take care of myself." I put my hands on my hips. "And don't call me babe."

"Yeah? What if those two hadn't been punk kids? What if they were two grown-ass men? What if one of them had a gun or a knife? Then what?"

Salem steps even closer and grabs the back of my head in a firm grip, forcing me to keep my eyes on his. "What if one of them decided to cut you up like that girl they found and then dump your body in the woods somewhere on the side of the road?"

My breath hitches as he spews his harsh words, and the dinner I ate a few hours ago, churns in my stomach.

"Or have you carelessly forgotten there is a man out there killin' pretty little things like you?"

"Stop," I whisper as tears start to pool in my eyes. Salem is right. What I did was stupid. But that doesn't give him the right to talk to me like he is.

I don't know if it's the way my body is trembling or the hurt in my voice, but there's a flash of something in Salem's eyes before he releases his hold on me. And the second his hand is gone, I turn and dash up the metal stairs that lead to my apartment.

9
SALEM

What the fuck was Sage thinking? The woman's lack of personal safety is infuriating. And that sassy mouth of hers...I'd like to fill that sweet mouth full of my cock is what I'd like to do. *Dammit, Ash, stop thinking with your dick right now.* She has me so fucking distracted. I continue keeping my eyes trained on Sage's backside as she's dashing up the stairs, still wearing my jacket. She enters her apartment above the salon then slams the door closed.

I turn my attention back to the dipshit kid sitting on the curb a few feet away and reach down, grabbing the punk by the collar of his flannel shirt. Now, paying closer attention to his face, I recognize him. "On your feet." Anger rolls off me in waves.

"Hey, don't fucking manhandle me, man."

"Your fuckin' balls haven't dropped enough to give me attitude. You'd better watch your mouth." My jaw ticks.

"Shit." He throws his hands up in defense. "I'm sorry, man. I swear. We were only havin' a little fun." Lucas rushes every word. "Don't kill me, bro."

My grip tightens on his collar, and I bring my face close to his. "First, I'm not your bro." I lift him higher, bringing the punk onto the tips of his toes. "Second, I'm not the one you owe an apology to."

I notice the police cruiser turn the corner near the end of the street before the red and blue lights flash and a short yelp of the siren sounds. The car rolls to a stop, and an officer steps out. "Salem."

I recognize the voice. "Officer Miller." For a cop, he's not a bad guy. His wife also works for me, waitressing at the club. Not your typical job for a cop's wife, but it works for them.

"Shit, dude. I don't want to go to jail." The kid struggles against my hold.

Miller looks between the kid and me, then at the shattered storefront window. "Is there a problem?" His eyes land back on the kid. "Lucas Cromwell," Miller sighs, then crosses his large arms across his chest. He glances around. "Where there's one, you'll find the other." Miller looks back at the kid. "Where's your, buddy, Ian?" The young man's lips tighten, but he doesn't speak. "What did the delinquents do?" Miller asks.

"They did some damage across the street at Belladonna's." I keep a tight grip on the shithead's shirt.

Miller looks at the kid. "This true?" Again, Lucas remains silent. "That's twice this week you and Ian caused trouble." Miller reaches out, grabbing Lucas by the arm, and I release my hold on him. "Let's take a ride to the station and call your parents."

Lucas turns ghost white, and I recognize the fear in his eyes. The kid is no older than sixteen and roams Salem's streets, causing trouble. There's more to his story. More going on behind closed doors at home. I'd bet money the scared look he's wearing has something to do with it. I know because I've been in his shoes. "Hold up," I interject. "I have a better idea."

"Salem, the kid just vandalized private property. I can't let that slide," Miller says.

"I won't let it slide, either." I widen my stance and cross my arms over my chest, staring down at the young man. "Give his ass to me for a few days." Lucas's eyes widen more than they already are. "I want his accomplice, too."

"For what purpose?" Miller eyes me with curious apprehension.

"I'll put their asses to work fixing the shit they vandalized tonight. And I'm sure I can find other jobs to work off some of the excess energy they've been utilizing to get in trouble," I explain and wait for Miller's reply.

Lucas looks at Miller, then at me, and he swallows hard. "Does my dad need to know?"

I take my eyes off the kid and jerk my head at Miller, motioning him to step away for a moment. Miller lets loose the kid's arm. "Don't get no hair up your ass and make me chase you," he warns Lucas, and the young man lowers himself to sit on the curb again. He places his elbows on his knee and hangs his head between his legs.

"What's his story?" I mutter.

Miller shifts on his feet and rests his hand on his utility belt. "Kid's dad is a piece of shit. He's been arrested multiple times on domestic violence charges, along with a few DUIs." My eyes stay on the kid, and I feel like I'm staring at myself. "Look, man. I get what you're hoping to achieve. I'd like nothing more than to see the kid break the cycle, also. But do you think your club getting involved is a good idea?"

"The kid needs direction, and you and I both know he won't find that at home or juvie." A beat of silence hangs.

"Alright. But if the store owner decides to press charges, what happens afterward is out of my hands," Miller says.

I step over to where Lucas is sitting. "On your feet." My tone is harsh. The kid stands and glances between Miller and me. "Your ass belongs to me." I level him with a hard stare.

Lucas swallows hard, nodding. "What about my parents?"

"No parents will be called," I say, and Lucas breathes a sigh of relief. "You know where the club's tattoo shop is down the street?" I ask him.

"Yeah."

"You are to report there at 11:00 am. Tell that buddy of yours if his ass doesn't show up too, one of my men will go lookin' for him." Lucas again nods. "I know that mouth of your works. Use your words, kid. I need to hear you understand what you're signing up for."

Lucas straightens his back, wipes his palm down the front of his ripped jeans, then holds out his hand. "I understand."

"Good." I shake his hand.

Lucas turns to Miller. "Could you drop me off near my house?"

"Sure, kid," Miller says. He gives me one last look, nods, then walks away. Lucas follows Miller, looking over his shoulder at me before ducking into the backseat of the patrol car.

I'm not a good role model for the kid—far from it. But sometimes, all you need is for one person to give a damn, to be given a chance to do better—be better. I'm no one's savior. What I'm doing for the kid I don't consider a deed that will wash away my sins. I'm allowing him to repent and maybe see there's more to his life. He doesn't have to accept the hell he's living in now.

Once Miller drives away, I glance up at Sage's apartment. Movement from a low-lit window catches my attention, and I recognize the silhouette backing away. A second later, the light in the room goes out, and Sage is watching me—again. My lip twitches as my thoughts drift to a few nights ago at the club. Then, just as quickly, I shake off the hold Sage has on me, remembering the unshed tears in her eyes tonight and the fact my harsh words put them there. I march across the street. Needing to lay eyes on her once more, I dash up the stairs. When I bang my knuckles against the door, it opens, and Sage stands doe-eyed in front of me, still wearing her barely-there pajamas.

"What do you want?" Sage whispers harshly.

You, I don't say, my eyes roaming over her curves. "You, okay?"

She huffs, steps outside, and closes the door. "You—the guy who criticized my lack of judgment for my own safety and made me feel like shit—want to know if I'm okay?" Sage folds her arms beneath her breasts. Fuck, her tits are perfect.

"Babe."

"Don't call me babe."

"I won't apologize for what I said. You inserted yourself into a situation that could have been dangerous," I say, and Sage turns her face away from me. Reaching out, I palm her cheek and bring her eyes back to mine. "But I am sorry my harsh words hurt your feelings." Sage leaves silence hanging between us until I break it. "Now, are you okay? You didn't hurt yourself tacklin' that kid, did you?"

"No, just a little scratch on my thigh from hitting the pavement." I watch a little fight leave Sage's body and the tension in her shoulders relax.

"What about Sukie's? I still need to call the police."

"I took care of it."

"How?" Sage asks.

"Don't worry about it."

She rolls her eyes. "The little shit deserved an ass-beating, you know. I would have given it to him, too, if you hadn't felt the need to take control. Believe it or not, I can take care of myself."

I smirk. She just can't help herself. I fight the urge to silence her with a kiss. Instead, I start to squat. "What are you doing?"

"Seein' how bad the scratch on your thigh is." I lower myself until I'm level with the lower half of her body. The scrape on her leg looks minor.

"Salem, I'm fine." She goes to move away, but her back hits the apartment door. I lean forward, press my lips against the abrasion, and feel her skin prickle. I'm so close to her pussy, I smell her arousal, and a hungry growl forms deep in my chest. "Ash. I want you to call me Ash."

"Ash." She repeats my name, and it's like an electric current straight to my cock.

I rise. Now we're face to face, breathing the same breath. "You want something?"

"Yes—I mean no." She shakes her head.

"I won't touch you unless you ask me to," I say, but won't deny how bad I want to explore every inch of her skin.

"Why are you here, Ash?" She tries disguising her desire with sass.

"Because of you," I shamelessly admit. I move in closer, pressing my palms against the door, caging her in. "Now ask me."

Sage remains quiet but I see the fight in her eyes slipping.

I run my nose along her jawline and growl, "Say it."

Finally, she gives in.

"Touch me, Ash."

The moment the words pass her lips, I drop one hand. "You're so fuckin' intoxicating." I caress her breast, dragging the pad of my thumb across her taut nipple covered by the satin camisole top she's wearing. Dipping my head, I kiss the side of her neck, and her hands find their way beneath the front of my shirt. She drags her nails across my torso.

"Ash, someone might see us," Sage whispers.

"You like that, don't you, babe?" My hand trails down her waist, slipping past the elastic waistline of her satin shorts. My dick hardens beyond comprehension at the feel of her arousal coating my fingertips. I rub circles around her clit. Sage softly moans as I work her bundle of nerves.

"Oh my god!" Sage buries her face in my neck to drown out her cries when I sink two fingers into her tightness. Her pussy clamps down around my finger. Hearing her moans of pleasure is almost my undoing, but I fight the need to fuck her. At least for now. This moment is all about her.

"Ash," Sage's fingernails dig into my side, and I know she's about to come.

"Let go," I command before covering her mouth with mine, swallowing her scream as her orgasm rips through her. I hold her body against mine until she's no longer trembling, then slip my hand out of her shorts.

"Here." Her hands fall to the button of my jeans. "Let me..."

"No." I stop her.

"But..." Sage's face falls, and she looks away. "Oh..." The euphoria she once had evaporates, and rejection takes its place.

"Look at me," I demand. Sage hesitates for a moment but finally cuts her eyes at me. "I want nothing more than to have your lips wrapped around my dick, babe. Trust me. I've been plagued with thoughts of having that sassy mouth of yours full of my cock. But not tonight. When I have you, all of you, it will be in my bed." Needing to taste her lips once more, I kiss her again. She tastes like salvation—my undoing. A cold wind swirls around us, and Sage shivers. "Get back inside."

"Ash." Sage chews her bottom lip, and I wait for her to say whatever's on her mind. Silence hangs between us.

I run my finger along her jawline. "Inside." Backing away, I wait for her to step inside her apartment, then close and lock the door, before descending the stairs and heading toward my bike.

I glance over my shoulder at Sage's apartment before driving away. "I'm screwed."

I drag ass into the tattoo shop, heading straight toward the back to where the coffee is located. "Thank fuck." I notice the pot is full and grab a mug, proceeding to fill it. I'm operating on two hours of sleep. I bring the cup to my lips and down my first dose of giving a fuck for the day. Instead of heading home hours ago, I rode out to the clubhouse after my encounter with Sage, and I needed to clear my mind. Wanting Sage is fucking with my head, but after making her come with my name on her lips, I can no longer fight the need to ride out whatever it is we're dancing around.

"Prez." Harlem strolls out of the supply room nearby. "What brings you?" He sets up his workstation.

I stride across the room, taking a seat on the leather sofa. "Got some business to handle." Before Harlem can question me further, there are three thuds against the shop's storefront window. He sets the ink bottles in his hands down and heads for the door. I lean back and chug more coffee down my throat.

Harlem opens the door. "We're not open, and anyone under eighteen needs guardian consent before ink hits the skin."

I eye Lucas and the young man standing beside him over the rim of my mug. His eyes dart from me back to Harlem, looming over them. "We were told to be here by 11:00 am."

"Let them in, brother," I say, resting the mug on my thigh. The two kids walk past Harlem with their hands shoved into their front pockets. "Lucas." I level him with a stern look, then give his buddy my attention. "What's your name, kid?"

His friend, with black shoulder-length hair and grunge style, glances at Harlem as he walks by. "Ian."

Harlem stops beside me. "What's with the kids?"

I look at the young men. "These two dipshits decided to bust out the window at Belladonna's, down the street."

"Sukie's place?" Harlem's face hardens.

"That's the one," I confirm. "These two are gonna repent by cleaning up the place, repairing what they can, and above all, apologizing to the store owner for their brainless actions."

"Would have gotten away with it too if Lucas wouldn't have gotten tackled by a half-dressed woman." Ian nudges his friend, holds his hands out over his chest like he's holding melons, and adds. "She had some big ole titties, though."

I slam my mug on the coffee table and fly off the couch and in his face before he draws another breath. "I'll wash the disrespect from your mouth if you speak of her that way again." My nostrils flare with anger. "You got me?"

Ian gulps. "Yes, sir." He shrinks to half his size.

"Good," I say, then look back at Harlem. "I'll catch up with you later."

"You know where to find me," Harlem says, then gets back to work.

I face the young men. "Let's go."

After a trip to the hardware store, Ian and Lucas walk down the sidewalk in front of me with a buttload of supplies. Approaching Belladonna's, we happen upon Sukie. With a broom and pan in her hand, she's sweeping broken glass off the concrete in front of her store. Then, Sage appears, walking out of the salon across the street.

"Ladies," I greet in what I thought was a friendly tone but I startle them anyway. Sukie stares at me, unmoving, with shell-shocked eyes. Sage, on the other hand, instantly blushes at the sight of me.

"What are you doing here?" Sage asks, sounding a bit frazzled, and I like it.

I smirk. "How's it goin'', babe. You look...refreshed." I watch Sage's pupils dilate and want nothing more than to relive the moment she came on my fingers.

"Come on, man, this shit is heavy," Ian complains.

Lucas throws a cutthroat stare in his friend's direction. "Shut up, Ian."

Sage looks between the two young men, noticing all the

supplies they hold, then focuses on me. "What's going on?" She sidesteps, bringing herself closer to Sukie.

I take a step toward Sukie. "Sukie."

Sukie looks to Sage, then up at me. Her forehead creases. "You know my name?"

I grin. "Yes." I hook my thumb over my shoulder. "These young men are here to clean up this mess."

Sukie tilts her head, looking around my body at Lucas and Ian. She then looks up at me. "Why?" she asks, soft-spoken.

"Because they caused it." I step to the side and usher the two culprits forward. Sukie looks at both kids quickly but struggles to maintain eye contact with anyone. She is nervous, and I'm positive that my being here is the cause of her anxiety right now. "Ian and Lucas here have something to say."

Lucas lifts his head, looking directly at Sukie. "I apologize for vandalizing your store."

Then Ian speaks. "Yeah, umm, like he said. Sorry for breaking your shit." His words hold no sincerity.

My jaw ticks, and by the look on Sage's face, she is holding back some choice words of her own. Sukie, on the other hand, shrugs. "It's no big deal."

"The hell it isn't," my voice booms, making Sukie jump. "Shit. I Didn't mean to scare ya, sweetheart." I take a breath then say, "No one has the right to trash someone else's property, and you sure as shit don't have to accept it, either. Don't allow anyone to walk all over you." Sukie stares at her feet for several seconds, then looks back at me. Her shoulders rise and fall with the deep breath she takes. I reach out and take the broomstick and dustpan from her hands. "Go. I promise they'll have this mess cleaned up soon."

Sage finally tears her eyes away from me long enough to turn to Sukie. "Want to have breakfast with me and Juniper at Supernatural Confections? My treat. They have a black cherry chocolate croissant I've been dying to try, and their coffee is amazing."

"Sure, I'll grab my things," Sukie agrees, then walks into her store.

I snap my fingers at the young men. "Move ass, and get this shit cleaned up."

Sage smiles. "It's nice what you're doing for Sukie. She deserves more than most people in this town are willing to give her." She moves closer to me, and on instinct, I place my hand on her hip, pulling her the rest of the way until her body is flush with mine. Sage glances around. "People will see."

"Let them." I dip my head and breathe her in.

"I don't want anyone getting the wrong impression."

"And what impression would that be, babe?"

Sage sighs. "That there's something between us."

"Fuck what others think." I bring my other hand up, brushing her hair back behind her ear.

"Ash."

"Shut up." My mouth crashes against hers in a brutally honest, *I've got to have you* kiss, leaving no room for misunderstanding.

10
SAGE

"Do you want to go out for lunch today?" I plop down in the chair and spin, facing Juniper. "Our next two appointments aren't until two o'clock. I've wanted to try that place a block over on Whitaker Street, and I heard they have the best lobster rolls."

"I'm down." Juniper jumps up from her chair. "Hey, why don't we go across the street and see if Sukie wants to go with us?"

I smile. "Great idea. And we can walk since it's not that far."

"How has Sukie been holding up since her place was vandalized?" Juniper asks, sliding on her coat.

"She seemed okay when I talked to her yesterday, just a little beaten down. She said stuff like that has happened before. I think she's become immune to the way people treat her, and it pisses me off. Nobody should be immune to being treated like shit and having their place of business vandalized."

When Juniper and I walk across the street to Sukie's place, we see the closed sign on the door, but we saw her go in this morning.

"You think she went home?" Juniper asks.

"I don't know." I bring my hands up, look through the glass on the door, and then knock. A few seconds later, I see Sukie walking up from the back of the store. Her steps falter, but then she smiles and makes her way toward us.

"Hey." Sukie smiles, opening the door. "Is everything okay?"

"Of course," Juniper answers.

"Yeah, we came by to see if you wanted to go to lunch with us?" I add.

Sukie's eyes flick back and forth between Juniper and me. "You...you want me to go to lunch with you?"

Juniper and I nod. "Are you okay with walking? We're going to that place on Whitaker with the delicious lobster rolls." I smile.

"Monty's?" Sukie asks.

"That's the one," Juniper chirps. "So, what do you say?"

Sukie fidgets with the hem of her sweater. "I...I guess I could go."

"Great!" Juniper's high-pitched voice makes Sukie jump, and I can't help giggling.

"Let me grab my coat." Sukie turns back toward the coat rack just inside the door and slips on her scarf, hat, and wool jacket.

On the walk to the restaurant, Juniper and I keep the conversation light, and neither of us brings up the incident from the other night.

"Are either of you going to ask?" Sukie's question comes out of nowhere a few minutes after we arrive at Monty's and are seated in a booth.

Juniper and I glance at each other. Sukie, however, is staring a hole through the menu lying on the table in front of her.

I soften my voice. "Sukie?"

"Did you all ask me to lunch so you can find out if the rumors are true or because you feel sorry for me?"

"No, we asked you to lunch because you're our friend. At least I hope you are."

Sukie's head pops up at my statement, and she opens and closes her mouth.

Reaching across the table, I take her hand. "Juniper and I don't give a shit what the people in this town have to say. We like you, Sukie, and there is no ulterior motive for inviting you to lunch other than we want to get to know our new friend a little better."

"But people will talk," Sukie says, her voice barely above a whisper.

"Yeah," Juniper cuts in. "And those people can suck my asshole."

At my best friend's comment, Sukie lets out a full-blown laugh. It's the first time I've heard her laugh, and I decide making Sukie laugh more will now be one of my life's missions. And as she wipes the tears from her eyes, I reach under the table beside me and squeeze Juniper's leg, giving her a silent thank you. But that's my friend for you. She has a gift for drawing people out of their shells and making them feel special.

"Now." Juniper picks her menu up. "Let's order."

The following day, I'm sitting on the sofa with a cup of coffee and my laptop, scouring social media and updating the salon's website with pictures Juniper and I took this week of some of our client's hair we'd done, when there's a knock at the door. Looking at the time, I wonder who could be at my door at ten o'clock in the morning on a Sunday. Setting my mug down on the coffee table and sliding the laptop over to the cushion beside me, I hop off the sofa and pad across the small living room to the door. When I swing it open and see who is standing there, I let out a loud shriek. "Daddy!" I throw myself in my dad's open arms.

"Shortcake." My dad picks me up and wraps me in a bear hug.

"Charles, put Sage down." My mom swats his arm and squeezes her way into our huddle.

"Hi, Mom."

"Hi, sweetheart. Give me a hug."

Dad finally lets go, and I'm pulled into my mom's embrace, where I take in the familiar scent of her perfume. When she releases me, I turn back to my dad. "How come you didn't tell me you were coming?"

"Your father wanted it to be a surprise."

"What's going on?" Juniper emerges from her bedroom, rubbing her sleep-filled eyes.

"Juju!" My dad booms.

Juniper drops her hand and blinks a few times. When she realizes what's going on, her face breaks out with a huge smile. "Mr. Briggs."

My dad wastes no time rewarding my best friend with one of his bear hugs.

"Where is your luggage?" I ask. "You guys are staying here, right?"

"It's down in the car," Mom tells me. "We weren't sure if you two had room. We can always stay at a hotel."

"No! You have to stay here. I can bunk with Juniper so you and Dad can take my room." I look at my friend. "You cool with that?"

Juniper is already nodding. "Cool with me."

"It's settled then." Dad claps his hands. "I'll go down to the car and get our bags."

"And I need the little girl's room," Mom says.

"Mom, Juniper will show you to the bathroom and to where you and Dad are sleeping. Dad, I'll come down and help with the bags."

"Thanks, Shortcake." Dad puts his arm around my shoulder and kisses the top of my head.

Mom goes to follow Juniper down the hall but stops and turns back. "Sage, be a doll and bring my makeup carrier to me when you get back. I'd like to freshen up."

"Will, do." I smile then turn back to my dad. "Come on," I say, feeling even giddier than I did five minutes ago.

"So, tell me, baby girl, how have you been?"

I set the suitcase I just pulled from the trunk of the car and set it down on the sidewalk beside me, then turn to my father. "I've been terrific, Dad," I say with honesty.

"You look it." He pulls me into his side, and I wrap my arms around his waist.

"I'm so happy you and Mom are here. I've missed you." I pull back and grin up at his handsome face. My dad is over six feet tall, has brown hair with a dusting of gray, and has blue eyes. He's always reminded me of Kevin Costner in the looks department. My mom even said that's why she said yes to their first date.

When Dad and I make it back up to the apartment, we find my mother has commandeered the kitchen, and the smell of bacon assaults my senses.

"Mom, what are you doing? You're a guest. Guests don't cook breakfast."

"I tried to tell her," Juniper says around a mouth full of bacon.

"Not so fast." Mom reaches across the kitchen island and smacks the crispy goodness from Dad's fingers when he goes to sneak a piece of bacon from the plate.

"Hey," he grumbles.

"Here." Mom sets down a bowl of oatmeal in front of him. "You know you can't have bacon, and that's for Sage and Juniper."

"But—" Dad protests.

"No buts. We had a deal. If you stick to your diet like the doctor said, then you get one cheat meal and some lite beer while we're here." After chastising my dad, my mom turns her attention to me. "Which reminds me, we need to go to the store. Your father wants to make you your favorite for dinner tonight."

"Really?" I clap my hands. And just like that, I turn into a kid again.

"You got it, Shortcake. Smothered chicken-fried steak and cheesy mashed potatoes."

"You're the best, Daddy." I kiss his cheek.

Later that afternoon, after showing my parents around the salon and taking them around Salem then stopping at the store to get the fixings for dinner, we wind up at Graves Wine & Spirits for some wine and Dad's lite beer. Although my dad seems to think he can slip a fast one on Mom by getting regular beer while Mom and Juniper wait in the car.

"Come on, Shortcake."

"Daddy, no. Put that back. We're getting the lite beer."

"Mom doesn't have to know." Dad holds onto the six-pack for dear life.

"This is Mom we're talking about. She knows everything. You have no chance of slipping by her." I grab the six-pack and wrench it from my father's grip. "Now give it here."

"Traitor," he grumbles like a two-year-old.

Suddenly, a throat clears from behind me, and when I turn around, I nearly drop the beer in my hands because standing there with a smirk on his face is Salem.

"Um...ahh...hi," I stammer, looking like an idiot. Although who would blame me. I haven't seen Salem in a couple of days, and the last time I saw him, he had his hand down my pants. And with just the thought of what he did to me, I can feel my face flush and the space between my legs tingle.

"You okay there, Shortcake?" my dad asks. "You're breathing funny, and you look a little red." He places his palm on my forehead. "Maybe you're getting sick. We should get you to a doctor."

Jesus Christ, this is not the time for my father to go all protective and start treating me like a baby. He's always done that when I get sick.

"No, Dad, I'm okay."

He doesn't look convinced. "You sure?"

"Yes, Dad," I hiss. I don't miss the chuckle coming from Salem.

Now the three of us just stand there in awkward silence. Well, I look uncomfortable, Dad looks curious, and Salem seems amused.

"You want to introduce me to your friend, Shortcake?"

I'm screaming no inside my head but reluctantly introduce Salem to my dad. "Dad, this is Salem. Salem, this is my father, Charles Briggs."

Salem and my dad shake hands.

"Your name is Salem? Like the town?" Dad asks.

"Nice to meet ya, sir. And Salem is my club name, but you can call me Ash."

Thankfully Dad doesn't question what Salem means by the club. At least not now. I'm sure he will grill me later.

"So, how do you two know each other?" This is my dad's second question.

"Uh...you know, just from around town," I answer. "I wouldn't exactly say we 'know' know each other."

"I don't know, babe." Salem runs his tongue along his bottom lip. "I'd say I know you pretty well."

Bastard.

"Well, it was good to see you." I grit my teeth, giving Salem the stink eye, which I know he finds even more amusing. Then I turn to my dad. "We should get going, and I'm sure Mom is wondering what's taking so long."

"You're probably right, sweetheart." Dad turns his attention back to Salem. "Say, since you are a friend of Sage's, why don't you come to dinner? I'm making my Shortcake's favorite chicken fried steak."

"Dad, no. I'm sure Salem is busy." I turn to Salem. "Right?"

Please say you're busy. Please say you're busy.

"I'm not about to turn down a homemade dinner, Mr. Briggs."

"Great. And please, call me Charles. How does six o'clock sound?"

Salem and my dad shake hands one last time. "I'll be there." Salem says the words to my dad but winks at me. Bastard. And why the hell is this asshole being so playful? Something tells me the man doesn't have a playful bone in his body. All he's ever been is a jerk except when he had his hand down my pants. But even that wasn't playful; it was more demanding.

I was right about my mom. As soon as we climb back in the car, she starts firing off questions.

"What took so long? And you better not have gotten anything you weren't supposed to, Charles."

"Jesus, woman. Stop hounding me," Dad grumps.

"Somebody has to hound you, or you'd end up in an early grave." Dad rolls his eyes at my mom's snippy retorts, though I see the smile he's trying to hide. My dad secretly likes my mother's sass, and it's why I firmly believe he purposely eggs her on. Men are so strange.

"We ran into one of Sage's friends," he informs Mom, effectively changing the subject.

Mom twists around in her seat. "Oh, really. What friend?"

"It was a man. I think he fancies my Shortcake."

"A man?" My mom gets excited.

"Yep. I invited him to dinner. His name is Ash."

"Wonderful." Mom claps her hands. "Let's stop back by the store. With Sage's man friend coming to dinner, I want to make something special for dessert."

"I know, sweetheart." Dad snaps his fingers. "You can make that chocolate mousse cake of yours."

"Perfect, Charles. I'm sure this Ash fellow will love it."

I groan from the back seat. This can't be happening. "Dad, he doesn't 'fancy' me. And can you please not say it like that anymore? As a matter of fact, can we not say he's my man friend, either." I screw my face up. "We're not really even friends. I don't know why you invited him."

"Whatever you say, sweetheart." Dad grins at me through the rear-view mirror. "Oh, look, there he is now." He points as Salem comes waltzing out of the store with only the kind of swagger and confidence a man like him could have. And I swear to Christ I just heard my mother whimper from the front seat.

"Oh my," she gushes. "He's a handsome one, Sage."

As if my luck couldn't get any worse, Salem looks this way. My dad waves at him like a loon while my mom clutches her imaginary pearls like some awe-struck schoolgirl. When Salem's gaze zeros in on me through the window, he tosses me a wink just before straddling his bike. "Kill me now," I mutter, making Juniper giggle.

At six o'clock sharp, there's a pounding on my door, shattering my hopes that today's earlier events were just a dream and Salem is not the man standing behind my front door.

"Shortcake, are you going to answer the door?" Dad eyes me from the kitchen, where he's finishing up the potatoes. "It's rude to keep our guest waiting like that."

"He's technically your guest, Dad, since you're the one who invited him."

"Yeah, but you're the reason he said yes," Dad counters.

"He said yes because food and beer are involved, and he's a typical man thinking with his stomach." I roll my eyes.

"That's not all he's thinking with," Juniper says low enough that only I can hear.

I give my best friend a look that I hope conveys my thoughts. And those thoughts are *payback is a bitch.*

"Shortcake, the door," Dad reminds me.

"I'm going, I'm going," I grumble, hopping down from the stool where I've been perched for the last hour while watching my dad cook.

And my best friend is no help. She just smirks and sips on her glass of wine. "Yeah, Sage, don't keep your guest waiting."

"Bitch," I mouth to her, making her snort into her glass of wine.

11
SALEM

Holding a paper bag with one hand, I knocked again on the door with the other. When it opens, a frazzled-looking Sage stands before me. She stares me down, then her eyes rake over my body, lingering on my jean-covered cock.

I clear my throat. "My eyes are up here, babe."

Sage rolls her eyes. "Ash, look, please don't lead my parents on with the illusion there's anything between us."

I step into her space. The air between us is electrifying. "That's not what your body was saying the other night."

"That was a one-time thing—a simple lapse of judgment."

"You gonna lie and say you don't feel this energy between us?"

Sage rolls her eyes. "It's called exasperation. You know, a feeling of intense irritation or annoyance?"

Always busting my balls. I reach out, brushing her long hair away from her face. "I like your spirit, babe. You're sexy when you get all fired up." I want badly to mark her with a kiss, but for now decide against it. "You gonna invite me in?"

Sage raises her brow. "Can I trust you?"

Why does that question feel like a knife to the chest? "I'll be on my best behavior." I make a cross over my heart. "Cross my heart." Sage steps aside to let me in.

"Ash." Sage's dad, Charles, approaches. "Good to see you again." He extends his hand, and I shake it.

"Likewise." I lift the bag I'm holding. "I brought wine and a bottle of scotch."

"You don't say?" Charles' face lights up. He takes the bag from my hand and walks toward the kitchen.

"Dad, you can't have that." Sage is on her dad's heels following him.

"Shortcake, our guest was thoughtful enough in contributing to tonight's delightful consumption. It would be rude not to partake in at least one small glass of this fine scotch." Charles pulls the bottle from the brown bag. "Good choice, son." He looks at me, grinning.

Sage glares at me then looks away. "Mom, a little help here."

A beautiful older woman appears from behind the opened refrigerator door. She and Sage share the same features. "Well, I suppose a small drink with your handsome friend won't hurt." She walks toward me. "You must be Ash." She smiles.

"Yes, Ma'am." I smile back.

She brings her hand to her chest. "A looker, and he has manners."

"Jesus, Mom." Sage palms her face, then says. "Salem—I mean, Ash, this is my mom, Mary."

I throw another smile at Sage's mom. "Nice to meet you, Mary. Or do you prefer Mrs. Briggs?"

Mary blushes, and I catch Sage rolling her eyes. "Mary is fine, hun." She leans into her daughter and whispers, but not too well, "That smile of his is a panty-dropper."

Sage develops a look of horror and cuts her eyes my way. I flash her the smile mentioned. "Kill me now," Sage groans, and I chuckle.

"I hope everyone is hungry. Dinner will be ready in ten more minutes," Mary says.

Charles, with the scotch in his grasp, looks at me. "We'll save this for after dinner. For now, how does a cold beer sound?"

"Perfect."

The tall blonde I always see with Sage sits at the small kitchen island with a glass of wine in her hand. "I'm Juniper, by the way." She places her drink on the counter, stands, retrieves a wine glass from the cabinet behind her, then returns. "The best friend, ball buster, and the woman who will turn you from a rooster to a hen if you hurt her friend." She smiles and proceeds to pull the bottle of white wine from the same bag the scotch was in while glaring hard at me.

I salute Juniper. "Message received."

"Juju." Sage sighs, cutting her eyes at her friend.

"What?" Juniper feigns innocence. "Just doing my job, now. Get over here and drink with me."

It's not long before the five of us are crammed in close around the small dining table. I'm seated beside Sage, whose sweet floral scent invades my senses. "I hope you're hungry," Mary says as she passes a large bowl of buttery mashed potatoes to Sage, who scoops a serving onto her plate then gives it to me. I make it a point to look into Sage's eyes when saying, "Starving." My words carry another meaning, and she gets the message, judging by how her pupils dilate.

"So, Ash." Charles takes a drink from the beer bottle in his hand then sets it down on the table. "If you don't mind, I'd like to get to know you a little better." He goes to pour a heavy amount of gravy on his plate, and Mary casually reaches over and prevents her husband from drowning the mountain of potatoes.

"Moderation, my love," Mary says softly, with a smile.

Charles sighs. "You're starving me, woman."

"Your health is more important than gravy," Mary states.

The way Sage's parents interact with one another is normal. Something I never knew growing up. Love in my childhood home looked vastly different than the picture painted here this evening.

"What would you like to know?" I stare down at the food-filled plate before me and begin digging in.

"How old are you?"

"Dad!" Sage cuts in.

I chuckle. "It's okay, babe." Then I look at Charles. "I'm forty."

Sage snaps her head back in shock. "Really? You don't look it."

"Appreciate that, baby." I wink.

Sage rolls her eyes as her father continues his interrogation. "How'd you meet my Shortcake?" Charles shoves a forkful of chicken fried steak into his mouth, his eyes on me, waiting for a reply. Beside me, Sage coughs. She sits her glass of wine down and side-eyes me.

"At my club." I wash my bite of food down with a swallow of beer.

"Your club?" Mary looks from me to Sage.

"Ash owns the club," Sage rushes.

"A business owner. Nice." Charles wipes his face with a napkin. "What kind of establishment, might I ask?"

"Strip joint," I answer while Sage responds with, "Nightclub."

Charles chuckles. "Well, which one is it?" He looks at his daughter with a grin.

I carefully gauge both her parent's faces, then tell them the truth. I have nothing to hide. "Technically, both."

Charles nods. "Interesting."

Mary looks at me, and her eyes are kind and non-judgmental. "Your vest there. Fallen Ravens MC. That's a motorcycle club, right?"

"Mom," Sage cuts in, sounding a tad nervous.

I reach down, place my hand on Sage's thigh, giving it a slight squeeze, and look at her. I've been waiting for this question since the moment I walked through the front door. "Babe, it's fine," I assure her. I then give my attention to Mary. "You are correct. Fallen Ravens MC is my club." I point to my name and rank on the front of the cut. "My road name is Salem, and I'm the club's President." I wait for disproving faces. They never come. Instead, the conversation moves forward as Mary asks another question.

"Have you always lived in Salem?" She takes a small casual bite of food.

"Born and raised. I've traveled many places, but this is and always will be home," I tell her, feeling more relaxed than I have in a long time.

"Do you live close by?" Charles asks after downing the last swallow of his beer.

"I live on the other side of town, on the coastline."

"Really?" Charles appears intrigued. "We plan on taking a drive over that way tomorrow afternoon."

I shovel a heaping amount of potatoes and gravy onto my fork. "You won't be disappointed. It's beautiful scenery, and I'm renovating and living in an old lighthouse out that way."

Sage turns to look at me. "You live in a lighthouse?"

I chuckle. "Yeah, babe. Where'd you think I lived, the club?"

"Well..." Sage shrugs.

"What about your parents, hun?" Mary asks. Her question is innocent, but it makes the chords in my neck tighten, and I develop an acidic taste in my mouth. Anger churns in my gut as my father's last words suddenly race through my mind.

A touch of Sage's hand on mine pulls me from the shadows of my past. I turn my head and lock eyes with her. "You, okay?" Her voice is sincere and full of genuine concern.

I don't deserve her. At this moment, as much as I want Sage, my past—my present—is a stark reminder that I shouldn't get too close.

"Yeah, Babe. I'm good." I flex my fingers against her thigh and continue keeping my hand there as an anchor. I feel the heavy stares of her parents and Juniper on us, but don't let it pull me from the safe space Sage unknowingly created. Finally, I look to her mother. "My parents are dead."

Mary's face falls. "Ash, I'm so sorry." She gives me a polite smile. "I'm sure they were lovely people, considering they raised a good man such as yourself."

Feeling an aversion to Mary's proclamation, I swallow the loathing words I want to say, telling her my mother, though she loved me, was a pill addict, and my father was an abusive piece of shit. Instead, I tamp it all down, keeping it to myself.

I'm thankful as the room falls awkwardly silent. It allows me to process my runaway thoughts, the prominent one being, why am I even here?

"Ash." Charles lays his fork down on his empty plate and gives me his full attention. "Epictetus once said, 'Man is troubled not by events, but the meaning he gives them.' "

I give thought to the Greek philosopher's quote for a beat, trying to believe the words. Charles leans back in his chair, patting his stomach. He lets out a heavy breath. "I don't know about you guys, but I'm fuller than a tick." He looks my way. "Ash, what do ya say we have that drink."

A few minutes later, I'm following Charles out the door with a drink in my hand. The two of us breathe in the crisp evening air as we stand side by side on the stair's landing just outside the front door. Setting my glass of scotch on top of the three-inch-wide railing, I reach inside my cut, retrieving a pack of smokes. Before tapping one out, I offer one to Charles and place the filtered end between my lips.

Charles waves the offer off. "Gave up smoking years ago."

I light the tobacco end of the cigarette. My lungs expand with the deep inhale of nicotine, then I release the smoke like a drag-on's breath through my nostrils. I lift the glass of scotch, taking a drink. The malty taste adds flavor to the tobacco, and the warmth coating my throat is a welcomed friend.

"My daughter is my world," Charles says.

"As she should be." I take another drink.

"I like you, Ash. But I'm no fool, and I suspect you're surrounded by darkness in your life." I stare out at the slow setting sun. "Don't hurt her," Charles warns, and it's the first time his tone is harsh.

Wanting Sage already puts her in danger. I'm not the good guy of the story. Far from it. I made his daughter moan my name and coat my fingers with her cum right where he's standing. Truth be told, the animal inside of me is hungry for more. "She's safe with me." I mean every word.

"That's all I needed to hear." Charles sips his scotch, then looks down toward the street in the direction my bike is parked by the curb. "She's yours?" He points to my ride.

I nod, welcoming the change in conversation. "Want to have a closer look?" I offer, and Charles lights up at the idea. The two of us make our way down the stairs and over to my bike. Charles strolls around her, admiring the all-black paint, paying extra attention to the raven airbrushed gas tank. "She's a 1998 Nightshade."

We both turn at the sound of footsteps to see Sage headed in our direction. She looks between her dad and me, lingering on my face for a moment before saying, "You two ready for dessert?"

"That's a loaded question." I hungrily stare at her.

Charles clears his throat, letting us know he's still there. "Ash was just showing me his bike. Have you been for a ride yet, Shortcake?"

Sage vigorously shakes her head. "No."

Charles faces me, his drink in hand. "Take her for a ride."

Sage quickly rejects the idea. "I couldn't. Besides, dessert is waiting on us, and I'm not cutting out on you and Mom when you drove all this way to visit, and that would be rude."

"Nonsense." Charles pushes the issues further. "It's a nice evening. Don't waste it stuck inside. Carpe diem."

Sage stares at my ride. "Is it safe? I mean, have you ever had someone my size on the back?"

I take a step toward Sage. "There's nothin' wrong with your size, babe, so don't even make that a factor. Every one of your curves is perfect. Got me?"

Sage sighs.

"And I do believe that is my cue to head back inside and get some of that dessert," Charles says. He stops briefly beside his daughter and kisses her temple. "Live a little, kid." Then he looks at me. "Remember what I said."

I nod. "Yes, sir."

Charles nods back, heads toward the stairs, and soon disappears inside the apartment.

"Remember what he said?" Sage tilts her head, raising a brow. "What did you two talk about?"

"That's between Charles and me, babe." I slip my arm around her waist and tug her closer to me.

"I wish you'd stop calling me babe. And this whole inserting yourself into my life is a bit odd, don't you think? We don't even know each other."

"Isn't that what we've been doing this evening, getting to know one other?" I ask, and Sage rolls her eyes, which she often does at my expense.

"Let's be real. You've been on a date with my parents, not me. This was all a ploy for them to get to know a man I'm attracted to." The moment the last few words leave her mouth, Sage slaps her palm over her mouth, and her face turns red.

I grin. "You like me, huh?"

Sage locks eyes with me. "I'm attracted to you. I never said I like you. If I'm being honest, you make my thoughts irrational and irritate me. To the point I can't think straight. You're bossy, arrogant—" I shut her up with my mouth crashing against hers. I kiss her hard and with fever until we're out of breath.

Sage is the one to pull away. "What is—what the hell are we doing, Ash?" She exhales.

"I don't know, babe, but I'm willin' to explore it if you are," I admit. Sage's silence engulfs the moment between us, and I become restless. "Take a ride with me," I say.

Her forehead creases while contemplating what her next move will be. Sage toys with a lock of her hair for a few seconds before pressing her palm to my chest. "Promise to go slow?"

I grin. "I can do slow, babe."

"Jesus, Ash. Why does everything you say sound sexual?" She rolls her eyes.

I smack her ass, then give it a firm squeeze, and Sage takes in a sharp breath. "Grab a jacket and tell ya folks not to wait up."

"There you go again, ordering me around." Sage turns around and heads for the stairs, giving me one last look before entering her apartment. "Try hanging a please on the command next time," she shouts, and I chuckle. I love the way she gives shit right back to me.

I watch her ass sway with each step she takes. "Please," I shout back, and Sage is quick to respond by extending her middle finger toward me. I snort. "God, she's fuckin' perfect."

I wait for several minutes. Just as it feels like she's bailing on me, Sage emerges. As she's approaching, she shrugs on a black leather jacket. She stops short of me being able to reach out and grab her once more and slips a hair tie from her wrist, then proceeds to loosely braid her long hair.

I straddle my bike then extend my hand for her to hold. Placing her hand in mine, Sage slides in behind me. There's too much distance between us. "Slide that sweet ass closer," I instruct. "Please," I add just for the hell of it.

I feel her tits press firmly against my back, and her thighs have me hugged just right. "Like this?" She asks.

Sage's body molds perfectly against mine. I bring the bike to life, twisting the throttle, warming the engine, and letting her feel the vibration between her legs. I ease away from the curb and take off down the road. Her arms wrap around my waist, her fingers splaying across my abs. As requested, I take it slow, letting Sage warm up to the ride. Once we're on an open stretch of road, I feel her relax. "More," she shouts with enthusiasm.

"More what, babe?" I shout.

"Speed!" Sage giggles and the sound makes me feel lighter than air.

I open the bike up, moving us faster down the road. The tires hum against the asphalt, and the cold air awakens the senses. In the side mirror, I watch Sage turn her face into the warmth of the sun and close her eyes. She smiles, radiating happiness. I reach back, wrapping my hand around the calf of her leg. An immense peace washes over me. A calm I can honestly say I've never felt. We cruise for a while longer before I take the exit to Winter Island.

I slow, approaching my home, bringing the bike to a stop beside my car. "This place is amazing," Sage glances around.

I help her off the bike then dismount as well. I take her by the hand. "We made it just in time." I start walking toward the house.

"Time for what?" Sage brushes several loose strands of hair from her face.

I look back at her while unlocking the front door. "You'll see." I jerk my head, ushering Sage to step inside. She walks past me into the house. "Welcome to my home." I toss my keys into the wooden bowl sitting on the nearby table.

"You live here?"

I chuckle. "Why so surprised?"

Sage shrugs. "I don't know. I guess I took you for a dungeon of death kind of guy."

We stroll through the living room. "I'll give you the penny tour." I take her hand in mine again. "Living room." I span the space with my free hand. "It's a work in progress." I point at the fireplace mantel, which has a can of stain and paint brush sitting on top of it.

"I like it. It's cozy." She smiles as we move across the room to a closed door and open it to a small bedroom.

"It's become a catch-all for my tools and supplies." I close it then we enter the kitchen. It isn't much square footage but more than enough for me, like the rest of the home. The bottom cabinets are sage gray, with white countertops and a white honeycomb backsplash. Instead of wall cabinets, I opted to install oak shelves, leaving the walls white for contrast.

"Did you do all of this yourself?" Sage strolls around.

"Yeah. I do what I can when I have the time."

Sage runs her hand across the kitchen island. "Did you make this too?" She admires the custom-built epoxy Olive Wood ultra-clear resin countertop.

"That is Laredo's handy work. Since the island doubles as a dining table, I wanted it to be a statement piece." I tell her.

"It's beautiful." Sage continues glancing around the kitchen. "There's so much natural light." She looks out the large window over the kitchen sink. "And the view is amazing."

I notice the sun sinking lower on the horizon. "I can do better than that." I tug her to follow me and lead us to the other side of the house where my bedroom and narrow winding staircase is located. "Ladies first." I wave her forward.

"Does this lead to the lighthouse tower?" Her face lights up.

"See for yourself." I find her happiness contagious and smile back. Sage bounds up the spiral staircase. The hatch is already open, and I wait for her to step up into the lantern room. "Wow.

That's a massive light bulb." She looks at me. "Does it still work?"

"Yep." I unlock the exterior door. A blast of cold air rushes in when I open it. I step out onto the deck and wait for her to join me.

Once outside, Sage takes it all in. She walks a few feet and stops. A breeze has Sage hugging herself. I stroll over, stand behind her, and use my body to shield her from the wind. "Ash, it's breathtaking." She presses her back to my chest, seeking the warmth I offer. "You think anything could be more beautiful?"

I wrap my arms around Sage. "I'm holding her."

Nothing more is said between us as we watch the sunset. Nature creates its own symphony as waves race to the shore, colliding against the rocks in a deep, slow rhythm only the sea can create. Above us, seagulls cry as they fly by. In the distance, a foghorn blows. The sky is on fire with vibrant shades of orange as the sun is swallowed by the sea.

We stand in silence for several minutes, just staring out at the harbor and city lights. The temperature outside is starting to drop, and a strong gust of wind causes Sage to shiver. "Let's get you inside where it's warm."

We make our way down the stairs and into the kitchen. "Drink?"

"What do you have?"

I point to a shelf lined with various bottles of liquor. "Take your pick."

"Not a wine person, huh?" Sage muses. She tilts her head, tapping her fingertip against her lip. "I'll have a shot of Irish whiskey."

I grin, snatch the bottle from the shelf, and then grab a couple of glasses. I pour Sage a shot before giving myself a double.

Sage sits on one of the barstools at the kitchen island. "Ash?" She swirls the pale amber liquid around in her glass.

I down my double in one go, savoring the malt flavor. "Yeah?"

"I've really misjudged you." She turns her head and looks away.

I reach out, touching her chin. "Look at me." Sage sighs but brings her blue eyes to mine. "Misjudged me how? That I'm trouble, a biker, a man who is capable of horrible things? That I'm arrogant, bossy, and possessive?" Sage takes in a deep breath. "You didn't misjudge me, babe. I'm not the good guy in anyone's story. I am all those things." My confession, if anything, is honest. "Does who I am frighten you?"

"I'd be a fool if it didn't." She brings the glass to her lips and downs her shot.

I brush the back of my knuckles along her jawline. Her breathing quickens as I press my hand to her throat. Sage's racing heartbeat pulsates against the pad of my thumb. "But I also excite you." I dip my head and nip at the flesh of her neck.

"You infuriate me," Sage moans.

"You want me," I throw back, and she huffs. I lift her from the seat she's on, and her legs hug my hips as I carry her toward my bedroom.

She threads her fingers through my hair, her nails scraping my scalp. Then she kisses my neck. Her touch lights my skin on fire, and a growl reverberates from deep within my chest. I enter my room and lower her to her feet. She kicks off her shoes and hastily removes her jacket, tossing it to the floor. I toe off my boots while tearing my coat off, followed by my cut and shirt, and throw them to the side. Reaching down, Sage grips the hem of her shirt and peels it up and over her head. I watch while she unclasps her bra and holds it in place.

"Show me your tits," I command, and she raises a brow at me. Her hands fall to her sides, and the fabric flutters to the floor. "Fuck." I move toward her, back her to the edge of the bed, and lower her to the mattress. "You're perfect." I palm her breast, taking her nipple into my greedy mouth, then switch, giving the other equal attention.

"Ash," Sage moans, bucking her hips against my cock.

"You need somethin', babe?" I grind against her. I work my way down her body, unbuttoning her jeans.

"You."

Standing, I peel the denim over her hips, down her thighs, and off her body, taking her panties with them. Sage moves to cover herself. "Don't ever hide from me." I reach down, gripping behind her ankles, and pull her ass to the edge of the bed. Like a feast fit for a God, my woman is laid out before me, and I'm fucking starving. I kneel, running my palms along her calf, staring at her pussy. "Your curves are perfect." I drape one of her legs over my shoulder and take my first taste and moan. "Your pussy is perfect." I swirl my tongue around her swollen clit.

"Oh my God!" Sage moans out, and I continue to devour her, working her bundle of nerves until her legs begin to quiver. I feast on her until her thighs have my head in a deathlock, while she screams my name. "Ash." An orgasm rips through her body.

Needing inside her pussy, I stand, undo my jeans, and free my cock. Sage recovers enough to look at me. I stroke myself while she stares. A woman has never turned me on as much as Sage does. She crawls backward, positioning herself in the center of the bed, then reaches between her thighs and plays with her clit. It takes all my control not to nut when she dips her finger into her pussy. I climb onto the bed and settle between her legs, the head of my cock pressing against her entrance. We lock eyes.

"Fuck me..." I sink into her slick pussy as she breathes my name.

Taking my time, I move in and out of her tight heat. Bringing my lips to hers, I kiss Sage like the sun kisses the sea. I don't just fuck her. I make love to my woman. Lifting her leg onto my shoulder, I deepen my strokes, helping her take more of my length. Her breath hitches and I feel her pussy flutter. "That's it, baby." My thrusts become needier as the pressure at the base of my spine builds. "Rub your clit, baby."

Sage does as she's told and slips her hand between our bodies to work her clit.

"You're mine, Sage," I groan.

Sage's lips leave mine, only to declare. "Yours, Ash." Her pussy tightens around my dick, and her body shudders beneath mine.

"Fuck, yes," I growl, and I continue working my cock in and out, riding the waves of her release. "Love how greedy your pussy is."

"Ash," Sage breathes against my mouth. Her nails digging into my flesh, marking me, are my undoing. With one final thrust, I sink into the sweetest pussy I've ever had and come.

12
SAGE

"What are ya doing there, Shortcake?"

My hand flies to my mouth, attempting to muffle my scream, and I whip around to face my father, who is sitting at the kitchen island in his plaid pajamas and a black t-shirt, with a coffee cup in hand.

"Jesus, Dad. You scared the crap out of me." I close my eyes and take a deep breath to calm my nerves at the fact my dad just caught me creeping into my apartment at five o'clock in the morning. Doing the walk of shame in front of my father is not something I ever thought I'd experience, yet here I am, my face burning with embarrassment. This is definitely one for the books.

"What are you doing up this early?" I try deflecting.

"I've been getting up at four-thirty every morning for the past twenty-five years, baby girl. You know that." He takes a sip of his coffee, and I see the mirth gleaming in his eyes over the rim of the mug. "The real question is, why are you sneaking into your own apartment?"

Groaning, I set my bag down on the counter and drape my coat over the stool. "Daddy."

My dad's shoulders shake with silent laughter.

"I'm glad you find my walk of shame amusing," I say drily as I plop down onto the stool beside him. My father leans over and kisses the side of my head. "Coffee?" he asks.

I rub my palms over my eyes and yawn. "Please."

Dad places a mug of coffee in front of me. "You know, Sage, you're all grown up now, and you shouldn't be embarrassed that I know you have sex."

My father says those words to me the moment I take a sip of coffee, and suddenly I'm sputtering and choking.

Dad delivers a hefty pounding to my back. "Breathe, honey."

I take the napkin he holds out to me and wipe the drool and coffee from my mouth and the wipe at the front of my shirt. "There is no way we are having this conversation."

"Why not?" He looks genuinely offended that I don't want to talk about my sex life with him.

"Dad, if you think for one second, I'm talking about...about." Jesus, I can't even say the words.

"Sage, sex is perfectly natural."

"I know!" I screech. "But I'm not discussing it with you, Dad." I can't help but shudder.

"Well, your mother and I—"

He doesn't get to finish his sentence before my cutting him off. "Nope." I shake my head. "Nope, nope, nope. I do not want to hear whatever was about to come out of your mouth, and just gross."

"Fine," he huffs. "But can I say one thing?"

"Oh, dear lord." I tip my head back and stare up at the ceiling.

"I just want to say that I like him. This Ash fella."

I snap my head back toward my dad. "What?"

"I'll admit he's a bit rough around the edges, but I like the way he looks at my baby girl."

"What?" I repeat myself like a fool. "How does he look at me?"

"Like he'd bring you the moon and stars if you asked him to."

I can't breathe.

"I'm not going to sit here and lie to you and say your mother and I don't have some concerns about Ash and the kind of lifestyle he leads, but as a man—as a father—Ash is the kind of man I can respect. There are no falsities, no bullshit words to sugarcoat who he is. And as long as he treats you with kindness and respect, then he will have mine."

"I love you, Daddy."

"I love you too, Sage."

<hr>

After spending the weekend with my parents, I'm sad to see them leaving Monday morning, and I'm also going to miss the distraction. I'm trying not to dwell on the fact Ash hasn't called or come by since our night together.

"I'll call you when we stop at a hotel for the night." Mom tucks a strand of hair behind my ear before kissing my cheek.

"Love you, Mom."

"Love you too, honey." She then does the same to Juniper. "Love you, sweetie. You and Sage don't get into too much trouble."

"I love you too, Mrs. Briggs. And I'm not making any promises," is Juniper's cheeky reply.

"I figured as much." Mom laughs.

I walk over to my dad, who has just finished loading the suitcases into the trunk of the car. "Daddy."

He opens his arm to me. "Come here, Shortcake."

Resting my head on his chest, I take in the scent of Old Spice. "I wish you didn't have to go."

"Me too, baby girl. You and Juniper should come home sometime, and Christmas is right around the corner."

I nod. "I'll talk with Juju, and her parents were asking her the other day when she was coming for a visit."

"Charles," Mom calls out. "If we want to make it to the hotel before dark, we need to get on the road."

"You better get going." I kiss his cheek. "Be safe, and I'll talk to you this evening."

"Love you, Sage."

"Love you too, Dad." I wave as he climbs into the car.

Juniper and I stand on the sidewalk outside the salon and watch as my parents drive off.

"I'm going to grab a coffee before we open. You want one?" Juniper asks.

I shake my head. "No. Thanks, though."

I can feel my best friend's eyes drilling a hole into the side of my head. "He still hasn't called?"

"Nope." I sigh. "It's fine. It's not like I thought just because we had sex that I was something special." I try to sound nonchalant, but Juniper knows me too well. I have never been the type to have casual sex.

Feelings have always been involved, and I have only ever had sex with men I was in a relationship with. "It's my own fault for going along with it. Ash did nothing wrong."

"You don't have to stand up for the asshole, Sage. What he did was a dick move."

"Yeah, but there were two participants." I pull myself out of my fog and turn toward the salon entrance. "It is what it is, and I fully intend to forget about Ash like he's clearly forgotten about me."

Later that afternoon, I'm on a ladder attempting to hang a mirror on the wall when the salon door opens, and Brandon walks in. He quickly jogs over and takes the large piece of glass I was clearly struggling with from my hands.

"I got that." He sets it down against the wall.

"Thanks," I breathe and step down. "I would have dropped it had you not helped.

Brandon grins. "It's a good thing I happened to be walking by and saw you through the window." His dimples make an appearance as his smile widens.

"Yeah, I have to admit, I didn't realize it was so heavy until I got up on the ladder."

"You should have taken me up on my offer to help."

"Probably." I chuckle.

"Well, I'm here now. Want a hand?" he asks.

"That would be great."

Brandon goes about inspecting the brackets in the wall. "You did a good job with these." Without using a ladder because he's taller than me, Brandon finishes mounting the mirror on the wall.

"I really appreciate this," I say again.

"It's no problem." He steps back. "Didn't you say you had another one?"

"Yeah, it's over here." I point to the wall at the back of the salon near the shampoo bowls.

"If I can use your tools, I'll have it up for you in no time."

"Oh, okay. Cool. I'll go grab them."

Fifteen minutes later, I watch Brandon level and mark the spots for the hangers when he asks, "So where is your friend? Is it Juniper?"

"It is, and she went upstairs to our apartment to make some calls. We don't have any clients until this afternoon, so we both decided to be productive with our break in between." I laugh. "Or at least I tried until you had to rescue me."

Brandon looks over his shoulder and winks. "Rescuing you is no hardship, trust me."

I feel my face flush with Brandon's blatant flirting.

"I don't know if you are busy or not, but would you like to get dinner with me sometime, Sage?"

Crap, I can handle the flirting, but I didn't think he'd ask me out. And it's not that I don't find Brandon attractive, because he very much is.

I'm just about to open my mouth to accept Brandon's invitation when a harsh "No" is growled from the other side of the room. Brandon and I turn to the voice to find Ash standing just inside the door, and one of his biker friends is with him. The look on his face causes my breath to get caught in my throat. And there is only one word to describe the energy radiating off him. Fury.

"Can we help you?" Brandon asks with ease, and I cringe inside. Ash's friend, however, snorts like he finds this tension-filled situation funny. And poor Brandon appears clueless to the fact this larger-than-life biker standing in my salon looks ready to spit nails.

"You can help by backing the fuck up from what's mine," Salem grinds out, his nostrils flaring.

Brandon blinks. "Excuse me?"

"Didn't stutter." Ash takes a step in my direction, and Brandon's reaction is to step in front of me, acting as a shield between me and the pissed-off biker.

"Aw fuck," Ash's friend hisses.

Needing to defuse the situation quickly, I sidestep Brandon, cutting Ash off by placing my palm against his chest. "Salem, stop."

"Sage, do you know this man?" Brandon asks.

"Yes," I sigh at the same time Ash says, "She's mine."

Ash's statement has me seeing red. Actually, this whole damn scene has me seeing red. I cut my eyes up at Ash. "I'm not your anything, and I'd appreciate it if you left."

Ash looks dead in my eyes when he says his following words.

"Pretty sure the moment your tight pussy came all over my cock, you became mine."

My mouth drops open on a gasp the same time Juniper decides to make an appearance.

"Looks like I got here just in time. All I'm missing is some popcorn."

I turn my murderous glare toward my best friend. "Zip it Juju. Now is not the time." Then turn back to Ash. "Leave," I order through clenched teeth. God, I can't believe he just said what he did. And in front of an audience.

"Baby." Ash hooks his arm around my waist, pulling me flush against his hard chest, making me shiver. Ash, of course, notices and has a knowing look in his eyes.

"You mad, baby?" he asks, nuzzling his face into the crook of my neck.

I try to struggle against his hold, but Ash refuses to let me go. The son of a bitch even chuckles low in his throat. He knows I'm pissed, and he knows why. You don't sleep with a woman, then ghost her and not know that will piss her off.

"Sage," I hear Brandon call from behind me. I almost forgot he was here. With Ash invading my space and senses, I can't think straight.

I see Brandon's jaw flex when Ash refuses to let me go as I turn back toward him. Now I feel like such a bitch for putting Brandon in this situation. He's a nice guy and doesn't deserve to have Ash acting like a dog and pissing all over me.

"Are you really with this guy?" he asks.

"Yes," Ash answers for me.

"Shut up," I hiss, elbowing Ash, then look back at Brandon. "Look, it's...complicated. I'm sorry you got pulled into whatever this was. I'm grateful for all your help today, though."

"Right," Brandon clips, grabbing his jacket that's draped on the back of the chair. "I just hope you know what you're getting yourself into."

"Sage is not your concern," Ash says in a tone that leaves no room for argument. Luckily, Brandon is smart enough to go on that note. He spares me one last glance before turning on his heel and walking out of the salon.

Once Brandon is gone, I whip around and jab my finger into Ash's chest. "Look here, you big jerk—" I'm cut off from my tirade when Ash captures my hand in his and suddenly we are on the move.

"Have fun, you two." Juniper giggles when Ash drags me past her and up the stairs to my apartment, where he opens the door, then slams it, cutting us off from the outside world.

"What the hell, Salem?"

"Ash."

Ash growls, spinning me around and forcing me backward until my legs hit the back of the sofa.

"What?" I breathe.

Ash leans down, bringing his face an inch away from mine. The smell of mint mixed with the whiskey on his breath invaded my senses. Oh, God, did I just whimper.

"I told you to call me Ash. Especially when I'm inside you."

My breasts swell, and my nipples harden at Ash's demand. Before I have the chance to come up with a retort, I find myself spun around and bent over the back of the sofa. And when I go to protest, a large hand presses down on my back, keeping me in place. "I came to see my woman and found her entertainin' another man."

"I wasn't—"

"Shut up," Ash snaps. Then I feel his free hand undoing the button of my jeans and shoving them down over my ass, followed by the sound of his belt buckle. "Now, I'm going to remind you who you belong to."

I gasp when the head of his cock glides through the seam of my pussy, making it clench.

"Fuckin' soaked," he growls, making my skin prickle. It feels wrong that I'm turned on by the way this man controls the situation and my body, but nothing else exists when I'm with Ash. Not logic, and not the control I should be having over my own body.

I don't care.

He's rough.

Even demanding.

But I feel safe.

I trust him to give me what my body craves while protecting it at the same time. There is this connection between us, one I can't explain.

"That's it, baby. Relax for me. You're going to take my cock and my seed into that tight pussy and let me show you who owns it."

"Yes," I pant.

Ash continues to tease me by rubbing the tip of his cock back and forth over my pussy. "Tell me, Sage. Tell me who's pussy this is."

"Yours, Ash. It's yours."

"Now tell me what you want."

A sob escapes past my lips when he pushes the tip past my entrance then stops.

"I want you to fuck me, Ash. Make me yours."

The second the last word leaves my mouth, Ash drives forward, burying himself inside me, and I cry out, *"Oh, god."*

"Fuck, I could live in this pussy. So goddamn good." Ash pulls out then slams back in. "So fuckin' good and all mine. Isn't that right?"

When I don't answer him, Ash grabs hold of my ponytail and pulls my head back, forcing me to look at him. His pupils are dilated and filled with hunger. "Answer me."

"Yes."

"Yes, what?"

"It's yours. My pussy is yours."

My words are like fuel to his fire, and it's the moment he's done talking. Instead, he starts pounding into me with abandon.

"Ash, I'm coming!" I cry out just before a scorching, tingling sensation washes through my body as my orgasm has all my senses spinning out of control.

"Jesus fuckin' Christ, your pussy is squeezing the hell out of my cock." Ash continues to work himself in and out of me while riding the wave of my orgasm. Finally, after three more thrusts, he jerks my head back, buries his face against my throat, and fills me with his release.

Neither of us is in a hurry to move, and I take the time to relish the feel of having him deep inside me. And the second he slips out, I feel his cum running down the inside of my thigh.

Then Ash does something that both shocks me and excites me. After tucking himself back inside his jeans, he goes down to one knee, and, with the kind of gentleness I didn't think he possessed, he tugs my panties back in place. "Don't clean up. I want you walkin' around the rest of the day with me inside you."

"Okay," I breathe.

"Good girl."

13
SALEM

I drum my fingers against the surface of the table. Shortly after bending my woman over and filling her pussy with my cock, I got a message from Ghost to inform me he's got some intel on the Demon Jokers. This is why I texted the men more than forty minutes ago, calling church.

I stare at the moisture seeping through the stone wall. If it weren't for the rustic metal chandelier hanging over the center of the table, it would be dark as night in the room. Our meeting room is located beneath the church. It smells of the earth, like the root cellar, although this room is larger and doesn't reek of death. It's also accessible from the inside, through a heavy wooden door with stone steps leading down, whereas the root cellar entrance is outside.

I close my eyes and try massaging the tension from my neck, and my thoughts drift back to Sage. Goddamn, sex with her is by far the best I've experienced. My mood darkens as soon as I think about that fucking dildo she was conversing with back at the salon. Hearing footsteps echoing down the stone steps, I turn my head, and Mystic walks into church, where I've been sitting alone waiting for my brothers to arrive. "Still sulkin' from earlier?" Mystic dips his head, and I want to wipe the smirk off his face.

"Fuck off," I huff. Reaching out in front of me, I snag the pack of cigarettes off the table, tap one loose, place it between my lips and pull it from the bag. I strike the lighter and watch the flame grow as I burn the cigarette tip.

Mystic sits at the table. "We've known one another pretty much our entire lives, ever since fuckin' kindergarten." He leans back against the chair and studies me for a beat. "I've never seen you worked up over a chick before. I mean, not since third grade when you gave Blake Timberland a black eye because he pushed Charlotte Pendergrass, making her cry." Mystic chuckles, and the memory makes me chuckle too.

"The little fuck deserved it." I fill my lungs with nicotine. "Sage..." I say, expelling smoke. "She's different."

Mystic nods. "So, it seems." My best friend stares me down like I'm part of an interrogation, wanting me to spill my guts. I can honestly say that I never considered being with one woman until crossing paths with Sage. Now, I find myself looking farther than tomorrow—with her. It's crazy thinking we've only known of each other's existence for a few weeks. But, going back to day-to-day life without her in it isn't an idea I want to entertain. None of this, though, I say out loud, because I'm still battling the way I feel about it all myself. Mystic looks at me knowingly, reading me like a book. "It's okay to fuckin' want someone, brother."

I say nothing in return.

The rumble of Harleys vibrates through the earth and stone of the basement walls. The sound is soon followed by heavy footsteps as the rest of the men file into the room, taking their seats at the table. Harlem sets a couple of six-packs of beer on the table, and every man reaches out to snatch one.

With the silver skull ring on my finger, I pop the tab off the bottle and down half.

Baja's bottle rattles against the surface of the table. "So, what did Ghost find out?"

"Bruin Whitlock." A baritone voice echoes throughout the room, causing Baja and Juneau to jump to their feet. I chuckle, seeing Ghost standing at the entrance of the room.

"Fuck, man. Why you always gotta sneak around like that?" Juneau takes his hand off his weapon.

Harlem shakes his head at Juneau. "You shit yourself, brother?"

"It's creepy as fuck is all I'm sayin'. The way he moves without making a sound. It's unnatural." Juneau over-exaggerates a body shiver.

I give Ghost my attention. "It's been a long time." Ghost walks over and flings a pack off his back. It smacks against the surface of the table. He then unzips the bag and pulls out a manila folder, handing it to me. "Bruin Whitlock," he repeats, and the last names sound familiar. "He's the Demon Joker's President. Goes by the name Warlock." I pull the contents from the folder, and the first image I'm faced with is a zoomed-in photo. It's like looking at a ghost. There's no way. The sides of the glossy paper crumple in my fisted hands. "He's the son of Jerry Whitlock, aka Mayhem." My eyes cut to Mystic. His face hardens like a stone, then he hurls his beer bottle across the table, and glass shatters against the wall.

"Numbers?" I turn my attention back to the contents in my hand and sift through the remaining images, mainly of the Demon Jokers' compound and evidence of reconstruction.

"Thirteen, which is three more than a week ago," Ghost says.

"So, they're actively recruiting," Laredo states, and Ghost acknowledges him with a nod.

I pass the images to Mystic on my right. He stares at the photo of Whitlock for several beats. I know where his head is at. We all know. It's hard not to relive the rage knowing the man he's fixated on; his father killed our family. Mystic takes a deep breath and passes the intel to Laredo.

"The arsenal they're acquiring is impressive." Laredo shuffles through the photographs.

"My sources informed me that Whitlock has a contract with Rian O' Dwyer," Ghost says, and all the blood drains from Laredo's face.

"Fuck." Harlem drags his palm down his face.

Fuck is an appropriate reaction. Rian O' Dwyer is the head of the largest crime syndicate in Boston. He also controls a massive share of firearms trade in and out of the States. O' Dwyer is not one to cross. You make a deal with him; you're making a deal with Lucifer himself. Fuck him over, and he'll not just take your life. He'll kill every name associated with you just to prove a point. Above all, O' Dwyer was once questioned about the disappearance of Laredo's kid sister a few years back. To this day, my brother hasn't spoken much on the subject. All I know is his sister has yet to be found, and the case is why he walked away from his FBI career.

"Any weaknesses you've observed?" I ask.

"They have numbers against you, but they aren't well-organized in the sense of teamwork or brotherhood. During my observation over a few days, I've found them to lack discipline," Ghost says.

"We can't mistake their incompetence for weakness," Baja adds.

I nod. "Agree. If anything, it makes the Demon Jokers more of a threat and unpredictable."

Juneau huffs. "If you ask me, it sounds like Whitlock doesn't know his ass from a hole in the ground."

Ghost is quick to add, "There's talk around their area. They fear some of the bikers may be connected to the recent death of a young woman a few weeks ago."

Laredo folds his arms across his chest. "We've had a woman killed here in Salem, as well."

Ghost cuts his eyes at Laredo. "I heard."

I let out a heavy sigh. "Anything else to add, my friend?" I scratch my stubbled jaw while staring at Ghost.

He slings his pack over his shoulder. "No."

"What's our next move?" Harlem asks.

"So long as they stay out of Salem, we don't do shit." I down the remains of my beer and stand. "Stay for a drink," I say to Ghost.

"I prefer drinkin' alone." He glances around the table. "No offense."

"None taken, brother." Ghost nods then takes his leave. "Alright, brothers. Church is over."

We congregate upstairs, everyone except for Mystic. "I gotta get goin'. I'm meeting the realtor in town to sign the lease on that building, but I need to swing by the warehouse first to grab the paperwork I left in the office."

"See ya tonight?" I ask as Mystic heads for the door.

"Naw, brother. Gotta spend time with my baby girl tonight." He pushes the door open. "You need me, call," he shouts as the door closes.

Mystic is a good man. Much better than I am. He's got someone else to live for besides himself. Lorelei may have turned his world upside down initially, but it was for the better.

I stride across the room and put my ass on the barstool.

Astrid, who also stays and works here at the clubhouse, saunters over, grabs a bottle of whiskey, then pours me a double. She slides the glass in front of me. "Penny for your thoughts?"

I down the shot. "Another." I slam the glass down.

"That bad, huh?" She pours me another, and I cut my eyes at her. She puts her hands up. "Okay, okay. Forget I asked."

"I'll take one of those," Laredo says, and sits down beside me. "It's only noon. You should slow down." He side-eyes me.

"I'm not getting' shit-faced," I grumble. "I just want to take the edge off."

"Of what? This bullshit with the other club, or a certain black-haired woman with ghostly eyes."

I grunt my response and feel Laredo's eyes burning a hole through the side of my head.

Letting the sleeping dog lie, he says no more.

Astrid smiles at Laredo and sets a glass in front of him. "Hey, cowboy." She pours the whiskey.

"How's your day goin'?" Laredo asks her.

Astrid sets the bottle on the bar top. "You happen to see the Range Rover parked outside?" She leans her hip against the counter.

"I did," Laredo says, taking a sip of his whiskey.

"It's all mine. Used but new to me. Paid for in full," Astrid says proudly.

I listen to Laredo and Astrid talk for a few minutes and massage my temples, trying to ignore the pressure of a migraine coming on. Grabbing the whiskey, I pour one more shot in my glass, down it, and stand. "You need me, I'll be in my room."

"You got it." Laredo lifts his glass at me, and I walk away and pass Baja and Harlem, playing a game of pool. They look up and nod, then keep on playing.

Juneau is sitting on a couch, with some random blonde perched on his lap, but is too occupied by a pair of tits to notice me breeze past him. I walk to the back of the cathedral and pull open a heavy wood door that takes me down a hall. I head straight for my room at the end and shut the door behind me when I step inside. I stride over and jerk the curtains together, blocking out the daylight, cloaking me in darkness. I stretch out on the bed, lying flat on my stomach, with the side of my face pressed against the cold pillow.

I close my eyes and take a few deep breaths, trying to relax my body and clear my fucking head. It's not long before I feel my body become heavy, and I'm drifting to sleep.

I'm woken by a knock on my bedroom door. "Prez," Harlem says, pounding on my door again.

"Fuckin' hell." I drag my ass out of bed and fling open the door.

"Mystic caught some prick breakin' into the warehouse."

"He still there?" I brush past him, stomping my way down the hall.

"He's on his way back to the clubhouse."

"And I'm just finding this shit out now?" I bark, bursting into the common room.

"He called you twice before getting in touch with me," Harlem says, his tone laced with irritation.

I pull the phone from my pocket, and, sure as shit, I have two missed calls from my brother. "Dammit," I hiss.

Juneau rushes through the front door. "He's here." Then jogs back out.

Laredo, Harlem, Baja, and I join Juneau outside just as a disheveled, bleeding Mystic climbs out of his car. "Blood yours?" I approach him.

"Some." Mystic walks to the back of his car and throws open the trunk lid. Inside is a Demon Joker, bound with boxing tape at his wrists and ankles. And in his mouth...

"Is that?" I ask, tilting my head.

"Rubber chicken?" Mystic nods, "Yeah. The asshole kept trying to bite my fuckin' arms while taping him up." Mystic grips the guy by the hair on his head, pulls him out and deposits him on the ground. The fucker squawks when his face smacks against the gravel at my feet.

"Christ." I rub the back of my neck and listen to my brothers lose their shit after Mystic puts the toe of his boot against the bastard's cheeks, applying pressure to make the rubber chicken squeal again. "Get him to the root cellar."

Mystic and Harlem lift the guy off the ground, carrying him to the side of the church. Juneau opens the double hatch doors leading beneath the earth's surface, and the biker is hauled into the damp darkness. A dim light flickers on. "String him up." I roll my neck as they hoist our company onto a hook and chains attached to one of the log ceiling rafters. "You check him?" I ask Mystic, who pulls a weapon tucked in the waist of his jeans and a phone from his back pocket.

"His weapon and cell." Mystic tosses the items on a metal cart that holds various tools.

"Cut off his clothes," I order, and Harlem pulls a large, serrated knife from a sheath at his side. His blade rips through the biker's cut, then shirt. The bastard cries out in pain as the knife tears at his flesh as well. Harlem tosses the ripped pieces of cloth to the ground. He twirls the knife handle in his hand before cutting into the denim covering the biker's legs. He rips parts of the jeans further with his hands, leaving the man's bottom half partially exposed. Harlem cuts his eyes at me, and I know what he wants. To inflict pain. I nod, giving him the go-ahead, and watch him kneel. He takes hold of the biker's thrashing leg and, like a knife cutting through butter, shoves the tip of the blade beneath the poor bastard's knee cap.

His wail is muffled behind the box tape wrapped around his head and mouth and further smothered by the fucking rubber duck halfway down his throat.

I pick up the Demon Joker's phone, flip through his contacts and find a number for his president. "Baja." I grab my brother's attention and toss the phone across the room at him. "Open the camera and press record." I look down at the cart and wrap my hand around a small propane torch. I twist the valve, releasing the gas, and squeeze the trigger, igniting the blue flame. The biker follows my movement as I take steps toward him.

"I'm not askin' questions. There's nothin' your man here has to say I'd want to hear. The motherfucker came into my town and made the unfortunate decision to trespass on private property— mine." I pull a cigarette from the inside pocket of my cut and light it with the torch flame. I breathe in a lungful of smoke, then blow it out. "I thought I made myself clear the first time." I approach the biker while Baja records my actions. "Either the warning went unheard, or you have no control over your men." I bring the fire close to the biker's skin. You can hear the sizzle and get a waft of dirty sulfuric odor as his chest hair becomes singed just before his flesh begins burning. The charcoal-like smell permeates the air as I burn off his right nipple. The asshole writhes in agony, his body thrashing, trying to escape the pain inflicted on him. "Laredo, hand me a screwdriver." My brother lifts the rusty tool from the cart, placing the twelve-inch device in my hand. I hold the steel rod over the torch's flame, waiting for the metal to turn red-hot.

Harlem peers at me again, his blade still held tightly in his hand. I nod, and he approaches the biker, who is breathing heavily through his nose. The Demon Joker's chest rises and falls while flails and sways. Harlem runs the tip of the blade between the biker's ribs before sinking into the meat of his flesh, leaving a gaping three-inch wound in the side of his ribcage. My brother takes a step back, only to wipe off and sheath his knife, walk over to a five-pound bucket sitting on the floor, and come back with a rusty tree branch cutter. Harlem spreads the shears the width of the gash he inflicted, shoving the rusty metal tips into the wound, then clamps down, followed by the sound of a rib bone cracking. The bastard gags on his screams. Piss runs down the fucker's leg, puddling on the floor beneath his feet, mixing with the blood dripping from the wounds on his body. I pass the torch for Laredo to hold, and Harlem steps away. Keeping the screwdriver steady, I position the tip directly over the guy's eye and look back into the camera lens of the phone Baja has pointed at me. "Make no mistake; I will kill every motherfucker you send my way." I shove the searing-hot rod through the bastard's eye socket, feeling the thin skull barrier behind it crunch.

The poor bastard jerks for a few minutes before life is gone from his body. Baja stops recording. "Get rid of the body," I order and take the phone from Baja. Waves of adrenaline continue to rush through my veins.

"You didn't even attempt to find out why the bastard broke into the warehouse," Mystic says, staring at Juneau and Harlem as they spread a tarp across the floor.

"Would it have changed the outcome?"

"No." Mystic rubs the back of his neck. "No, it wouldn't have."

I look down at the phone gripped in my hand and swipe the screen, pulling up the text thread labeled Prez and attaching the video. "He knows where to find us." I press send, then toss the phone to Mystic. "Make sure the body is buried deep," I tell him, then turn toward the exit.

"Where are you off to?" Mystic asks.

"To clear my head."

Once the fresh air hits my face, I breathe it in, trying to rid the stench of death from my nostrils. I head across the yard toward my bike. The engine rumbles, and I take off down the road, shrouded by outreaching branches casting ghostly shadows on the surface of the road. I drive to declutter the clusterfuck inside my head. This shit with Demon Jokers is becoming a bigger problem than I would like.

I ride for a solid hour before my drive leads me straight to Sage's apartment. I contemplate for a moment whether I should even be here before turning off the engine and dismounting my bike.

"Ash?" Sage walks out of the salon along with Juniper. She passes the keys in her hand to her friend, says something, then walks in my direction. "Something wrong? You look...tense." She stops, leaving a bit of space between us.

I reach out, snagging her by the waistband of her jeans, and pull her to me. Her hands slip beneath my cut, and she wraps her arms around my waist, pressing her cheek against my chest. "Just needed to feel ya, babe."

"Okay." Sage holds on a little tighter, and it's just what I need to wash my current worries away.

"Um." Juniper stops a few feet away. "Sage, I'll see you upstairs."

"I'll bring her home soon." I look at Juniper, and Sage wrenches her head back to gaze up at me.

"And where am I going?"

"Anywhere. As long as I'm with you." I brush the hair from her face.

She raises her brow. "Anywhere?"

"Got someplace in mind, babe?" I'm hoping she says my bed.

"The clubhouse."

I turn Sage loose to retrieve the phone from my pocket and shoot a text to Mystic.

Me: Shit clean?

Mystic: The trash is being disposed of.

Me: Good. Heads up, I'm bringing Sage to the clubhouse.

Mystic: Are you in LOVE?

I shake my head.

Me: Fuck you

Mystic: We'll be on our best behavior

"Yeah, right," I mutter, then look at Sage. "Ready?"

"Now?" She looks down at herself. "Let me freshen up first."

"You're beautiful, babe." I snag the helmet strapped to the back of my ride, and place it on her head. I fasten the strap beneath her chin, then kiss her. "Tell your friend I'll have you home in a few hours."

Sage turns to Juniper, who's been waiting. "I'll be home in a bit."

"That dick better be worth ditching your best friend, wine, a pint of ice cream, and reruns of Supernatural." Juniper blows a kiss and smiles. "Be safe bitch," she says most affectionately, then climbs the stairs. I wait for her to enter the apartment before climbing on and helping Sage slide in behind me and slip her arms around my waist.

"Hold tight," I say.

"Always," Sage replies just before I drive off.

A short time later, we're rolling onto the Fallen Ravens compound. I park alongside the other bikes and climb off my bike. Sage is already removing the helmet as she glances around. "Aside from the creep factor of the old headstone in that field over there —" she points "—the building itself is beautiful. How old is it?"

"One hundred eighty-three years old."

"Wow." Sage takes it all in as we walk up the few stone steps leading to the entrance. I push open the door and usher her in.

"This is the commons. It's where we relax, unwind, and party." Sage looks across the room, her eyes landing on Astrid, who spots us from her seat at the bar.

"Hi," Astrid waves, and we walk in her direction. She looks between Sage and me. "Mystic said to tell you he and the others should be back within the hour."

"Thanks."

"Would either of you like a drink?" Astrid asks.

"Have a bottle waiting for me. I'm gonna show Sage around." I look at Sage, who hasn't taken her eyes off Astrid. "You want anything, babe?"

"I'll have whatever you'll be drinking." She takes hold of my hand.

Astrid smiles. "You got it."

I tug on Sage, and we continue walking across the room. "Does she live here?" she asks, and I cut my eyes at her.

"Yeah, babe."

"Do you sleep with her?"

My feet stop moving. "Babe."

Sage sighs, then brings her eyes to mine. "I'm no fool, Ash. I know enough to realize what MC club girls do, and neither of us was celibate before." She waves her hand between us. "Whatever we are calling this. I just want to know if you're entertaining more women besides me. Because..."

I stop her right there and close the small gap between us. "Have I fucked her, or am I fuckin' her?"

"Ash." Sage turns her face away.

"Look at me." I touch her chin and bring her eyes forward. "You are the only woman I'm fuckin'. It's only been you since the night I first laid eyes on you, babe," I confess. Sage's lips part on a small gasp as I grip the back of her head, fisting her hair. I tilt her head back. "You're mine." I touch my mouth to hers.

Whistling and clapping break our heated connection. "Fuckin hell, brother. I feel the heat of that kiss all the way over here," Juneau bellows, and Sage buries her face in my chest. Across the room, my men are walking through the door, and they scatter about the room.

After the introductions, I take Sage by the hand again, and I push through the doorway leading to the back end of the clubhouse. To our right, I push open another door. "Kitchen." We enter, and Sage looks around. "Through that door over there is a small laundry room."

"You turned this old church into a real home." Sage sounds impressed.

"A couple of us have outside homes, but the clubhouse is the heart of it all. These walls hold a lot of history, and have seen a lot of shit."

"How long has this place been Fallen Ravens?" Sage asks.

"Our original President, Chicago, founded the club. He was Mystic's old man."

"So, there are more of you?"

"Naw, babe. Only the ones you've met."

"How many are gone, and where are they now?"

I feel the sting and taste the bitterness of their deaths like it happened yesterday. "Dead." I pause a beat. "They were good men." I jerk my head. "Let's finish the tour." We keep moving toward a hallway that wraps around into another, going past several closed doors. "These are all bedrooms that were once a large open space because this church doubled as a small orphanage."

Sage presses her palm against a nearby windowpane, glancing outside. "If these walls could talk, huh?"

I'm glad they don't.

"Ready for that drink?"

Sage glances back at me. "Absolutely."

We make our way back to the commons, where music plays, and find my brothers gathered around a table. Cigarette smoke drifts above their heads, whiskey is poured, and a deck of cards is shuffled. They've decided to unwind with a game of poker. I lead the way over toward them, pull the empty chair out for my woman to sit, then drag another chair from nearby across the floor and sit beside her. "Deal me in," I say to Harlem, who is dishing out cards.

Laredo directs his attention to Sage. "You play?"

Sage smiles. "A little. My dad would play penny poker with me when I was a kid, but it's been a while."

Laredo cuts his eyes over to Harlem. "Deal her in."

Sage notices cash sitting in the center of the table and the folds of money each brother has in front of him and laughs. "Those aren't pennies."

"You don't have to play, babe." I grab the whiskey bottle sitting on the table and pour some into a couple of empty shot glasses.

Sage eyes the men who are looking back at her. "What's the buy-in?"

Something tells me Sage knows more about the game than she's letting on. Wanting to see where the evening goes, I stay quiet.

Baja tokes the cigar resting between his fingers. "Hundred bucks." Sage looks apprehensive but then reaches down the front of her shirt, pulling cash from between her breasts.

Sage looks at me, and my eyes go from the wad of money to her cleavage. "What?" She shrugs, unfolds the bills, and tosses five twenties onto the pile of cash at the center of the table. She then lifts the shot glass full of whiskey before she throws her head back and down the liquor. Sage shakes her head, blowing the fire from her throat, then rubs her hands together. "Let's play."

Almost two hours later, we call it quits, and my woman is sitting beside me counting her winnings. "I can't believe you hustled us." Juneau laughs off the fact he lost a few hundred bucks.

"I told you I knew how to play. I've just never played with big money before," Sage quips, doing a little happy wiggle in her seat.

Mystic stands. "It's getting late. I'll catch y'all tomorrow," he says, and we all reply *catch you later*, or *safe travels*.

Within no more than a few moments of Mystic walking out the door, he is strolling back in with a thin blonde woman, soaking wet from head to toe. "Who the hell is this?" I come out of my seat, and the woman flinches.

"Ash." Sage stands. "Jesus. Can't you see she's terrified?" Sage narrows her eyes at me.

I look at Astrid, who's relaxing on the sofa. "Get her somethin' to dry off with." Sage moves past me toward the woman. While she comforts her, Mystic approaches me. "She said what the hell she wants?" I ask him?

"She said she needs help and was told this was where she could find it." Mystic glances back at the woman standing near the front door, then Astrid appears with a towel, handing it to the drenched woman.

"Lock it up and take her downstairs," I order, and Mystic heads back to gather the young woman. He takes her by the arm, leading her across the room. I eye the rest of the men, and they follow Mystic.

Sage comes to my side. "What's happening? Who is she?" She shows concern for the stranger.

"I'm about to find out." I kiss Sage on the forehead. "Come with me." I pull her by the hand, leading her to the back where the bedrooms are located.

"Ash, slow down." She tugs against me, but I keep moving. With the shit going on with Demon Jokers, I can't trust anyone. Not even a defenseless-looking woman. I throw open the door to my room. "The hell, Ash? One minute we're having a great time. Next, you're hauling off a scared, helpless woman and dragging me in here."

"Stay put until I come back."

"I don't like this." There's a hint of panic in her voice, enough for me to pause.

I dial my actions back. "Babe." I sit her on the mattress, then kneel in front of her. "We won't hurt her, but I need to find out what she's doing here, understand?"

"But—"

"No buts, Sage. Stay put." My voice is a hint harder this time.

Sage crosses her arms and huffs. "Fine."

I kiss my woman's stubborn ass then leave her sitting on the side of my bed.

In the basement, the men have the woman sitting in a chair, wrapped in a blanket, sipping on a steamy cup of coffee. I waste no time getting down to business and drag a chair across the floor, placing it directly in front of our trespasser. "Who sent you?"

Even though she still breathes, the young woman's eyes are devoid of life. "I was told you could help me."

"What is it you think we can help you with?"

Her eyes set on mine. "Murder."

I lean back, cross my arms over my chest and study her for a moment. "I don't think you have a clue what you're askin' to get tangled in, girl." I lean forward. "Could you live with knowing someone is dead because of you?"

"Every night when I close my eyes, I see him. I relive what he did to me—what he stole. I want to breathe again. I want to walk the streets of my hometown no longer terrified that he's lurking around every corner." The young woman straightens her back. "To answer your question, I'd live knowing my rapist and a dozen other women's rapist would no longer hurt another living soul again."

I pull my attention from the woman to look around the room at my men. They don't need to say a word for me to know they will gladly put the son of a bitch in the cold hard ground. The young woman reaches into the deep pockets of her coat and pulls out two thick white envelopes. She sets them on the table.

The sleeves of her coat ride up her arms as she slides the envelopes to the center of the table, exposing raised scars on her inner wrists, the one on her left more pinkish than the other revealing the self-harm inflicted on herself is not very old. "I don't know what your fee is, but this is all I have—everything."

I cut my eyes at Mystic, who takes the envelopes and peers at the contents, counting the cash inside. He pulls out a folded piece of paper, opens it, passes it to me, then sits them back on the table. "Five grand."

I look at the paper in my hands, on it all the information I need on the man she wants dead. Judge Jack Westgrove from Boston. There is corruption in all walks of life, including those who claim to uphold the law. "Five grand all you got?" Her eyes shift between Mystic and me, and she swallows hard. Tears fall from her eyes to the tabletop.

"Yes." She wipes the tears away with the sleeve of her coat. "I'm sorry for wasting your time." She goes to stand.

"Sit." I keep my voice neutral, and she lowers back onto the chair. I look at Mystic and jerk my chin. Knowing what I want, my brother slides the money back in front of the young woman. "I don't want your money," I say, and she drops her eyes to the envelopes. "What's your name?" I ask, which isn't typically something I would do.

She lifts her head and hesitates before answering, "Aya."

"Give me the name of your monster, Aya."

Aya sucks in a deep breath, closing her eyes. "Jack..."

I interrupt her. "Open your eyes when you say his name Aya. Don't give your power to anyone."

Her eyes pop open. "Jack Westgrove."

I nod my approval at hearing the strength of her voice. I fold the paper containing our target's information and pass it over to Laredo. "Baja," I call my brother over and look at Aya. "My man here will see to it you get home safely." Baja steps to our visitor's side and waits for her to stand. "Don't forget your money," I tell her, and she places the envelopes back into her coat pockets.

"He'll do it again." Aya hugs herself. "Men like him will continue to prey on women and get away with it." Those are her last parting words before Baja leads her out of the room.

I feel my brother's eyes on me, but it's Harlem who speaks. "You should have taken the money and killed the judge."

"She needs the money more than the club does." I push away from the table and stand. "I have every intention of killing the judge, but Aya didn't need to know that. She's got enough demons to battle with and doesn't need his death on her conscience. The least we can do for her is to rid her life of one less monster. And I'll take pleasure in doing so."

With the current situation taken care of, I leave my men and head back to my room for now. When I get there, Sage is missing. "Dammit," I hiss, turn on my heel and go hunting. I look all over the clubhouse before continuing my search outside, which leads me toward the back of the property. I spot her near the crumbled mausoleum, sitting on the throne of rubble with Nimbus lying peacefully on her lap. "What part of stay put do you not understand?" The woman is defiant as the day is long.

Sage looks at me, not the least bit fazed by my anger. "I don't see the harm in getting some fresh air." The cat purrs his approval as she scratches behind his ear. The fucking traitor. "He's so sweet. I wonder where he came from?"

"His name is Nimbus." I suck in a breath through my nose, trying to tamp down my frustration. "Put the cat down, and let's go."

Sage stops stroking the cat. Sensing the storm, Nimbus looks up at me, then jumps to the ground and trots toward the trees. "You even scare off your own cat." She shakes her head and sighs. "Did I listen to you? No. But come on, Ash. It's not like I was spying on you or getting into trouble. I simply took a walk outside."

I growl my frustration. "You defied me."

Sage's eyes widen, and she stands. "Defied you." Her hand goes to her hip, and she pokes at my chest with the tip of her finger. "Who do you think you are? You don't own me, Ash. And you sure as shit don't get to control me, either."

She's fucking cute thinking she's not mine. I press my hand to her neck, tilting her head back further to keep her eyes locked on mine as I push my body into hers. "I've tasted that sweet nectar between your thighs. My cock has been buried deep in that tight pussy of yours." I lean down, give her neck a squeeze, and brush my lips against hers. "I've claimed every inch of you, babe." When Sage breathes out, I breathe it in. "You are mine." I feel my pulse quicken. "Got nothin' to say?" I drag my lips along her jawline before releasing my hold on her and stepping back. Sage looks at me with lust-filled eyes. "Since that mouth of yours likes a good workout, I'm gonna fill it with my cock." I undo my belt buckle, then unfasten my jeans, and Sage kneels in front of me. Reaching out, she pulls my cock free. She flicks the tip of her tongue against my piercing, and my dick throbs in her hand. Sage takes half of my dick into her mouth, keeping her blue eyes locked with mine. I moan at the warm contact, and the muscles in my thighs flex with every stroke her tongue makes against my flesh. Sage moans, and I feel the vibration travel up my spine. "Fuck, yes," I growl, fisting her hair, and watch my woman suck me off. Heat spreads across my skin, and my pulse quickens as intense energy builds in my body. Sage squeezes the base of my shaft then releases just before I explode with the most insane orgasm I've ever experienced. My mind goes blank, and my body shudders through the euphoria as her mouth continues taking my cock. Sage swallows every fucking drop before finishing me off with one final lap of her tongue.

I pull Sage to her feet. "Who do you belong to?"

"I've had your cock in my mouth, babe." She smirks. "That makes you mine."

How can I argue with that? "Damn right I am."

14
SAGE

"Where are you off to?" Juniper sits up and peers at me over the top of the sofa.

"I'm going to go track down Brandon and apologize for the other day," I say, pulling on my coat.

"Really? Does Salem know you're going?" Juniper eyes me. "I mean, after that little pissing contest he put on downstairs, I'd think you'd leave well enough alone."

"Why would I do that? Salem was rude, and Brandon has been nothing but nice. Besides, Salem doesn't own me," I snip.

Juniper puts her hands up in front of her. "Hey, I wasn't saying I agree with him. Just wondering if going to see Brandon is a smart move. You said he asked you out. Do you think going to see him would give him the idea you're interested in him?"

I slip my keys in my purse and ponder Juniper's question, then shake my head. "I don't think so. I think Salem made it clear that he and I are together." I sigh. "I just feel bad for how things went down. Even though I'm not interested in Brandon beyond being friends, I do believe he's owed an apology."

"In that case, good luck." Juniper plops back on the sofa then adds, "Because if your scary, alpha biker boyfriend catches wind of you so much as breathing the same air as another man, he'll probably lose his shit." She peeks back over the edge at me. "He's hot as all get out, but scary as hell."

I roll my eyes. "It'll be fine. Besides, it's not like he'll find out. And if he does," I shrug, "so what."

Juniper gets a wicked gleam in her eyes and smirks. "Or maybe you want to piss your man off so he can punish you again."

"Oh, shut up, you wench." I laugh. "I knew I never should have told you what he did to me when he dragged me up here after he was done pissing on me in front of Brandon."

"Whatever," Juniper tosses back. "We're best friends, and best friends are supposed to tell each other all the juicy deets. It would be a crime against the best friend's law to keep such details from me."

"Yeah, yeah." I wave over my shoulder on my way out the door.

When I pull up in front of the hardware store and park, I look down at my phone sitting in the cup holder and see Ash's number flashing on the screen. I decide to let the call go to voicemail. If I answer, and he asks where I am, I won't be able to lie. And though I don't feel like I'm doing anything wrong by seeing Brandon, Ash would undoubtedly disagree.

"She's back again," Billy booms when I walk in the store. "Yours is one face I could get used to seeing every day."

"Good morning, Billy."

"What can I help you with today, sweetheart?"

"Actually, I'm here to see Brandon. Is he around?"

"He sure is. He's in the office doing the books. He knows how much I hate numbers. You can go on back. It's the first door on your left."

"Thanks." I smile and make my way down the tool aisle and past a row of ladders until I come upon a door that's sitting slightly ajar where I see Brandon seated at a desk, his attention on the computer in front of him. He looks up when I knock, and I do my best to give him a friendly smile. For a second, he looks shocked to see me standing in front of him, but it's quickly replaced with a smile of his own, to my relief.

"Sage." Brandon stands and opens the door further for me to come inside. "What are you doing here?"

"Hi, Brandon. I hope it's okay that I stopped by like this. If you're busy, I can come back."

"No. no. It's fine." He moves a stack of papers from the chair sitting across the desk. "Here, have a seat."

"Thanks." I sit down. "I just wanted to come here and apologize for what happened the other day."

Brandon shakes his head. "Sage, it's fine."

I cut him off. "No, you were there helping me and being nice. What happened with Salem was rude."

The corner of Brandon's mouth lifts into a small smile. "Sage, I appreciate you coming down here, but really, it's okay. I'm a big boy."

I hang my head, and my shoulders sag with relief. "Good."

"Sage."

I lift my head when Brandon continues. I notice he looks a little uncomfortable as he shifts in his seat.

"I know I already asked this, but do you really know what you're getting into with that man?"

I don't miss the sour expression taking over Brandon's face at the mention of Ash, and I also don't like it.

"Yes." I look directly into Brandon's eyes when I draw out my answer.

"So, you are aware of the kind of people he and his club are?"

"I don't know everything about Salem and his club, but he

also doesn't know everything about me, as we're still getting to know one another."

"Sage, those men..."

Before Brandon can finish his sentence, I hold my hand up. "I'm going to stop you right there. I get what you're trying to do, Brandon, and trust me when I say I appreciate it. You're a great guy, and I can tell you're trying to look out for me, but your efforts are not needed. Now, I know what some people see when looking at Salem and his club. They see a bunch of criminals. But let me tell you what I know about Salem." I make sure to enunciate that last word. "Salem, though he can be scary and rough around the edges, is also kind and gentle. He's the kind of man that cares for and respects his friends, who from what I can gather, he thinks of as family. Salem is also the kind of man that when some punk kids get the bright idea to vandalize Sukie's store, he chases them down and holds them responsible for their actions by making them work and replace the property they destroyed. And that is why I'm making a choice to continue seeing Salem, regardless of what rumors have to say."

The expression on Brandon's face is a tell-tale sign he didn't like what I had to say, but the tight nod I get in return says he's accepted it.

I stand and turn to leave when Brandon stops me. "Sage."

I peer over my shoulder.

"I want you to know I heard what you said. I can't say I'm not disappointed, and I sure hope this guy knows what he's got."

I nod. "Thanks."

"Friends?" He holds out his hand.

I smile. "Friends." I shake his hand.

"Come on, I'll walk you out."

Brandon walks with me back to the front of the store. "See you later Billy," I call out to his uncle.

"Later, sweetheart."

I turn to Brandon. "Bye."

"Take it easy, Sage." He jerks his chin.

When I step out on the sidewalk, I'm knocked backward and nearly fall to my butt before a pair of hands grip my upper arms to keep me from kissing the pavement.

"Oh goodness. I'm so sorry."

"No worries."

Once I right myself, I look into the face of the man who just spoke, and for some inexplicable reason, a sense of unease washes over me. The man in front of me is at least six feet tall, has dark, almost-black hair shaved close to his scalp, and tattoos peeking up from the collar of his jacket along his neck, along with an assortment of random face tattoos, one being a spider on the right side of his forehead. It's his dark soulless eyes that have a shiver running down my spine.

"Oh, well, again, I'm sorry for running into you." I go to side-step the man only to have him cut me off by stepping in my way.

"Where ya off in such a hurry there?"

"I'm sorry, but I don't think that's any of your business, and I need to be going." I try again to leave.

"That's no way to treat someone who just saved you from taking a spill. Why don't you tell me your name, sexy?"

My heart rate picks up as the strange man increasingly turns aggressive. "Look, I thanked you already, so if you will excuse me." I try to escape the uncomfortable situation for the third time.

"And I asked you what your name is. No reason to be a bitch."

My back goes straight, and I narrow my eyes. "Not wanting to give a strange man my name doesn't make me a bitch. But it does is make you a fucking creep."

"You're a nasty little cunt, aren't you? You know what happens to bitches like you?"

My breath gets caught in my throat when the man looks like

he's about to grab me, but luckily that doesn't happen because we're interrupted.

"Is everything all right out here?" Brandon and his uncle step out onto the sidewalk.

"We're fine," the asshole replies.

"No, we most certainly are not fine." I take three steps back toward Brandon and his uncle, putting some much-needed space between me and the creep who had the nerve to call me a cunt and a bitch in one go. "This man is bothering me."

"You hear that fella," Billy says. "The young lady doesn't want you here. Maybe you should go on about your business."

"Yeah. Maybe you should haul your ass back inside, old man, and stay the fuck out of mine."

The situation is two seconds away from turning ugly when the rumble of a motorcycle catches my attention. Not only does it catch my attention, but also the asshole in front of me.

Without saying a word, he turns on his heel and hustles down the block before disappearing around the corner of the brick building at the end of the street.

A moment later, the bike pulls up in front of the hardware store. When the man removes his shades, I recognize him as Harlem. My body instantly relaxes. Harlem, however, is tense. His sharpened gaze flickers between me, Brandon, and Billy. He climbs off his bike. "What's goin' on?"

"Hi, Harlem. Nothing, just a run-in with some asshole. No biggie."

Harlem's eyes bore into mine, and I can tell he knows I'm full of shit. Probably because I'm still trembling, and my words came out shaky.

"Don't move," he orders. Then I watch him put his phone to his ear. "Prez, I'm outside of Billy's with Sage. Somethin's up." He listens a moment before hanging up. "Salem will be here in five."

"Harlem, you didn't have to call Salem. I told you everything is fine. I had a run-in with some jerk, but then Brandon and Billy stepped in, and he left."

Harlem shakes his head. "It's done. We wait for Prez."

I blow out a breath and groan when I hear another rumble followed by Ash parking next to Harlem's bike. His eyes never leave mine as he swings his leg over, and his feet eat up the distance between us. "Baby." His voice is low and gentle once he steps into my space.

"I told Harlem I was fine. He shouldn't have called you down here."

"Tell me."

"Ash," I breathe.

"Tell me, Sage."

Knowing there's no way out of this, I give him what he wants. I tell him word for word what happened. And with each syllable out of my mouth, Ash grows tenser. There is no denying the heat rolling off him in waves.

"Stay here." Ash leaves me standing with Harlem, and I watch as he makes his way over to where Brandon and his uncle are standing. I can't hear what's said, but I look on as the three men have words. I don't miss the tick in Ash's jaw as Brandon speaks. Something tells me he doesn't like what he's hearing. When Ash turns back toward me, I go to ask what's happening but shut my mouth when he cuts me off. "Keys."

I blink. "What?"

"Give me your keys?"

"Why?" I ask.

"You're on the back of my bike."

"What about my car?"

"Harlem will drop it at your place."

Without another question, I hand Ash my keys and he, in return, tosses them to Harlem. "Take her car back to her place then meet us at the club."

"You got it, Prez."

Ash brings his eyes back to me as he straddles his bike. "Let's go."

"Go where?"

"Babe, let's go."

"Go where?" I ask again.

"Jesus Christ, do you always have to be this difficult?"

I put my hand on my hip. "I'm not trying to be difficult. I only asked you where we're going."

"I got shit to sort out at the club, and you're coming with me because some of that shit I have to sort out is you."

I narrow my eyes. "Are you saying I'm allowed in your club now? And I don't need sorting out, Ash."

"Sage." Ash's lip twitches. "If you don't get your ass on the back of my bike, I'm going to put you over my knee," he orders in a no-nonsense tone.

"Fine," I grumble as I climb on behind him.

After we arrived at The Fallen, Salem dumped me at a table near the stage and told me to wait for him, then he disappeared into the back.

Three of the men I met yesterday at the clubhouse came in five minutes after that. Baja, Laredo and Mystic. They spotted me sitting at the table, and each acknowledged me with a nod before heading toward the back where Salem had disappeared.

"Hey there."

I tear my eyes away from the hall where Ash disappeared down to the woman standing at the edge of the table. I remember her from the clubhouse last night. Much different from the first time I lay eyes on her. Meaning she has clothes on, and her mouth is devoid of Ash's dick.

Yep, standing in front of me wearing a pair of skin-tight jeans, leather boots, and a crop top sweater, holding two bottles of water, is the very woman I saw giving Ash a blow job that first unforgettable night I was here.

"You don't mind if I sit, do you?" The woman asks but sits across from me anyway before I have a chance to protest. "I thought you could use the company while the guys are tending to business." She passes me a bottle of water. "I can get you a beer if you prefer. Aspen is not in yet, and I'm shit at mixing drinks. The best I can do is water or beer." Her smile is warm and welcoming and not in the least bit catty. Which confuses me.

I take the offered water and offer a hesitant smile of my own. "Water is fine. Thanks."

"No problem. I'm Astrid, by the way."

"I'm—" I go to introduce myself, but apparently, introductions are not needed.

"You're Sage. I know. We've all heard about you. You're Salem's woman."

Shocked, I ask, "How do you know about me?"

"The boss hasn't had any of the girls here take care of him since the night you and your friend came in, and when he found Misty, one of the other dancers, naked on the couch in his office earlier today, he kicked her out and told her not to do that shit again. When Misty asked why, he said he has a woman who tends to his dick now and that he wasn't interested in her snatch."

My mouth hangs open at Astrid's blunt recount. I also don't like that women are offering their bodies to Ash.

"Is...is that something that happens often around here?"

Astrid shrugs. "Yeah. The guys like pussy, and the women here have no problem giving it." Then she turns serious. "But we don't prostitute if that's what you're thinking. The club doesn't sell pussy. And not all the girls that work here have sex with club members. And they don't make us. We all have an itch that needs to be scratched from time to time." She shrugs.

I'm starting to second-guess my coming here. I never had any preconceived notion that Ash is a saint. I know he's had women, and I got an idea what type of woman he's used to the night I first laid eyes on him in this very club, but to have it blatantly in my face is another thing altogether.

I also didn't miss that Ash had a naked woman in his office today. Hell, he could've had sex with her, and I would be none the wiser. Is Ash the kind of man who can commit to one woman? Am I enough to keep his interest when he's used to variety?

"Hey." Astrid pulls me out of my wandering thoughts. "You should know Salem is crazy about you. I knew he was gone over you the first time he laid eyes on you, and he's been different, too."

"Different how?" I ask.

"I don't know, just less of an asshole. Lighter, and I even caught him crack a smile or two." Astrid laughs. "And I saw the way you looked when you realized I live at the clubhouse. I want you to know, you have nothing to worry about," Astrid says sincerely. I'm about to reply when we're interrupted by a woman dressed in a red silk robe barely hiding her bare breasts and matching red garters. She has blonde hair cut into a short bob, and despite the heavy makeup caked on her face, I can tell she's a beautiful woman. And she's tall. In heels, she'd tower over me. I've tried not to feel insecure about my short stature and the bit of extra weight I carry around my midsection and my butt and thighs, but being side-by-side with this woman is bringing it out.

"Need something, Misty?" Astrid asks, her tone laced with irritation.

And there she is. Misty. The very woman Astrid was telling me about. The woman who a short while ago offered herself to my man. Something unwelcome sizzles in the air, telling me this woman was butthurt and being rejected was something she didn't take kindly to, and because she heard about me and heard I was here, she wanted to show out. You don't grow up around catty bitches and not learn a thing or two on how they operate. Luckily, I'm an expert at dealing with a woman like Misty. Women like Misty, who look like her, will always look their noses down on women like me; the women they think are less-than. Because I'm not tall, or skinny, or have the kind of in-your-face beauty. Women like Misty are all the same.

"I just thought I'd come by to say hi to Salem's..." She looks me up and down "Friend."

"Woman," I correct. "I'm Ash's woman." I purposely use Ash's name and turn internal cartwheels when I see Misty flinch. Take that bitch.

Misty quickly recovers, schooling her features. "That's okay. Salem will get bored fucking that fat chick soon enough, and when he does, I'll be back to sucking and riding his big cock." Misty smirks as if she's won some sort of victory. Too bad for her, I am not one to eat shit.

"I'd rather be a fat chick than a nameless cum dumpster that allows a bunch of men into my used-up pussy, only to have them toss me aside when they're finished getting off. What you had with Ash is past tense. He's mine now. I'm the one riding on the back of his bike, sleeping in his bed and taking his cock." When I finish, Misty looks ready to spit nails.

"You fucking, bitch." She launches herself at me, but Astrid is out of her seat in a flash, catching Misty by the hair and shoving her to the floor.

"You just fucked up," Astrid tells Misty.

Ash chooses that moment to make an appearance. "What the fuck is goin' on?" he barks.

I stand and glare up at Ash. "You let your dog off her leash."

Someone behind Ash chokes out a laugh.

"Fuck you," Misty spits from her place on the floor.

Ash ignores my jab and instead looks at Astrid. "Explain."

"Misty came out here and tried to lay claim to you and your dick. She got in your woman's face. Sage handles herself beautifully, though." Astrid grins.

Ash turns his murderous glare to Misty, who has now picked herself up off the floor. "Told you this mornin' I wasn't interested in your cunt." Ash takes a step closer to Misty, causing her to shrink. This time when he speaks, his tone is low and menacing. "Clue in. You never had a shot claimin' me or my dick. My woman was right. You're nothin' but a nameless hole. You fucked up by getting' in Sage's face and disrespectin' her in my club. You have five minutes to get your shit and get gone." Then he jerks his chin at Astrid. "Go with her. Make sure she does as she's told."

"You got it." Astrid smiles at me. "Later, babe."

"Uh...later." I wave.

Baja, Laredo, and Mystic scatter when Ash sets his sights on me. We stand there staring at each other, not saying a word. When the uncomfortable silence gets to be too much, I speak. "So...how much of that did you hear?"

I'll admit I'm a tad embarrassed by some of the things I said. I don't usually have such a crude vocabulary.

Salem's lip twitches. "Cum dumpster?"

My cheeks heat. "I heard it in a movie once."

"Get over here," he rumbles.

I go to him, and when I'm within reach, he hooks his arm around my waist, pulling me against his chest. "You good?"

I nod.

"What she said," Ash goes to explain.

"It's fine," I stop him. "I get it. You've had other women before me. That's not something I can or will hold against you. But I will stand up for myself when it blows back in my face like today."

"That kind of shit won't happen again, baby. You have my word."

I'm silent for a beat as I contemplate asking my next question.

Ash, being in tune with the expression on my face, asks, "You got somethin' to add, babe?"

"You said I'm yours, right? Does that mean you're mine? That as long as we're doing whatever this is, there is no other woman?"

"The fuck, babe? I thought I made myself clear the other night out at the clubhouse." Ash's head jerks back. "I'm not wettin' my dick anywhere else." I bite my bottom lip to keep from smiling like a loon. Ash leans in close, and I can smell the whisky on his breath. "As long as you're in my bed and on the back of my bike, there will be no other woman. Got it?"

"Yes," I breathe.

"Good. Now give me your mouth."

15
SALEM

Sage putting Misty in her place has my dick hard as a fucking rock and I'm itching to throw her sweet ass over my shoulder, take her upstairs to my office, and reward her with my cock buried deep inside her sweet pussy. My palms slide over the flare of her hips and onto her backside. I grab her ass cheeks in my hands, pull her flush against my body, and pry my mouth from hers, very aware we have an audience. "You drive me fuckin' crazy." Sage opens her eyes, and I feel myself falling. She has no clue of the storm brewing. If something were to happen to her, I could never forgive myself.

"Trust me, the feeling is mutual," Sage says in a light-hearted voice. She clears her throat, her fingers fiddling with the President patch on my cut. "So..." There's a twinkle in her eyes. "You talk about me?" She smiles with a glint of mischief.

I growl. "I'm about two seconds from hauling your ass up those stairs and lettin' you screamin' my name do all the talkin' for me, babe," I confess, and Sage's pupils dilate.

"Fuck, yeah. Now that's what I'm talkin' about," Juneau boasts. "Nothin' like hearin' a woman getting' a good dickin'.

You're a damn lucky man, Prez." He lowers his ass into an empty seat nearby, holding a beer in his hand.

I smile at Sage, who laughs at my brother's banter. "Come here." I move around her and take a seat, pulling her on my lap.

"Ash. There are perfectly good chairs I can sit on." Sage wiggles her ass.

"Woman." I grip her hips, keeping her still. "Stop rubbin' that sweet ass on my dick."

Sage flips her hair and looks at me. "All the more reason I should have my own seat."

"This is your seat," I growl, as she goes to move but I keep her in place. "Stay put."

She sighs heavily. "We have got to talk about this bossy behavior."

Mystic laughs as he parks his ass in the chair beside me. "Good luck." My other brothers, Laredo, Baja, and Harlem, chuckle at Mystic's remark while joining us at the table.

One of our waitresses, Ashley, appears with a tray full of drinks in her hand. She sets six beers, an entire bottle of whiskey, and six shot glasses on the table. Then she places a martini in front of Sage and smiles. "Aspen said you like them extra dry." Sage looks across the room, her eyes landing on Aspen at the bar, giving her a wave and appreciative smile.

"I like her." Sage takes a sip of her drink.

"You're mine." I slip my hand between her thighs, leaving it to rest there while lifting my beer with the other to down part of it.

"Are you serious right now?" Sage giggles. "Aspen is a beautiful woman, but I'm all about the D." She pops a green olive in her mouth.

Baja grabs the whiskey bottle from the center of the table and pours every man a shot. I down mine. My thoughts shift back to why Sage is with me at the club in the first place. "Babe, I need a detailed description of the fucker who approached you earlier.

Anything that stood out." My bitter tone garners my brothers' attention.

"Aside from his rancid breath?" Sage murmurs, taking another sip of her martini.

"Babe," I groan.

"Really, I don't see why one asshole of a man is becoming a big deal. I handled it; he's gone. End of story." Sage brushes the entire incident off.

Harlem, who's usually the quiet one of the bunch, cuts his eyes at me before he speaks. "We only have the short description Billy and Brandon gave us: tall, dark hair, and tattoos."

Fuck, you might as well be describing those of us sitting around this damn table right now.

Harlem turns his focus on Sage with a severe look on his face. "This bastard disrespected you." His eyes are narrowed at my woman, and Sage leans back into my chest. "You're Prez's woman, which means the bastard also disrespected my brother," he states, and the rest of my men agree with nods and a few damn rights being said.

Pride fills my chest, and I lift my beer to them, knowing they have my back but, most importantly, their respect. I rub my palm up and down Sage's thigh. "Think, babe."

"Fine," she huffs. "Just don't go getting yourselves hurt or arrested over some gutter trash. The asshole isn't worth the effort." Sage looks around the table. "He was dressed plainly: jeans and a black shirt. Oh, and an MC cut like yours. Only it said Demon Jokers. You know them?"

My blood runs cold. One of those motherfuckers approached my woman in my town. The worst part about the ordeal is the Demon Jokers knowing Sage is mine.

"What about tattoos? Can you describe what they looked like?" I ask.

Sage nods while sipping her drink again, then sets it on the table. "A spider. He had several smaller face tattoos, but the spider tattoo—" Sage touches the side of her neck "—stood out. It looked so real."

"Catch which direction he took off?" Laredo asks her.

"No, he walked off before Harlem rolled up on the scene." Sage twists her body to face me. "Ash. Just let it be. The guy is gone, and I'm fine, I swear."

Before the conversation can go any further, Mystic clears his throat. "We have company." He lifts his chin in the direction of the front door. Strolling our direction is Sheriff Huxley, along with another officer walking behind him. Judging by the intense look on his face, this visit isn't a casual one.

"Pour me a shot, babe." I draw circles on her leg, not the least bit affected by Huxley's presence. Sage reaches for the bottle and pours the whiskey into my glass without hesitation. Huxley stops at the table, standing between Harlem and Baja, with his hand resting easily on his holstered firearm at his side. I greet him with, "There a problem?"

Huxley eyes each of us then sets his attention on me. "I need the whereabouts of you and your men last night."

"What the fuck for?"

"Have another murder. Her body was found on the outskirts of town." Huxley's words cause Sage's body to tense.

"Oh my god," Sage gasps, covering her mouth with her hand.

"If you're expectin' us to know anything, you're barkin' up the wrong tree, Sheriff." I make no attempts to hide my contempt that he's even suggesting we have any involvement.

"The young woman's body was found in the middle of an overgrown field less than a mile from your clubhouse," Huxley states, and the little nugget of information has not just me but my brothers' full attention.

"Ash?" Sage looks at me, and I don't like the concern and fear in her eyes.

I stand, bringing Sage to her feet as well, then kiss her forehead. "Wait for me upstairs."

"But..."

"Now, babe." Listening, Sage remains silent, gives a quick glance back at Huxley, then moves toward the stairs off to the far side of the club. I wait until she's in the loft area out of view before turning my attention to our guest. "Myself nor my men had nothing to do with the death of any woman."

"And for the record, I must ask you and your men to prove your whereabouts between the hours of 2:00 am and 3:00 am this morning," Huxley reiterates. The officer behind him steps to the side. Now I understand why he didn't waltz in here alone. Huxley needs a witness to his questioning.

"All of us were at the clubhouse, in fuckin' bed. Except for Mystic, who, as you know, has a young daughter and would be at home with her." I take my seat. "You want proof? I'll gladly show you camera footage backing up the fact that not one of my men left the compound until around 6:00 am."

Huxley continues eyeing me for a beat, then shifts his attention to Mystic. "This true?"

"Like Salem said, I was at home," Mystic says, clearly agitated.

A moment of silence hangs between Huxley and the rest of us before he nods, then looks over his shoulder. "Go sit in the car. I'll be out in a minute," he tells the officer, who doesn't question his boss's actions and takes his leave. Huxley turns back to face the table. "Mind if I sit?"

I spread my arms. "By all means."

Huxley relaxes in the chair. "I'd like your help."

I grunt. "I don't see what the club can do about a couple of dead women."

Huxley pinches the bridge of his nose. "The FBI is involved, and the dipshit they sent plays by the book. I don't want another young girl found dead in my town, which means the rules some-times need bending."

"I sure as shit don't like the loss of innocent lives either, but someone steppin' on your toes is of no concern to me." I fold my arms across my chest.

"Are they investigating these as serial homicide cases?" Laredo asks.

Huxley licks his lips, nodding. "The murders in Salem, along with the one a couple towns over, appear to have the same M.O. as some killings that took place almost two years ago in Texas, and they've garnered some attention."

"Who's the agent?" Laredo leans forward in his seat, becoming more interested in the details.

"Shawn Procter." The second Huxley says the name Laredo's lips thin. "You know him?"

"I do." Laredo's jaw ticks.

"He's a cocky son of a bitch." Huxley shakes his head. "If it's not in that FBI handbook he's got shoved up his ass, then he's not doing it." Out of frustration, Huxley sighs and scrubs a palm down his face. "Laredo, I need—"

Laredo throws a hand up. "I'm gonna stop you right there." He shakes his head. "I don't work for the law anymore. I hung up those spurs years ago."

"I'm only asking that you look at some files, nothing more. Not a soul needs to know. Just the men at this table." Huxley pauses, leaving a moment of silence lingering.

"What if that agent comes around askin' questions? The club doesn't need no FBI butt-sniffer poking his nose where it doesn't belong." Juneau says the very words I was thinking.

"I'll deal with Procter. I'm here because Laredo was the best damn profiler in the state of Texas, and I want someone not looking to impress his bosses to help me find some answers, before another woman ends up dead." Huxley sets his sights back on Laredo. "All I want is your knowledge. Look at the files and point me in the right direction."

Laredo says nothing, but we can all see him battling with what Huxley is asking him to do. The Sheriff pushes the chair from the table and stands. "I best be on my way. You know where I am should you decide to lend your skills." He turns and heads across the room.

"Fuckin' hell," Laredo mutters, then his eyes hone in on Huxley. "I'll do it," he shouts. Huxley stops, looks back at Laredo, nods once, then turns back around and walks out the door. Laredo reaches out and grabs the whiskey bottle, then he pours himself a drink and downs it.

"You sure you wanna do this?" I ask, knowing that once he opens that door again, mainly due to the nature of the cases, it will mess with his head.

Laredo cuts his eyes at me, and I see the storm brewing inside. "What if I don't?" is all he asks, and the question is no different than the single bullet of a loaded weapon in a game of Russian roulette.

"I hate to add more on the plate, but are we doing anything about the biker who approached your woman?" Mystic raises awareness of our problem from earlier.

I'm done with the bullshit. "I want to meet the bastards. Face to face. I want to look Warlock in his eyes and let him know his days are numbered." I rise from my chair and look up at the loft where Sage is waiting.

"I say we ride in, put them all in an early grave, and be rid of the headache," Juneau throws in.

"We need to be more calculated. The Demon Jokers outnumber us. We go in guns blazin', there is a higher possibility we don't walk out." I glance at Harlem. "Get word to the Demon Jokers. I want a sit-down. I'll be waiting at a neutral location: Pale Horse." Then I look at Mystic. "Call Lycidas and set shit up." I eye the rest of my men. "We ride out when the sun rises, so enjoy yourselves tonight but get some sleep." I look back up at my office. "You know where to find me." I waste no time walking away.

Upstairs, I find Sage sitting on the sofa with one leg crossed over the other, her foot flicking up and down. Her blue eyes fix on my face. "Ash, what the hell is going on?" It's not fear in her eyes but a tremble in her voice that stabs at my heart. "Another killing?" She hugs herself. I sit down beside her and pull her into my side. "And why would he think you could..." She doesn't finish her sentence and picks at the frayed rip on the knee of her jeans.

"Huxley knows the club had nothin' to do with the deaths, babe." I pull back and bring her face to mine. "Do you have doubts?" I search her eyes for any signs of uncertainty.

"You may be a lot of things—do a lot of things—Ash, but you didn't kill those poor women. Neither did those men downstairs." She rests her hand on my thigh and exhales. "Although I admit, another murder in town makes me extremely uneasy, and it changes my perspective on the run-in with the stranger at the hardware store today." She hangs her head. "I was stupid to act so passively about it."

Sage bringing up the encounter makes my blood boil. "Until further notice, you won't go anywhere without me or one of my men nearby at all times."

Sage tilts her head back, and for a second I think she's gearing up to give me pushback on the matter. "I won't fight you on it," she says submissively, and I grin. "What? You expected a fight?"

"I did."

Sage's hand slides a little further up my leg, and my dick swells, anticipating the feel of her fingers, but she stops short. "Usually, our disagreements lead to other activities. Was that what you were hoping for?" My little vixen leans into me, her lips barely brushing against mine. She was right. Our arguments always end with my dick inside her sweet pussy. My woman has my blood pumping for an entirely different reason now, and I plan on acting on it.

I stand, and Sage's eyes go straight to my dick. "Let's go." I extend my hand to her, and she takes hold of it. I pull her off the sofa.

"Where?"

"My place so I can fuck you proper."

The following morning, my men and I are sitting in an empty bar, minus Harlem, who is back home watching over Sage. I relax against the back of my seat and smoke my cigarette while admiring the bar's décor. The Pale Horse, which feels like we're sitting at the table in Dracula's castle, is owned by Lycidas Cross. Stone gargoyles placed throughout the bar hold vintage Victorian lamps, bathing the bar with amber lighting. The walls are painted a deep moss green, complementing all the ornate gilt mirrors and framed pieces of his artwork on display throughout the bar. Lycidas is gifted with a camera and a paintbrush. His works are of beautiful, mostly naked women. It's not just the curves of their bodies that are mesmerizing. It's the women's eyes that draw you in. Lycidas captures more than the sensual moment between artist and muse. He's able to capture what the woman is feeling. Each piece reflects a different emotion.

Lycidas himself makes an appearance, strolling up to us with a bottle of Scotch in one hand and stacked shot glasses in his other hand. His long, black hair is braided, draped over one shoulder, and he's in his usual attire, which can only be described as Victorian Goth. "Looks like your appointment is a no-show." He takes a seat with us and pops the cork from the expensive liquor bottle.

"It appears that way." I watch Lycidas pour the shots. "Talks here today could have kept him and his men from certain death."

"One of those Demon Jokers was caught in my bar, slippin' shit in a woman's drink last week," Lycidas says, and my mind goes back to the night I met Sage. He looks at me. "I hear you had a similar run-in?"

"I did." I nod. "He's been disposed of." I down my whiskey. *Fuck, that shit is good.*

"I heard that too." Lycidas lifts the shot glass to his lips and throws his head back. He slams the glass down against the surface of the table. My men drink theirs, and Lycidas pours us one more. He raises his glass. "Here's to you killing the mother-fuckers." He winks. "Minus one, whose corpse is rotting in a shallow grave in an undisclosed location." His lips twist into a sinister grin, and I know he personally ended the life of one Demon Joker.

I respect Lycidas and lift my drink to him before pouring it down my throat.

Lycidas stands. "Not to be a dick, but I have a business to run. You can see yourselves out." He eyes me for a moment, nods, then walks off. "Keep the bottle," he says before disappearing down a dark hallway.

"You think he has a dungeon below the bar where he sleeps in a coffin?" Juneau jests. "Fuck, I'm serious." He pushes from the table and glances at each of us. "You mean to tell me he doesn't give you vamp vibes?"

"Shut up," Baja grumps.

"Sounds like someone needs a nap," Juneau pokes back at Baja.

We walk outside, and my eyes need to adjust to the sun's brightness. We're no closer to ridding ourselves of the Demon Jokers.

"What's our next move?" Mystic asks, swinging his leg over his bike seat.

"Kill them all, if that's what it takes."

16

SAGE

"Spread your legs wider, baby." Ash's palm comes down on my right ass cheek. "I want all the way in there." Then I feel something heavy between my shoulder blades, pressing my upper body into the mattress as he continues to drill me from behind. "Fuck," he rasps. "That's it." My biker grabs two handfuls of my flesh and squeezes. "Best goddamn ass I ever had my hands on." His thrusts become more powerful, leaving me no choice but to grip the headboard above my head.

"Ash," I breathe, peering up at him over my shoulder. Ash in his usual worn jeans, black boots, t-shirt, and cut is a sight to behold. Still, Ash Crawford, naked, his bare chest slick with sweat, pure lust shining in his eyes, on his knees behind me with his cock buried deep inside—touching me in a way no man before him has, and I pray never will get the chance to try—can only be described as glorious.

"You're going to take what I give you, aren't you, baby?"

My mouth opens on a gasp, but I cannot form words. The only thing I can concentrate on is how good Salem being inside me feels and how I don't ever want this to end. Until he suddenly pulls out. "Ash," I cry out at the loss of him, and when I go to move, his hand on my back stops me, keeping me in place with my face turned to the side and my cheek pressed against the gray sheet.

"I asked you a question."

"Yes," I sob, needing his cock back inside me.

"Yes, what?" His chest heaves, and his pupils dilate, turning the color of coal.

"Ash, please," I go to say, but the plea dies on my lips, and I cry out instead when the next smack that he delivers is across my pussy.

"Give me the words, Sage, and I'll let you come on my cock."

"I'm going to take whatever you give me," I pant.

"You're going to take my cock and my cum, aren't you?"

"Yes!" I cry. "I'm going to take it all. Now please, I need to come." I'm barely able to utter the last syllables before he is there, filling me, stretching me, and giving me exactly what I crave. *"Ash!"* I scream his name as my orgasm rises out of nowhere, lighting my entire body on fire. And the heat of my release is all it takes to push him over the edge with me.

"Sage," Ash growls, and I watch the cords of his neck strain as he slams into me with one final push, taking what he demands of my body yet giving more in return. And when he collapses against my back, giving me his weight, I take that as well. Ash rolls to the side when he exhales, taking me with him, then he tags his arm around my waist and settles his leg between my thighs. He doesn't speak for a long while. We're both content at the moment. Soon, his body goes lax, and I can feel his warm breath on the back of my neck, letting me know he's out. As for me, I can't get my brain to shut down long enough to find sleep.

With each passing day I spend with Ash, I become more and more attached. There is a draw between us, one I am confident he feels, too. My internal conflict stems from what I'm learning about his club and him. Though I'm certain he hasn't told me all there is to know about him, the dangers surrounding him are not lost on me. That's the part of Ash that terrifies me. He didn't say as much, but I feel that the man who approached me outside the hardware store is somehow connected to the club. There's no other reason he and the guys acted the way they did about the incident. This, too, has me worried. But I'm in deep and can no longer see the surface of the once black-and-white my life was before Ash. Sure, my life was great, but now I see in color. I think that alone is worth taking on whatever risks come with this thing building between us. I fall asleep with my heart deciding to take a leap of faith.

I wake sometime in the middle of the night to an empty bed. Reaching out, I take in the cold sheets, a sign Ash's side has been vacant for a while. Tossing the blanket aside, I slide out of bed and shiver when cool air touches my bare skin. Finding his flannel on the floor, I pick it up and slip it on over my shoulders, quickly working the buttons while looking around in the dark for my sleep shorts.

I make a mental note to pack warmer pajamas when staying over at the clubhouse. The old building is drafty. Once I'm dressed, I open the bedroom door to a dark, silent hallway. Though I've been here a few times, I still haven't gotten the lay of the land. The clubhouse is pretty big. Ash mentioned the old church was once an orphanage, too. I find the history behind the place interesting, but it's the architecture that fascinates me the most. Though the building has had some updates, much of the original structure remains. Vaulted ceilings, arched windows, and they even kept some of the old church pews.

Clearing the hall, I pad into the main room of the clubhouse, the space I've noticed all the guys hang together.

I'm startled by a door slamming, followed by footsteps. A moment later, I turn to find Ash, Mystic, Baja, and a man I've never seen before walking in through the door from outside. None of the men notice me, and I take a step back into the shadow of the hallway when the man I don't recognize starts to speak.

The guy is of average height, slim, light brown hair, and wears glasses. Standing next to Ash, Mystic, and Baja, he looks out of place. I know I shouldn't be listening, but a man like him in a place like this compels me to stay rooted in place.

"Please, I want this done as soon as possible. That man kidnapped my little girl, held her for three days before the police found him, and now he's getting out of prison. Seven years was not enough for that scum. It took my Annie years of therapy to get to a place of peace. I can't let Harry Carpenter rob that from her."

My heart rate starts to pick up at this father's plea for his daughter. Why is he here? Why is he telling Ash this? Why does he think the club can help him?

Then I watch with rapt attention as Ash stops and turns to the man. "I told you once, Mr. Andrews, we don't discuss business such as this out in the open. If I have to remind you again, consider this meeting and any future meetings void," he rumbles, his tone low.

My gaze bounces back to the man, and even from across the room I can see his posture waver. I'm so focused on the scared, desperate man that I don't notice the pair of eyes that have clocked me until it's too late.

When I shift my attention once more, I find Ash staring right at me. He doesn't look pleased, and I swallow past the lump in my throat but hold his gaze. It's not until he releases mine that I turn and run down the hall back to his room.

Safely inside, my shaky legs carry me over to the edge of the bed, where I collapse. I sit unmoving, for I don't know how long. Minutes turn into hours. The sun is starting to peek through the curtains of the window when the bedroom door opens, and Ash strolls in, his eyes glued to me and his face devoid of emotion, making it difficult to get a read on him. Considering he caught me eavesdropping, it's safe to assume he pissed. It's the silence stretching between us that's making me nervous, though. He's just standing there, not saying a word. Therefore, neither am I.

"The next time you decide to go for a midnight stroll, and you find yourself in the middle of business that doesn't concern you, it would be in your best interest to turn your ass around and walk the fuck away," he warns in an acid tone that makes my insides twist. But just because Ash's current demeanor is on the scary side, it doesn't stop the words that fly out of my mouth. I might be many things, but someone without a backbone is not one of them.

"Or," I hiss through clenched teeth, "I can get my shit and go home. That way, if I wake up in the middle of the night and find myself wanting to take a midnight stroll...I can do so." Not waiting for Ash's response, I stand and march into the bathroom, where my overnight bag sits on the floor beside the bathtub. Snatching it up, I start tossing my things inside. Toothbrush, lotion, hairbrush. Then I stomp over to the shower, where I retrieve my shampoo and body wash.

"The fuck you doin'?" Ash walks up behind me.

"What's it look like I'm doing? I'm getting my stuff and going home." I angle past him with my bag in hand and start looking around on the floor for the clothes I had on last night. Only, my panties are nowhere in sight. Screw it. I pick up my jeans and tug them on over my silk sleep shorts. Then I decide to keep Ash's shirt on and shove my sweater into the bag.

"You're not goin' anywhere."

"Yes, I am. Just as soon as I find my shoes."

"Sage," Ash calls my name, but I ignore him.

Yes! Found my shoes. Now I can get out of here. Sitting on the edge of the bed, I shove my feet into them.

"Sage," Ash grinds out a second time. This time I don't ignore him.

"Look, I get that I heard something you obviously didn't want me to hear, but instead of coming to me and having a conversation about it, you come at me with your asshole, bullshit demands. I might not live in the world you live in, and I get there are things about you and your club that you might not want me to know, but under no circumstances does that give you the right to talk to me like you just did. All I did was wake up alone to an empty bed and wonder where you had gone. I didn't walk out of this room with the intent to spy on you."

I don't wait for a reply. Instead, I hike my bag over my shoulder and head for the door. I don't make it three feet before my bag is ripped from my grasp and Ash's arm is around my waist, and I'm airborne.

"What the hell. Put me down." I struggle against his hold.

"I told you; you aren't leavin'."

"You can't stop me."

"The fuck I can't," he growls against my ear.

A second later, my back hits the bed, and Ash's large frame looms above me, caging me in.

"Get off me," I grind out.

"No."

"I swear to god..."

"His daughter was kidnapped and raped."

My following words get caught in my throat at Ash's statement. "Wh...what?" I stammer.

"The man you saw me with tonight. He came to the club because his daughter's kidnapper is being released from prison this week."

I take a deep breath as I try to force back the bile rising in my throat.

"Wh...why did he come to you?" I ask the question, but I know what the answer will be, deep down.

Ash's eyes bore into mine for a beat before he speaks. "He wants me to kill the piece of shit."

He doesn't say more, and I know it's because he's waiting for what I'm undoubtedly going to ask next. "Are you?"

Without hesitation, Ash answers, "Yes."

I search his eyes for the truth, but I don't have to look very long. "Have you done that before?"

Again, he answers, "Yes."

Ash's confession is made with no hint of regret or remorse, and his face is again devoid of emotion. Instead, in its place is something dark and cold. It's like the Grim Reaper himself is hovering above me, saying these things as casually as someone reciting their grocery list. And yet, I'm still not afraid of him.

"So, you're like a hitman?"

"Yes."

"And these people, like the man that came here tonight, do they pay you to kill for them?"

"Yes."

I look up at Ash's beautiful face for a beat before I say, "Okay."

Suddenly, there it is. A chink in his armor opens, and Ash's head rears back as he blinks down at me. "Okay. That's all you have to say?"

"What?" I ask.

Ash's nostrils flare. "I tell you that people hire me to kill for them, that I take hits in exchange for cash, and all you have to fuckin' say is, okay?"

I gaze at Ash, but when I touch his face, he jerks away. "Don't," he says.

"Ash," I whisper.

"I'm a murderer, Sage. I kill people for money," he tells me through clenched teeth. "That's the kind of man I am. It's the kind of man I will always be."

I know he's trying to scare me, but it's not working. When he sees my own truth shining through my eyes, he shakes his head. "Jesus."

"What kind of people do you kill? Do you go after innocent men? How about women and children, Ash?"

"Fuck no. We only go after worthless pieces of shit. I've slit the throats of men who have raped women, men who have killed innocent fathers that were driving home from work because they thought killing someone would be, in their words, *fun*. I've tortured the lowest of the low, men who put their filthy hands on children. I've put bullets in the heads of the corrupt who knowingly let a man who tortured, raped, and nearly killed a teenage girl at a party go free." Salem stares at me like he's trying to figure me out. "Fuck," he hisses, then shakes his head, his fingers digging into the flesh at my sides. "Fucking fuck me."

"Ash," I breathe.

"No way you're fucking real," he cuts me off.

I try again to touch him, and this time he lets me. I thread my fingers through his hair, and it's his undoing. Ash's mouth comes crashing down on mine, and suddenly we're in a race to get each other's clothes off.

"Need to fuck you," he grunts, tugging my jeans down past my hips, taking my sleep shorts with them.

I bite his bottom lip while fumbling with his belt buckle. "Yes."

Rid of all barriers between us, Ash hooks my leg over his back then surges in.

My nails dig into his back as I cry out, *"Oh god."*

Ash's palm glides up between my breasts before latching onto my throat. "You're not allowed to keep this pussy from me. It's mine."

"Yes. Yours, Ash." I buck my hips, meeting his thrusts.

The hold around my neck tightens. Not enough to cut off my air, but enough to force my eyes to snap open and meet his gaze.

"Don't ever threaten to fuckin' leave me again."

Thrust.

"You belong to me."

Thrust.

"Never."

Thrust.

I didn't see it before, but I see it now. Ash keeping stuff from me wasn't because he was hiding who he was. It's because he was afraid I'd leave him once I found out.

Not taking my eyes off him, I give Ash the only thing I know I can provide. Myself. "Never. I promise."

***

It's been a week since the blowup with Ash, after I witnessed the exchange between him and the man. Or should I say, client? Hell, I don't know what terminology is appropriate, but I'm not about to ask, either. In fact, the topic hasn't been brought up again. Things between Ash and I have gone back to normal, whatever that is. The only difference is he insists I sleep in his bed every night except for last night. I told him yesterday I'd been neglecting my best friend and owed her a girls' night. Juniper hasn't complained. In fact, she's been nothing but happy for me, but I could tell she missed me. The truth is, I've missed her too.

"What's the deal with your private security?" Juniper tips her head toward the sidewalk in front of the salon where Baja is leaning against his bike smoking a cigarette.

I roll my eyes. "Ash has been having one of the guys follow me around ever since the creep approached me last week. I told him it wasn't necessary. He's just being overprotective."

"I think it's romantic." The woman getting her hair colored by Juniper fans her face, adding, "Who wouldn't want a big strong biker going all alpha on them."

I laugh. "It's annoying, is what it is."

"Why, if I was twenty years younger, I'd give one of those hunky bikers a run for their money."

"You should go for it, Meg." Juniper winks at the older woman, making her giggle like a schoolgirl.

"Oh, heavens no. I wouldn't know what to do with a man like that."

We all look over at Baja, who has just walked inside the salon. He pauses when he notices three sets of eyes on him. As if he knows we were talking about him, he gives us his best panty-dropping grin. "Ladies."

"How's it going, Baja?" I smile.

"Can't complain, darlin'." He looks at Juniper, tips his head, and then looks at Meg and winks, making the old woman blush. "I need to hit the head."

I flick my hand over my shoulder. "Knock yourself out."

Thirty minutes later, Juniper and I watch Meg walk out of the salon with her fresh cut and color and a smile on her face, and her arm linked with Baja's as he escorts her to her car.

"Know what's funny?" I ask Juniper as I watch Baja with Meg, working his charm.

"What?" Juniper tips her head toward me.

"Most people in this town are scared of the MC. They believe they're nothing more than criminals. They think those things without even getting to know them. Yet if those same people would take the time to open their eyes, they'd witness stuff like this. Big bad biker helping an old woman to her car and probably making her whole year by doing so. Or when those punk kids destroyed Sukie's window and how the club made them fix it."

"Yeah, well, most people are mindless idiots," Juniper retorts.

Isn't that the truth?

Juniper sighs. "I have about twenty minutes before my next client shows. I'm going to go fold some towels. What about you? Are you heading out since that one lady rescheduled?"

"Naw. I'm going to catch up on some paperwork before heading to the clubhouse."

Juniper smirks. "Tell your boyfriend I appreciate him letting you up for air at least one night to spend some time with your bestie."

Even though her comment was meant to tease me, I can't help feeling bad because I have been neglecting my friend. As if she can read my thoughts, Juniper quickly squashes them.

"I know what you're thinking, Sage, and I want you to stop."

"Juju."

Juniper walks over and wraps her arms around me. "I'm happy for you, Sage. I like Salem, and more so, I like the way he makes you smile and laugh and the way your face lights up when you mention his name. I don't ever want you to feel like you have to choose between the two of us. Now, go have some naked fun with your man."

I burst out laughing. "I love you, Juju."

"I love you, heifer."

While on the way to the clubhouse, my cell rings. Reaching out toward the cup holder, I smile when I see Ash's name flash across the screen and tap to answer on speaker. "Hey, you."

"Baby, where you at?"

"I just left the salon and am on my way to the clubhouse. Why?"

"Where's Baja?"

I glance in the rearview mirror to see the man in question trailing behind me on his bike. "He's following behind." I sigh. "I still don't think the bodyguard is necessary. I haven't even seen that guy since that day outside of the hardware store."

Ash lets out an exasperated, "Babe."

"Fine," I huff. "I guess having Baja looming around the shop all day isn't so bad. The ladies like eye candy, anyway."

The sound of Ash's booming laugh does something funny to my stomach. "I'm sure Baja is eatin' that shit up, too," he remarks.

I giggle. "That man could charm the panties off a sixty-five-year-old woman. Just ask Meg."

"Who's Meg?"

"A sixty-five-year-old woman Baja was putting the moves on today at the salon."

Another bark of laughter rings through the line. I don't miss the hint of mischief behind his laugh, either. One that says that Ash is for sure going to give Baja shit.

"Anyways, is there a particular reason you called?" I ask.

"Yeah, baby." Ash's voice warms. "I'm going to be a little late gettin' to the clubhouse. There's some shit I'm dealin' with."

"Oh. I can just turn around and go back home if you're busy. No biggie."

"No. You'll carry your sweet ass to the clubhouse and wait for me. You weren't in my bed last night, but your ass will be in it tonight."

"Okay, Ash. I'll wait for you."

"That's my girl."

And there are those damn butterflies again.

"Later, baby."

"Later, Ash."

.   .   .

I'm about three miles out from the clubhouse when I spot a truck pulled over to the side of the road with its hazard lights on. I ease off the gas to slow down, and that's when I recognize the person standing beside the truck. Brandon. I pull my car over to the shoulder and park behind his vehicle.

Sticking my head out the window, I call out, "Need some help?"

Brandon pops his head out from under the hood and smiles when he sees me. "Hey."

I climb out of the car the same time Baja pulls his bike in between my car and Brandon's truck. Brandon's steps falter along with his smile, but he quickly schools his features.

Baja cuts the engine to his bike. "There a problem?"

"Yeah, my damn truck died on me. It needs a new battery." Brandon turns his attention back to me. "Mind giving me a jump?"

"Sure," I say. As I go to turn back to my car, Baja stops me.

"I got it." He holds out his hand. "Go wait over by my bike, darlin'."

"I got it, Baja. I don't—"

He cuts me off by shaking his head. "Go wait by my bike."

Deciding not to argue, I toss my keys to Baja and do as I'm told. Brandon watches the exchange but says nothing. Instead, he turns and climbs in behind the wheel of his truck and waits for Baja to give him a jump. Luckily, they get his vehicle started in no time. When Brandon jumps down from the cab and rounds the hood to close it, I notice him and Baja speaking. I hope Baja isn't being an ass. Brandon is a friend, and that's just something they'll have to get used to.

. . .

When Baja and I walk into the clubhouse, my ears are immediately assaulted by the sound of a loud screech, followed by a flash of puffy pink tulle.

"Uncle Baja!" A little girl no older than four, wearing a black Harley t-shirt, a pink tutu, and black motorcycle boots, runs toward us and throws herself into Baja, who has already dropped down to one knee, arms open and ready for impact.

"How's my favorite princess?" he asks the little girl while tickling her belly.

"Stop! That tickles." She giggles.

Suddenly a woman appears from the back of the clubhouse with an apron on and a dish towel in her hand. She looks frazzled. "Lorelei."

"It's okay, Ophelia. I got her," Baja tells her.

The woman, Ophelia, looks back and forth between Baja and me like she's waiting for an introduction, but Baja is too engrossed in his tickle war with the little girl. "Are you going to just stand there and be rude, Baja, or are you going to introduce me to your friend."

"Oh, sorry, Ophelia. This is Sage."

"Oh my goodness." Ophelia's face brightens, and she quickly makes her way over to me. "You're Salem's Sage. I've heard so much about you." As soon as I'm within arm's reach, I'm pulled in for a hug. "I'm Mystic's momma."

"It's nice to meet you, Ophelia."

Ophelia pulls back and takes a long look at me. "You are just as beautiful as Salem described."

Ash told me he and Mystic are close and grew up together, so I'm not surprised at how close he and Ophelia are. Ash has never mentioned her, though it feels weird that she knows all about me.

"And this little monster is Lorelei." Ophelia points to the little girl. "She's my granddaughter."

Wow. Mystic has a kid.

Just then, the door to the clubhouse opens, and Mystic walks in.

"Daddy!" Lorelei abandons Baja and runs to Mystic, and he wastes no time scooping her up into his arms.

"Hey, baby girl. You have a good time with Grandma today?"

"Yes. We went to see Grandpa and Mrs. Crawford at the cemetery, and we gave them pretty white flowers."

Wait. Did she say Crawford? That's Ash's last name.

"Hey, sweetie," Ophelia says over my shoulder. And when I turn, I see Ash standing just inside the door.

17
SALEM

As I walk into the clubhouse, I overhear Mystic's daughter, Lorelei, talking about visiting my mother's grave. My mood instantly shifts, and I feel my body tense. Memories resurface, and I see his drunk raging face again. I see his fists pummeling my mom's face again, and swear I feel the sting of another backhand across the cheek.

"Ash." Sage calling my name pulls me from my torment. My gut feels tight, and my mouth is dry. Sage takes a small step forward. "Ash." She says my name as if she's walking on broken glass. I pull in a breath of air, then blow it out. I keep my eyes focused on my woman, grounding myself. The intense grip the past has on me starts subsiding.

"Uncle Ash!" Lorelei wiggles from Mystic's arms and rushes at me. I scoop her up. She smells like candy.

"Hey, Squirt. You find my stash of jelly beans again?" I bop the tip of her nose, and she giggles.

"Maybe you should hide them better."

I tickle her side. "You little jelly bean bandit."

Lorelei reaches her tiny hand into the little pocket on the front of her Harley Davidson shirt that sports the Born Free logo and pulls out two red jelly beans. "I saved them 'cause they're your favorite." I hold out my hand, and she places it on my palm. I pop the warm candy in my mouth lint and all, because her gesture is too fucking adorable.

"You're the best girl a guy could have." I smile and kiss the top of her head before setting her back on her feet.

Lorelei looks up at me, then looks over at Sage. "Is she your girl, too?"

"She is," I say, and Lorelei peeks at Sage again and is quiet for a second.

Lorelei smiles. "Okay." Then she skips off to go play.

My eyes land back on Sage.

"Salem." Ophelia moves into the frame, coming to stand beside Sage. She gives me a smile that wavers a bit. "I'm so sorry. I didn't mean any harm." She smiles, but it doesn't quite reach her eyes, which become misty. She wrings the towel in her hands and drops her eyes to the floor. "Chicago and I would have celebrated twenty-seven years today, which is why Lorelei and I visited the gravesite this morning." Ophelia pulls in a deep breath.

Shit. I feel like a dick. I stroll up to Ophelia and wrap her in a hug. "No harm done. Just threw me off guard for a moment is all." Ophelia is like a second mother to me—always has been. In all the ways my mom wasn't a mother, Ophelia stepped in and filled the role. I love and respect the woman. At least I know where the flowers on my mom's grave are coming from. I pull back. "So, you're the one leaving the lilies."

"Guilty." Ophelia reaches up and touches her palm to my cheek. "I'm not even sure why I started. It's just I pass by their headstones each time I pay my husband a visit, and one day, I bought an extra bouquet of flowers and placed them on your momma's headstone. I've been doing it since." Ophelia looks at me with caring eyes. I press my lips together with nothing to say.

I'm not mad, just indifferent. Ophelia smiles then backs away. "I need to pull the pie out of the oven." She claps her hands together.

I sling my arm around Sage and we follow Ophelia into the kitchen.

Juneau strolls in. "When do we eat?" He walks over to the table and plucks a fried chicken leg off the platter. "I'm starvin'," he says, with a mouthful as he munches down on the chicken.

Ophelia lifts the platter from the table and hands it to Juneau. "Why don't you put some other muscles besides your mouth to work and carry something to the tables you men set up earlier?" Juneau grins around the gnawed-on chicken leg hanging between his lips. He holds the food platter in one hand, salutes Mystic's mom with the other, and then strides out of the kitchen.

"I'll help set the tables." Sage moves to pick up a bowl of mashed potatoes, but before she can, I snake my arm around her waist and pull her to me.

"Hey." I look down at her. Having her close in my arms settles my afflicted soul.

"Hey." She rises on her toes, placing her lips to mine. "You, okay?" Her words drag like feathers against my lips as she continues to kiss me.

I breathe her in. "Yeah, babe," I lie, and do my best to shove the remaining residue of my plagued emotions into the pits of hell, where they belong.

For a moment, as we sit around the table, I listen to the conversation flow and feel a sense of normalcy. If brief, it feels good to push aside all the bullshit surrounding the club and focus on family. I watch Sage's interaction with Lorelei and easily picture having a child of our own. Wanting kids never entered my thoughts before this moment. My heart beats harder against my chest.

Ophelia, who is seated at my left, leans in close. "She's a

keeper, Ash," she whispers. "Be careful, though. As strong as she is, she's fragile, too."

Again, I say nothing. But the truth is, Ophelia is right. Sage is a strong woman. My thoughts drift to all the shit with Demon Jokers looming over our heads and the real threat of more bloodshed. I keep my eyes on Sage as she laughs at a joke Juneau says. Her smile warms my cold insides. How could I ever live without that feeling again? Can I give her everything she needs to keep her happy like she is now? Will my lifestyle corrupt all that is pure and good about Sage? Is her light bright enough to withstand my darkness?

"Wait, wait," Juneau shouts. He throws his head back, downing a swallow of beer, then wipes his mouth with the back of his hand. "I got another one for ya." He points at Sage, who is still smiling from the last joke. "What's long, green, and smells like bacon?" Juneau looks like he's about to burst.

"I'm afraid to find out." Sage giggles.

Juneau grins. "Kermit's fingers!"

Even I chuckle at that one.

Sage throws her head back in laughter. "That's disgusting." She turns her head and looks at me, her face beaming with amusement.

I find myself paralyzed, captured in the glow of her light. An electric current shoots through me like a comet streaking across the night sky. "How is it possible for you to become even more fuckin' beautiful?" The words flow past my lips the instant I think of them. Reaching out, I grip the back of her neck and pull her close, then crash my lips against hers.

"Damn, who knew a green frog finger-bangin' some pork bacon could be such a turn on?" Juneau cracks. "But hey, we all have our kinks, right?" Sage's lips lift in a smile against mine. Not able to hold back, she giggles at my brother's comment.

Extending my middle finger, I give my brother the one-finger salute.

"That's what the frog said." Juneau delivers another joke, and this time I chuckle.

"Fuckin' hell." I press my forehead against Sage's.

"You have the best family, Ash," Sage murmurs.

Later that night, Sage and I are sitting on the observation deck, her in my lap, with a blanket wrapped around us, watching the sun go down. "I had a wonderful time today." Sage snuggles closer.

"It was a good day."

"I like Ophelia. The two of you seem close."

"She's the mom mine never was." Something tells me Sage is leading up to something. She's silent for a moment.

"Would you tell me about them—your parents?"

And there it is. Deep down, I knew she'd be asking the question. I can't fault her for wanting to know. It's the last bit of truth she doesn't know about my life, and part of me is fighting against telling her. Fuck it. Sage knows more than I've ever told anyone outside my club family. "My childhood is nothin' to sing about, babe. My father was a drunk who beat his wife and kid."

"Jesus, Ash. I'm so sorry. We don't have to—"

I interrupt her, because if I don't say it now, I may never. "You should know everything I'm about to confess, babe, so let me say it." I pause long enough to feel the churning in my gut that I always get when I return to the past. I lick my lips, suddenly feeling thirsty and wishing I had a bottle in my hand. "My mom used to shine brighter than the sun. She was beautiful inside and out. When I was around five, maybe six, years old, all that began to change. My dad would come home smellin' like whiskey and another woman's perfume. My mom confronted him once, and it was the first time I witnessed seeing his fist smash into her face." My body tenses. "As I got a bit older, I would try to intervene and protect my mom from another strike." I swallow hard, and my voice deepens. "Step to me like a man, I'll beat you like a man." My nostrils flare with every breath I take, doing my best to control the anger building inside. "And he did."

Sage stays facing forward, her eyes on the orange and red sky, but takes my hand in hers.

"Mom's means of escape were through the pills she ate daily. Instead of leavin' his sorry ass, she numbed herself to the abuse. Her choice to stay is still something I struggle with. I can't wrap my head around her reasoning not to walk away."

"I'm sure she loved you," Sage says softly.

"She loved me, babe. But it wasn't enough to overcome her addictions, not only to the pills, but to my father." I take a deep breath.

"It's hard to grasp what someone else must have seen or gone through when we only experience life through our own eyes and emotions. Looking in is far different than looking out," Sage says, and I kiss her neck. The sun begins sinking into the sea and soon disappears completely before another word is said between us. "How did your parents die?"

Her question feels like a loaded gun in her hand. I only hope what I say next doesn't change how she looks at me. "My father killed my mother." Sage gasps, her hand tightening around mine. "I walked in on him after he had finished drowning her in the bathtub."

Sage twists her body so that we're face to face. "Ash, I'm so sorry you witnessed such a thing." Her palm rests against my chest, and I'm confident she feels my heart pounding. I want nothing more than to detach from the emotion coursing through my body, but I stay connected with the anger and pain.

"Don't feel sorry for me, babe. I don't deserve it." I lock eyes with Sage. "He killed my mother that day, then I killed him. I took his life—watched the last breath leave his body—and felt no remorse doing it," I admit.

Sage's eyes widen, but not with fear. She seems shocked, yet she's unmoving, with her palm still resting over my heart, and I wonder if she knows it only beats for her. "I'm not going anywhere," she says. "I see you for what you truly are, Ash."

"And what's that?" My voice is rough and raw.

"Mine."

18
SAGE

"You look great!" I beam at my best friend. "Do you know where Kyle is taking you on your date tonight?" I peer over my shoulder at Juniper as I finish sweeping the floor around my chair. A few days ago, this guy down at the gym Juniper joined asked her out. She said they started chatting during one of her workout sessions and hit it off. It's been nice to see my best friend get excited about a guy. She disappeared upstairs after her last client, over an hour ago, to get ready. Tonight, she's wearing a pair of ripped black jeans, a burgundy slouchy sweater, wedged boots, and a black leather jacket.

"Kyle's taking me to a concert in Boston, but we're going to stop for something to eat first."

"Boston? Wow, that's almost an hour's drive."

"Yeah, but we're going to see East of Addiction, so the drive will be worth it." Juniper shrugs.

"What?" I gasp. "You lucky heifer. Those tickets have been sold out for months."

"I know, right? Rumor has it, the lead singer has cut back on touring ever since he met this girl. I saw an interview where he said he wanted to take more time off to focus on his personal life."

I nod because I get it. I don't envy celebrities. It has to be difficult balancing your career and personal life. I admire the ones who can put the people they love first.

"Don't worry." Juniper smirks. "I'll be sure to take a bunch of photos and send them to you."

A car honking sounds from outside, and I turn to see a tall, handsome man with black hair step out and jog up to the sidewalk outside the shop.

"That's Kyle." Juniper slings her purse over her shoulder and walks past Harlem, who has been sitting silently on the sofa.

"Have fun, Juju," I call out.

Juniper waves. "Bye."

Following Juniper, I lock the door once she's out and flip the open sign over to closed. When I shift back, I notice Harlem staring out the window, his face hard and his hands resting on his thighs, clenched. I follow his line of sight and at first think he's looking at Juniper and her date, but when they drive off, I realize Harlem's attention is on Sukie, who is across the street unloading boxes from her car and carrying them into her store. For a minute, I want to ask him what the hell his problem with my friend is, but then it dawns on me. "You could go over there and give her a hand."

My sudden statement knocks Harlem out of his stupor, and his head snaps toward me, his dark eyes flare, and he clenches and unclenches his fist.

"Why would I do some shit like that?"

I roll my eyes. When I first started hanging around Harlem, I found him the most intimidating out of all of Ash's brothers. The man is at least six feet, five inches tall, has dark hair, dark eyes, and is covered in tattoos. He's also a man of few words.

"Uh, because you like her?" I say it like it's obvious.

Harlem's lip curls like he's disgusted, and his expression has me compelled to stick up for the sweet shy woman who works across the street.

"You can wipe that look off your face, Harlem." I cock my hip and point my finger at him. "I'll warn you; Sukie is my friend. So, if you were about to let some asshole remark fly from that gob of yours, I suggest you think twice." Then because I must be a glutton for punishment, I add, "All I'm saying is I see the way you've been looking at her, and it wouldn't be the worst thing in the world to go over there and talk to her."

Harlem and I face off in a staring contest for a beat, and I can tell he's mustering up all the self-control he can to keep from going off on me. Instead, he grinds out, "You about done, so we can get the hell out of here?"

I huff and, with great restraint, keep from stomping my foot at the stubborn man. "Yeah, let me take the trash out, and then we can go."

"I'll do it." Harlem climbs to his feet. The sofa makes a creaking noise when he shifts his weight. I swear I was holding my breath all day that the small sofa would accommodate his large frame. The man is a mountain of solid muscle, and I'm thankful the cheap legs Juniper and I replaced on there were sturdy enough to hold him. Seriously, one of Harlem's biceps is bigger than my head.

"Stay inside," he orders.

I shake my head as he follows me toward the back. "We had some deliveries today, so there are several empty boxes. If we both do it, we can get everything in one haul."

I get a grunt in return.

I gather the two trash bags while Harlem wrangles the boxes. When we get to the back exit, I use my foot to hold open the door to allow him to pass through. Just as I turn my back to him to toss the trash into the dumpster, I'm shoved to the ground and land on my hip with a hard thud. It was Harlem who pushed me. "Hey, what the heck you do that for?" I cup my hurt elbow. And when I shake my hair from my face, I realize why he pushed me down, because out of nowhere, there is what sounds like a loud fire-cracker followed by a bullet ricocheting off the dumpster, right above my head. Harlem then goes down to one knee, placing his body in front of mine, shielding me as more gunfire erupts, mostly on his end. I scream as I cover my head with my arms and tuck myself into a ball. It feels like the shooting goes on forever when actually it's mere seconds. When it does stop, I look up to see two bodies lying on the ground in a pool of blood about twenty feet away from me. Then I watch as Harlem stands.

"Let's go," he orders.

I nod and scramble to my feet. "What's happening?"

Harlem grabs my upper arm. "We need to get to the clubhouse —" Another blast cuts his words off, and his body jerks backward. He loses his footing and bumps into me. I grab hold of him to try and steady his footing. That's when I notice blood seeping from a hole in his shoulder.

"Oh my god, you've been shot!"

Harlem ignores me and instead raises his gun and fires back. I look in the direction he's pointing his weapon and see a truck stopped at the end of the alley. There are two men inside the vehicle and three standing beside it. All five of them have their guns aimed at us. Harlem fires again, striking one of the men in his chest, and I watch as he goes down. But before he can get another shot off, Harlem is jumped from behind. My eyes widen, and I recognize him as the biker who approached me that day outside the hardware store. I scream, "No!" At the same time I catch a flash of metal, and I watch as he sinks a blade into Harlem's back, one, two, three times. That doesn't stop Harlem. Acting as if he hasn't been shot and stabbed three times, he whips his large body around and elbows the man in the side of his head.

The guy quickly recovers and delivers an uppercut to Harlem's chin.

Deciding I'm not going to just stand here, I look around for something, anything, I can use as a weapon. That's when I spot my keys lying on the ground next to the dumpster. And on my keyring is my pepper spray. Picking it up, I run over to Harlem, and the guy throws punches.

"Hey asshole," I call out, gaining both their attention, and when the piece of shit who stabbed Harlem looks my way, I douse his face.

"You fuckin', cunt!" He roars in pain and proceeds to claw at his face.

Just when I think we've gotten the upper hand, I'm proven wrong when I'm grabbed from behind and forced to witness Harlem get jumped by three more men.

"Let me go!" I struggle and kick my feet against the man who has his arms around me. All the while, I'm horrified at the sight before me. I watch helplessly as Harlem puts everything he has into fighting off those men, but I can see the strength draining from him with each passing second. "No!" I scream, and buck against my captor when one of the assholes pulls his gun from the inside of his jacket and points it at Harlem's head. My body flinches when he pulls the trigger, only nothing happens. He pulls the trigger again, and still nothing.

"Fuck," he hisses, then looks around. He spots a metal bar lying in the grass behind the dumpster.

"You gettin' this?" the man holding the piece of metal in his hand asks.

I look over to see who he's talking to, to find a tall, lanky guy with a buzz cut, sunken-in eyes, and a broken smile, holding up the phone he just took from Harlem's pocket. Wait, is he recording?

"Yeah, I'm gettin' it." The skinny guy smiles.

A moment later, the metal bar comes down over the back of Harlem's head, knocking him to the ground.

"Harlem!" I cry out. Only he doesn't move.

"Finish taking the trash out," the bastard holding me orders, and his minions pick up Harlem's lifeless body and toss him in the dumpster.

"You can't do this!" I continue to kick and fight. "Let me go!"

"Shut the fuck up, bitch." The hold on me tightens as the man starts to drag me down the alley. I dig my heels into the gravel then throw my head back, clocking the guy in the nose. His hold on me loosens, and I take advantage of that by ducking out of his arms altogether. I don't make it two feet before I'm grabbed by my ponytail and flung backward.

"Not so fast, you stupid, cunt," the guy barks.

"Ahhh." My hand wraps around his and I try to pry his greasy fingers from my hair. "Let me go, asshole!"

I see the fist coming at me from the corner of my eye, but I don't dodge it fast enough. And for the first time ever in my life, I'm punched in the face. The blow feels almost numbing for a split second before a burning sensation explodes over my eye, followed by immediate throbbing.

"Put her in the fuckin' truck and tie her up so we can get the hell out of here." I'm tossed into the hands of another jerk, who then pushes me into the truck.

SUKIE

I duck down in the driver's seat of my car when one of the men holding a gun looks back over his shoulder in my direction. My breaths are labored, and my heart feels like it's going to beat out of my chest. Five minutes ago, I was unloading boxes out of my car, carrying them into the store, and the next, a truck pulled up and stopped in the middle of the road. Then I watched as several men jogged down the alley toward the back of Sage and Juniper's salon. As soon as I heard the first gunshot, I ducked into the front seat of my car.

Now, taking a chance, I lift my head and peek out the window. I have to cover my mouth with my hand to silence the gasp escaping past my lips. I watch in shock and horror as two men manhandle a struggling Sage as they drag her unwilling body toward the truck parked in the road, then shove her inside before peeling off down the street. Once the truck is out of sight, I scramble out of my car and force my shaky legs to carry me inside my store, where I run to retrieve my phone sitting on the counter beside the register. My hands tremble as I type the numbers 911. Only my finger hesitates over the send button, because it suddenly dawns on me. Where is Harlem? He's been at the salon all day. For whatever reason, there has been a Fallen Raven at the salon every day for the past couple of weeks. I don't know why, and I haven't asked. I do know Sage is dating their president, Salem. Most days, it's been Juneau hanging out there, but today it was Harlem. No way he would let Sage get kidnapped.

"Oh my god!" I cry.

Bursting out the door, I run across the street into the alley behind the salon. I must be crazy running into the unknown, but my gut tells me to keep going. My steps falter when I come around the corner. My eyes dart around the darkened alley, not seeing anything. I rush toward the back door that leads inside the salon, finding it slightly ajar. The only noise I hear is the sound of my beating heart whooshing in my ears.

A bang followed by a grunt causes me to startle. When I turn, I don't see anything. There's another bang. Fear has me rooted in place. My legs feel like lead. The noise is coming from the dumpster. Harlem!

Again, I don't think; I just run. When I get up to the dumpster, I pry back the side opening and will never in my life be able to forget the image in front of me for as long as I live. "Oh no. Oh, god."

Harlem lies on a pile of garbage, beaten and covered in blood. I reach my hand in to touch him when his eyes snap open, making me jump.

"Har...Harlem." My voice shakes.

He blinks up at me as if he doesn't know where or what's going on.

"You need a hospital. I'm going to call nine-one-one."

That seemed to snap him out of whatever daze he was in. "No."

I blink down at him. He's obviously delirious. "Harlem, you're hurt really bad. I need to call for help." I go to dig my phone from my back pocket when he snaps at me.

"I said no."

He then proceeds to try to heft his large frame out of the dumpster. When he loses his grip on the edge of the opening, I reach out and wrap both hands around his bicep and pull. "I got you," I say, my face inches away from his. "Lean into me," I tell him, then try to take as much of his weight as I can, which is no easy task. I'm five foot two on a good day, and Harlem is a giant.

With my arms supporting him around his chest, I take a deep breath, and with all the strength I have, I pull. Harlem growls in pain. I lose my footing when I trip over a metal bar lying on the ground, and the two of us fall to a heap on the ground.

Harlem rolls off me. His breathing is labored, and even through the blood and swelling on his face, I can see he's losing color. I also don't miss the oozing hole in his shoulder.

"Harlem, we have to call the police. Those men took Sage, and you need a hospital."

"I already said no fuckin' cops." He reaches into his leather vest. "Fuck," he grits through clenched teeth. "Those fuckers took my phone. Give me yours."

I dig my phone from my back pocket to find the screen cracked. I turn it toward him. "It must have broken when I fell."

He curses under his breath and makes a pained face when he shifts his body.

"Harlem," I try again. "Look, I don't mean to beat a dead horse, but did you not hear me when I said Sage was kidnapped."

"I fuckin' heard you," he snaps, making me flinch.

Harlem tries to climb to his feet but fails, so I stand to try and help him. His head rests on my shoulder, and I can feel his heavy breathing against my neck. I get him to a seated position where he can rest his back against the dumpster. He looks at me, his chest rising and falling with each breath he struggles to take. "Get your car."

This time I don't hesitate. Nodding, I run back down the alley and across the street to my car. I reach for my keys sitting in the cup holder and pause when I catch sight of my hands. They are covered in blood... Harlem's blood. Bile rises in my throat, but I swallow, forcing it back down. Then I shake off the shock of what's happening and start my car.

When I pull up in the alley, Harlem is in the same position I left him. Jumping from the car, I run around to the passenger side and open the door. Turning back, I rush to Harlem. My breath catches in my throat when I see his head cocked to the side and his eyes closed. "Harlem." My voice wavers when I call out his name. At the sound of my voice, his eyes open. The relief that washes over me is indescribable.

It takes great effort, but I finally get Harlem in the car and start it. He recites a set of directions for me. "Once you hit Waverly, take a left about a quarter-mile down. After that, just drive."

My eyes dart back and forth between the road and Harlem, whose breathing has become shallower. "Harlem, where are we going?"

"Clubhouse," he forces out between breaths.

My body goes stiff. I have never been anywhere near the Fallen Ravens clubhouse.

"No matter what, make sure we get to the clubhouse," Harlem says.

Confused, I ask, "What?"

"Make sure you tell Prez everything you saw. Understand?"

I nod. "Yes."

Harlem's head lolls to the side, his dark eyes bore into mine. "I'm going to need you to step on that gas, babe." His eyes close.

"Harlem," I call out. He doesn't answer, and I take one hand off the wheel and shake him. "Harlem?"

Still nothing. Oh god.

Eyes back on the road, I step on the gas.

SAGE

It's impossible to keep my mind from running wild as I'm being forced to trudge through a cemetery with nothing but the moonlight and uncertainty shining down on me. Back at the truck, I was gagged and had my hands bound at the wrists with rope. Then I had to sit and listen to these assholes go on and on about how the Fallen Ravens would get what's coming to them. Then they started laughing at what they'd done to Harlem. Listening to them relive how they had stabbed him and about how good it felt to crack his skull open made me want to vomit.

"Pick up the fuckin' pace. Prez is waitin' on us," the guy up ahead of us barks.

"Man, I would, but Salem's chubby fuckin' whore is draggin' her feet." The asshole behind me presses his palm against my back, shoving me. His actions cause me to trip over my feet, and I fall face-first onto the cold, damp ground. This causes all the men to laugh at my expense.

"You stupid shits done fuckin' around?" A new voice enters the scene. A tall, dark-haired man steps out of the shadows with menacing brown eyes. The patch on the front of his vest says, President Warlock.

Picking myself up off the ground, I come face to face with the Demon Jokers President. He takes a long drag from his cigarette while his seedy gaze roams over every inch of my body. "You're not what I expected." He blows the smoke out through his nose. "I don't get why Salem has a hard-on for you when he's got a variety of pussy at that club of his."

My eyes narrow, making him smile.

"Must have a tight snatch." He takes another drag. "Maybe I should find out." The son of a bitch reaches out and rubs a lock of my hair between his grimy fingers.

I jerk my head away and take two steps back, only to bump into one of the other assholes. And it just happens to be the jerk from the hardware store.

"That sounds like a good idea, Prez." He slings his arm around my chest, pulling me against him, my back to his front. And when he does, I can feel something hard against my ass as he pushes his groin into me.

Screw these sick assholes. Taking the man holding me off guard, I elbow him in the gut, knocking the wind from his lungs, twist out of his grip, take one step back, lift my leg, then kick him in the dick as hard as I can and watch him go down like a sack of potatoes. My father would be proud. My glory moment is short-lived when the president of Demon Jokers swiftly backhands me across the face. Then he turns to the man whose dick I hope is broken.

"If you're done cryin' like a pussy, get your ass up. We got shit to do." He turns his attention back to me. "Move." He jerks his head toward the mausoleum to my right, covered in many years' worth of green moss and black grime. On the rooftop of the concrete structure sits the broken statue of a weeping angel. The president shoves me forward as one of the other men opens the door. There is no way he's taking me in there. I start to panic and scream through the gag in my mouth.

"Pitch, Hook, grab her," the president orders, and I'm shoved inside. Once inside, the man called Hook takes out a cell phone and starts recording.

19
SALEM

I lift my phone off the table and look at the time. She should be here by now.

I tap the screen, calling Sage. It rings, going straight to her voicemail. I wait a couple of minutes to see if she returns my call, with no luck. Feeling off about it, I pull up Harlem's number, only to get the same response—nothing. My body tenses.

"What's wrong?" Laredo asks, his tone alert.

"I can't get in touch with Sage or Harlem." I shove my phone in the inside pocket of my cut. Laredo pulls out his phone, swipes the screen, and places it to his ear. He's soon shaking his head. "It's going straight to voicemail." Laredo furrows his brows. "It's not like him. Harlem always answers on the second ring without fail."

Baja suddenly bursts through the front door. "We got company, and they're comin' in hot!"

The rest of us jump to our feet, draw our weapons, and run outside where a small car is speeding toward us. Whoever is behind the wheel slams on the breaks, locking the wheels up. The car skids, throwing loose dirt and rock into the air, stopping a couple yards short of where my brothers and I stand.

Once the dust settles, the driver's door swings open. We take aim, ready to put bullets through the dumb motherfucker. The fuck? "Sukie?" I lower my weapon, but the others keep theirs raised. I take in her rapid breathing. She's terrified.

"They took Sage." Sukie's voice trembles, and my gut wrenches.

I rush toward Sukie, causing her to backpedal, and she stumbles. Reaching out, I grab her by the arm before she hits the ground. "Who?" I growl, making Sukie flinch.

She swallows hard, then opens her mouth, but a deep moaning from inside her car snatches my attention. I turn my head and peer through the car's opened door. There, in the passenger's seat, is Harlem and he's covered in blood. "Shit." I look back at my men. "It's Harlem." They all rush toward the car as I duck down and reach over the console. There's blood everywhere. The passenger door swings open, and Juneau is at his side, his hands all over Harlem's body, lifting his shirt, looking for the source of his bleeding. "Christ. He's been stabbed multiple times." Harlem's head lolls to one side as Juneau checks his pulse. "He's not doin' good. Get him inside." The urgency in Juneau's voices has the others lifting Harlem from the seat and rushing him inside the clubhouse to the back, where we have our own infirmary. "Put him on the bed and get those fuckin' clothes off him," Juneau barks while he gives his hands a quick wash in the sink, then pulls on a pair of blue surgical gloves. Being an ex-army medic, Juneau has proven beneficial to the club on more than one occasion since he's been with the brotherhood. Let's hope tonight he will save Harlem.

With my hand still attached to Sukie's arm, I have her tagging alongside me. She watches the men move around the room, gathering everything Juneau needs to hopefully fix our brother. While the men are tending to Harlem, I spin around to face her. "Why the fuck did you waste time bringing him all the way out here, Sukie?" I'm fuming and invading her space even more. "And where the fuck is my woman?" I'm about to lose my shit.

"Harlem told me to bring him here." Sukie jerks her arm, and I release my hold. "I don't know who took Sage. These men dragged her from the alley and shoved her inside a truck and took off. It all happened so fast." She hugs herself, and her body starts to shake uncontrollably. Her eyes shift to where the men have Harlem laid out on a bed while Juneau barks orders, doing his best to make sure our brother doesn't lose his life today. "Is he going to die?"

"I don't know." I breathe deeply and attempt to better grasp the chaos to find out precisely what the hell is going on and where Sage is. I keep trained on Sukie. At the moment, she holds all the answers we need to put this fucked up puzzle together. "Sukie, I know this is scaring the hell out of you, but it took a lot of fuckin courage to get this far." Her gaze drops to her feet. "Hey, I need you to look at me and focus," I say, and she slowly lifts her head, bringing her eyes to mine. "Sage is your friend. You can do this. Take a deep breath, then tell me everything."

Sukie's shoulders rise and fall with the three deep breaths she takes. She closes her eyes and proceeds to recount what went down. "I was loading my car in front of the store when it happened." She licks her lips, swallowing hard. "A bunch of men wearing vests like yours but with Demon Jokers on them rushed down the alley and grabbed Sage." My blood runs ice-cold at the mention of the Demon Jokers, and my fists clench at my sides, fighting against the need to rush out and find the motherfuckers responsible. I still myself and finish listening to what Sukie watched. She inhales through her nose. "I ducked down, hiding, hoping they wouldn't notice me." Sukie slowly shakes her head. Her eyes begin to fill with emotions, and tears flow down her cheeks as she relives the moment.

"How many men were there?"

"Five, I think. But I saw two of them lying on the ground in the alley." Sukie wipes her eyes with the back of her coat sleeve. "Sage was crying, trying to scream, but the man holding her kept his palm over her mouth." Sukie sniffles. "When they drove off, I remembered Harlem was with Sage all day. I ran down the alley and found him in the dumpster. Harlem wasn't moving at all. I thought he was dead. When I realized he wasn't, I helped him out of the dumpster. He was too weak to walk, so he told me to get my car. After I helped him in the car, he told me to come straight here."

This is all my fault. "Did you happen to see which direction the vehicle went?"

Sukie shakes her head. "No."

"You did good," I tell Sukie. "And the loyalty you showed here tonight won't go unnoticed."

Sukie wipes her eyes again. "You guys have always been kind to me." She lifts her chin. "Sage is my friend." Her lips tremble while holding back more tears. "Please find her."

"Prez," Baja snags my attention, and I look back at him. He's standing beside the bed near Harlem. Leaving Sukie where she stands, I cross the floor toward the rest of my men. Baja looks back at her.

I look down at my brother. "Juneau, fill me in."

Juneau packs gauze into a stab wound then dresses it with tape to keep it in place. Harlem looks extremely pale. "He's goddamn lucky. The blade missed any vital areas. The stab wound on his back..." Juneau shakes his head. "If it would have been an inch further to the right, it would have hit his kidney. Infection is a cause for concern, and he has two cracked ribs. But the gunshot is minor." Juneau sighs. "They busted our brother up pretty damn good."

Harlem's hand shoots out, gripping my pant leg. "Get me out of this fuckin' bed." He attempts to pull himself up.

"Your ass is stayin' put." Juneau pushes against Harlem's shoulders, pressing him back to the bed.

"You're not killin' those motherfuckers without me," Harlem grumbles, struggling against Juneau's hold. "Turn me loose," he growls, grabbing at his side, clenching his teeth through the pain. With all he's been through, my brother still has fight in him yet.

Juneau looks at me. "I'll have to sedate the big son of a bitch, so he doesn't hurt himself further."

Without hesitation, I say, "Do it." Then I look down at Harlem. "Not this time, brother. You are to remain here at the clubhouse, and that's a fuckin' order," I bark, knowing a direct order is the only way his hard head may listen. Then Juneau inserts the sedative through Harlem's IV line. Within a matter of seconds, our brother drifts into a comfortable sleep.

My phone pings. I pull it from my pocket and see a notification of a couple text messages from Harlem. What the fuck? I swipe the screen and go to the message. It's a video. I tap Play. The screen is dark for a few seconds before Sage's face comes into focus. She's being held by a biker, then it pans over to three men beating the hell out of Harlem. I can hear Sage fighting against her captor. The camera shakes as the person holding it takes a turn at striking my brother. My gut ties in knots watching them toss Harlem's lifeless-looking body into the dumpster. Then it's nothing but ground view until the phone is pointed at Sage once again at the precise moment one of the bastards rears back and hits Sage. He's a dead man. The video goes black. I open the last message sent from Harlem's phone and play the video.

We watch Sage being led into a stone structure. A concrete casket sits in the center of the small interior room, the lid halfway pushed to one side. The phone pans to the right, and there, staring into the camera lens, is Warlock.

"It seems I have something that belongs to you." He places his dirty hands on Sage. "You want her, come and get her." Warlock turns to Sage and points a gun at her face. "Get in." He orders her into the casket. Sage's body begins shaking, and silent tears roll down her cheeks. She steps into the concrete box. "Lay down," Warlock barks and she lowers herself onto her side. "On your back, cunt," the motherfucker growls. Sage shakes her head.

Warlock presses the end of the gun at Sage's temple. "On your fuckin' back," he orders, and Sage complies. I die inside as her blue eyes stare into the camera being held above her. Then the stone lid slowly causes her face to disappear.

My grip tightens around the phone, and the case cracks. Blood will spill tonight. Silence encapsulates me as the video ends. My vision darkens, but for a much different reason. I hear every breath in the room and the blood rushing through my veins. The bastard took her. "There are half a dozen cemeteries in town. We'll have to split up and search each one to eliminate time."

"No you won't." Sukie's voice is low, almost a whisper.

"What?" I ask.

Sukie's nose scrunches. "I'm sorry, but can you go to the beginning, right when they make her walk inside the mausoleum?" I hesitate to watch it for a second time. "Salem, please," she begs, so I play it again, feeling the anguish and rage inside my body building once more. "Pause it," Sukie orders and points at the phone screen.

"What am I supposed to see?" I search the still image.

"That headstone, right there." She shows me on the left side of the image. I take a screenshot then zoom into the area Sukie is referring to. On the weathered headstone, I read the name Agnus Pierce "That's my three times great grandmother." Sukie looks up at my face, her eyes filled with hope. "I know where Sage is. It's this old cemetery on the outskirts of town. It's located on private property. Oddly enough, not many townspeople know about it."

I look from Sukie then at my brothers. You don't live in Salem and not know where all the cemeteries are. I look back at Sukie. "I need the exact location." Sukie rattles off the whereabouts. "I'm gonna need you to stay put."

"I want to help." Sukie wrings her hands together.

"You've helped enough." I cut my eyes at Harlem, who needed to be sedated and is resting. "I need you to stay here and look after Harlem. Think you can do that for us?"

Sukie glances at Harlem then looks back at me. She nods. "Yes."

"Good." I face Laredo. "Give her a weapon, something she can handle in case of trouble."

"Wait." Sukie throws her hands up. "I...I don't know how to use a gun."

Laredo leaves the room, only to return a minute later, holding a 9mm handgun. "It's fully loaded. This—" he shows her "—is your safety. Make sure it's disengaged before you pull the trigger here." He places the gun in her tiny hands, showing her how to hold it. "Point and shoot. Only pull the trigger if you intend to kill or seriously injure someone. Got it?" he explains, giving her a watered-down crash course on operating a weapon.

"I got it. I think." Sukie's hands tremble. Laredo guides her to the side of the bed Harlem is laid out on, and she sits on the edge.

Juneau steps up to Sukie, whose wide eyes stare down at the gun she's holding on her lap. He hands her a cell phone. "Any number will put you in touch with one of us."

"Sukie." I snag her attention, and she whips her head to look at me. "You got this. Take care of my brother."

Sukie glances back at Harlem, closes her eyes while taking a deep breath, and then blows it out. When she locks eyes with me again, there's less fear in her eyes as she nods.

Across the room is a wall of lockers where we store an arsenal of weapons. Baja and the rest of my men begin loading up on ammo along with other extra firepower. I stride across the room to do the same, pocketing a couple of fully-loaded magazines for my 9 mm. I spot Chicago's Peacemaker, a single-action revolver, toward the back of the locker and wrap my hand around the handle of the old-school, cowboy-style handgun. The barrel opens with a flick of my wrist, and I begin loading the chambers. The last time I held Chicago's gun was when I used it to kill Mayhem, the former Demon Jokers President. Only seems fitting I use it again when taking his son's life. Beside me, Mystic loads his late father's handgun, a 44. Magnum, nicknamed Widowmaker, which he always carries on him.

After securing my weapons, I slam the locker door shut. Nearby, Laredo holds a sawed-off shotgun in one hand. Juneau has an extra pistol strapped to his outer thigh, one at his hip and another he's got tucked away inside his cut. Baja slams the locker door in front of him, holding a small black duffle bag. I don't have to guess what he has inside. Given the opportunity, the man likes to blow shit up.

He looks at me and pats the bag, shrugging. "I have an idea." We listen as Baja suggests he ride out to the Demon Jokers and light their shit up like the fourth of July. It's a risky move, but I agree to his plan to eradicate Warlock's men and significantly decrease their manpower.

I look at my men, all waiting and willing to die tonight if that's what it takes to get my woman back. "Let's ride."

We speed down the road; Juneau, Mystic, Laredo, and I go in one direction while Baja takes off the opposite. The cold night air makes my skin as numb as my insides. My mind is waging a war of its own against my heart. I'm a fool to believe a man like me could have the love of a good woman. Being with me will only continue to put her in dangerous situations. She's mine. How could I go on breathing without her? My gut churns, unsettled by the real possibility of Sage being better off without me. My inner voice screams inside my head as I lock my deep-seated torments away. "Get out of your fuckin' head." I grit my teeth and throttle the gas, speeding faster down the road. No matter what happens tonight, a decision needs to be made.

I channel all my emotions into one.

Rage.

I let it consume me until a vast nothingness remains.

I'm hollow.

All that's left behind is death.

Twenty minutes later, the directions Sukie gave me have us approaching a dirt road, with overgrown grass nearly making it unnoticeable. The property is heavily wooded, which works in our favor. Cautious and alert, we roll to a stop, gravel rock crunching beneath our bikes' tires, loud enough to wake the dead. "We hoof it from here," I say, and we leave our bikes hidden behind clusters of large thorn bushes.

"Keep your eyes open," I whisper before disappearing amongst the covering of the trees outlining the perimeter of the property. We're going in knowing we don't have the element of surprise and the odds are stacked against us. These fuckers are waiting for our arrival. Armed and at the ready, we trudge across the soggy leaf-covered forest floor. The air is thick, feeling heavy in the lungs.

I throw my hand up and point to two shadowy figures hunching between two trees several yards ahead. Juneau raises his rifle and steadies himself. As he pulls the trigger, we also give away our precise location. Spreading out, we take cover behind the trunks of trees, shielding our bodies from the battle about to commence. Juneau glances at me, and, nodding, I give him the go-ahead. He fires two rounds, hitting their marks and the dark figures fall. Laredo moves toward the targets. Stopping, he kneels, then soon looks back, giving us the thumbs up.

Two down. Several to go.

As suspected, gunfire cracks all around us, splintering the bark on the trees and pelting the ground. Warlock's men are useless idiots. We wait them out, not returning fire, letting the dumb fucks waste their rounds.

As the gunfire ceases, the forest falls silent. I peek around the tree, noticing four bodies moving at a fast pace about twenty yards beyond our location, and I alert my men, pointing toward the bikers fleeing. We all take aim in their direction and open fire. One by one, each man falls.

I'm done playing games. "Fuck it." I step into the open, making myself visible. "You want me, motherfucker?" I shout, marching across overgrown plots and crumbled headstones. I risk being shot, but I'm not here to hide. "Show yourself, Warlock."

"We're easy targets," Mystic warns, keeping his arm raised and weapon ready. "Fuck!" he hisses before pulling his trigger. In front of us, a Demon Joker stumbles, grips his chest where the bullet pierced his body, and falls to the ground. I glance down at the man's lifeless body, continuing forward across the unkempt grounds, only noticing the blood soaking his shirt that looks like a blot of black ink.

Darkness shrouds the graveyard, the only light coming from the moon hanging low in the night sky, partially curtained by light gray clouds. There's no talking between my men as we tread across the hallowed grounds. We stay alert, with our weapons raised, ready to put bullets in any Demon Jokers while dodging moss-covered tombstones. The old oak trees scattered about the property cast shadows that dance across the grassy graves as the wind blows, making all of us jumpy as fuck. The temperature is dropping, becoming cold enough to see clouds of vapor as we breathe. Several yards away, a stone statue of an angel weeping with broken wings standing high atop a mausoleum finally comes into view.

"Help!" I hear the faint muffled scream.

"Sage." My pace quickens, and the beating of my heart drowns out all thought. "Ash!" she screams, and it feels like a bullet ripping straight through my heart. I put her in this mess.

A twig snaps. "That's far enough," a disembodied voice says. I recognize the speaker. Warlock. He steps out of the shadows, followed by the biker with the spider inked on his face. I look around, searching the darkness for other men but failing to find any.

"Keep your eyes open for others." I speak low, for only my men to hear, then speak directly to the Demon Jokers President. "Warlock." My sinister tone is laced with murderous intent. I want to inflict pain on him. In the background, Sage continues pleading for help. "You got what you asked for." I give Warlock my undivided attention. "Seems you're unprepared and outnumbered." I harden my stare. "Now release her."

Warlock cocks his head. "You figured it out much faster than I anticipated." His beady eyes look me up and down, followed by the spreading of his arms. "The man. The myth. The fuckin' legend of Witch City stands before me, begging for the life of a woman." His rough voice drags across my skin like nails across a chalkboard. "She thinks you're a goddamn saint. Does the cunt know she's spreadin' her legs for a killer and fuckin' soon-to-be-dead man?" He spits at the ground in my direction, sneering as he stares me down. "Look at you now. Salem, leader of Fallen Ravens, beggin' for a bitch's life. Just like my father killed your former President," Warlock's taunts, eyes cutting to Mystic who stands at my side, "and the rest of his men." He attempts to get a reaction from my brother, but Mystic stands tall, unfazed. "I plan on ridding this town of you and your men, then taking over."

"Careful, Warlock. I think your envy is showin'." My hand flexes against the cold metal of my gun.

"I'm a fuckin God. I envy no man. Especially a man who makes himself vulnerable because of a cunt." He smirks, and I want nothing more than to wipe it from his ugly face. "That juicy piece of ass you've been fuckin' is your Achilles heel. I knew taking her would give me the one thing I've wanted for a long time. An empire. I'll become the alpha and omega in this town." His eyes narrow. "And most of all, I'll see you, dead."

I show no signs of his words penetrating my skin. "It sounds like you have a major hard-on for me, Warlock." My finger itches to pull the trigger.

The man standing to his right snickers at my comment, and Warlock's face contorts with rage. He lifts the hand his gun is in one swift movement, shooting the poor son of a bitch. The bullet rips through his man's head, and his body falls to the ground.

"You're not too bright." I keep my gun trained on Warlock. "Killin' your own man?" I make a dig at his incompetence.

Warlock squares his shoulders. "What makes you think I don't have men in the shadows, with their weapons, pointed at your heads. If I want you dead, all I need to do is snap my fingers. My men are willin' to die for me." Warlock points his weapon at the biker's lifeless body. "That's what respect looks like. One call, and I'll have more men roll up on these hallowed grounds willing to do the same."

"You mean the men you left to watch over your inheritance?" I pause a beat, enjoying the cocky smirk falling from Warlock's face. "By now, the remainder of your men are nothin' more than ash and bone, buried beneath the burning rubble of what used to be the Demon Jokers clubhouse." I watch Warlock's nostrils flare before adding, "But, I won't give you the luxury of dying so easily."

Warlock regains the composure he had before finding out

everything he attempted to rebuild is gone. He reaches into his cut, pulling out a small square-shaped box. "Monsters think alike," he boasts. "Seems you underestimated your enemy, Salem. All I need to do is press this button and poof" Warlock —raises his arms in the air "—the bitch is dead."

I'm not sure what my next move is, for once in my life. My men and I are in a standoff against one man wielding the power to change my life. Sage screams my name again, and I know I must do something. I'm more than ready to die tonight. So are my men. Somehow, I need to get to Sage or the detonator in Warlock's hand. I toss my gun to the ground. "My life for hers." I willingly sacrifice myself to save Sage and step away from my men.

"Goddammit," Mystic whispers. "Let me shoot the mother-fucker," my best friend urges, but my mind is made up.

Warlock takes aim at my face, staring me down for several seconds, giving his best attempt at intimidation. "You're a fool." He moves forward until the barrel end of his weapon is pressed against my forehead. "Tell your men to stand down."

I clench my teeth. "Back off," I order.

"Prez." Juneau has his rifle raised. "Let me put him down."

"No," I assert. "I won't risk that button beneath his thumb being pressed before the bullet hits its mark. Now. Stand. Down," I repeat and hope like hell my men follow the command and trust in the decision I'm making.

My brothers back away and lower their weapons.

"Turn around and face your men," Warlock orders, and I slowly twist on my heels. Facing my brothers, I hold my head high. Warlock presses the barrel again at the back of my head.

So, this is how it ends. The executioner is executed in front of his men. I suppose it's only fair if I go out this way. An eye for an eye. Karma is a cruel bitch.

Out of the corner of my eye, I can see the detonator, the line between life or death for Sage in his left hand, dangling at his side.

Suddenly, I no longer feel the gun against my head. Instead, it's replaced with the cold steel edge of a blade against my neck. "I'll kill you the same way my father killed your former President." Warlock loses his grip on the ignitor in a foolish move to fist my hair and wrench my head back. I feel the blade digging into my skin at the exact moment I twist my body, reaching for the detonator that's now lying on the ground at my knee. Fire spreads across the flesh of my neck, but the sensation becomes an afterthought the instant I take hold of the little black box. Shifting my weight into his knee, I feel Warlock's leg buckle. He lands on one knee and swings the knife to defend himself as I rush at him. The blade slices across my right shoulder, but I feel nothing.

He's quick to stand. Warlock is screwed, and better yet, he knows it. I stretch out my arm for one of my men to take the detonator, and Laredo steps forward. He also hands me my weapon. I turn back to Warlock and take aim. "Drop it motherfucker."

Not listening, Warlock lets out a battle cry and rushes at me. I pull the trigger but avoid a fatal shot, hitting him in the shoulder. The knife falls to the grass-covered ground at his feet, and when he attempts to pick it up, I fire another round that explodes through the back of his hand. Warlock breathes heavily, his useless arm and hand dangling at his side. "Kill me, you piece of shit!" he rages, spittle flying from his mouth.

I stroll up to him and whip the bastard across the cheek with the side of my weapon. "You know better than to believe it will be that easy for you." I point my gun at the back of his head and jerk my chin toward the mausoleum. "Move your fuckin' feet," I order. When he doesn't budge, I crack him across the back of the head. Laredo and Mystic come up and flank both sides of the son of a bitch and drag him the few yards keeping me from Sage.

I enter the stone structure with Juneau. "Sage," I call out loudly to let her know I'm here.

"Ash?" there are several thuds against the concrete covering from the inside. "I'm in here. Oh my god. Please get me out!" she shouts. I can hear the fear in her tone, and it's crushing my soul. Juneau carefully removes the bomb lying on top of the concrete casket and quickly takes care of disconnecting wires to assure it doesn't blow us up. "Help!" Sage's voice is rough from screaming.

"I'm here, baby," I grunt, pushing against the heavy covering separating me from my woman. Juneau stands beside me and aids in removing the lid. Concrete scrapes against concrete as we push the cover from the casket. The moonlight breaking through a small window reflects off the tears glistening in my woman's eyes as she comes into view, staring up at me from inside.

"Ash," she cries and wraps her arms around my neck as I lift her from the tomb. I sit her on the edge of the casket.

My hands are everywhere, looking for injuries. I'm careful when touching the bruises on her cheek and eye area. "You hurt anywhere else?"

"No." She blinks away the tears wetting her lashes. "They just smacked me across the face really hard." Her hand covers mine, which is pressed against her cheek. Her eyes widen. "Oh my God, Ash." She touches the hollow of my neck, and it stings to the touch. Sage pulls back her hand, and her fingertips are covered in blood. It's where Warlock attempted to cut my throat, but I feel no pain right now. Sage then touches my shoulder. "You're bleeding here too."

I kiss her forehead. "The only person who matters is you." I tuck her into my side and guide her out of the mausoleum. Sage takes a deep breath when the cool night air hits her face. She then spots her tormentor being held by Laredo and Mystic. Sage's face hardens, and she breaks away from me. Sage stops turning to look at Juneau. "You mind?" She gestures toward my brother's rifle. Juneau eyes me, and I nod, so he lets Sage take the weapon from his hands. She holds the gun like a skilled marksman and marches right up to Warlock. For a moment, I believe she is about to put a bullet in the bastard. Instead, she engages the safety, slides her palms down the gun barrel, and holds the rifle in her hands like a baseball bat. Rearing back, she swings with all the force of her body weight behind it, cracking Warlock in the nuts with the stock of the weapon. The fucker's face contorts from the pain and he gags from his ball sack being shoved clear up into his throat. Sage turns and casually walks back to Juneau, gives the rifle to him, and returns to my side.

"Stay here with Juneau. I've got something I need to do." I look down at Sage, feeling mixed up on the inside. Her eyes are appraising for a second as if she sees a battle brewing inside me. She nods, then steps away. I turn to Laredo and Mystic, jerk my head, and they walk back into the mausoleum with me, dragging Warlock with them.

I still myself and focus all my energy on the Demon Joker standing before me. "Get in," I order.

"Fuck you." He spits at my face, which earns him a bit of pain from Mystic, who grips the back of the bastard's head and slams his face against the stone wall. The sound of his nose crunching beneath the forceful blow gives Mystic a satisfied grin.

"Get in the box, motherfucker." Laredo grabs and tosses Warlock over into the concrete casket. The back of Warlock's head smacks against the bottom, dazing him further. I lift my leg over, stepping into the coffin with him, pressing my knees and the weight of my body against his chest, forcing the air from his lungs.

I reach inside my cut, pulling out Chicago's pistol. "Seems fitting to use the weapon I killed your father with."

Warlock laughs manically. His fate is sealed, and he has nothing to lose but his life here tonight. His eyes bulge with rage as he screams one final, *"Fuck you!"* Then he adds, "You're going the same place I'm going, which is straight to hell."

Reaching down, I pry his mouth open, shoving the barrel down his throat. "Tell Lucifer I said hello." I pull the fucking trigger.

Blood splatters, painting the inside of the casket and seeping from beneath his shattered skull.

His cold, dead eyes stare back at me.

I feel nothing.

He was nothing.

I rise and step out of the grave, and Laredo and Mystic slide the heavy lid back into place. I look at my brothers. "Let's go home." Then I walk out, tuck Sage into my side, and walk away from Warlock's final resting place.

It's just before sunrise, and I haven't slept since we arrived here at the clubhouse more than eight hours ago. Instead, I've watched Sage resting peacefully in my bed. My eyes keep fixating on her bruised cheek, and my mind keeps replaying the fear in her eyes the moment we opened the casket Warlock's corpse is now rotting in.

I lift the bottle of liquor to my lips and take another swig. There isn't enough whiskey in the world to drown out the anguish I feel for putting her in danger. I know what needs to be done. My mind is made up. I stand from the seat my ass has been parked in, swaying a bit as the room spins. Shaking it off, I stride across the room and kneel beside the bed. I gently brush my lips against hers, knowing this time will be the last, then rise and walk out of the room.

I stumble my way to the front of the clubhouse, with the bottle of booze still in my hand, and fall onto the sofa. My eyes burn from lack of sleep, but I fight against the drowsy effects the whiskey is causing and wait.

It's not long before the rest of the men wake and venture out into the commons. All of them eye me with concern, but it's Mystic who says something about my drunken state. He glances around. "Sage go home?"

"No." I stare at the same spot on the wall I've been fixated on for the past hour.

"You drink that whole bottle alone?" he asks, and I hear the disapproval in his tone. I ignore him.

Across the room, Sukie appears. "I, uh, I hope you don't mind that I used the kitchen." She's holding a plate of food in her hands. The smells of sweet maple and greasy bacon waft in the air. "I figured Harlem would need something when he woke."

"Sukie?" Sage's voice stirs my insides, bringing some life back into my body, and my eyes find her standing behind her friend. "I'm so..." Sage says, looking confused. "What are you doing here?" she asks Sukie.

"Well, I helped the guys find you," Sukie says, her voice almost a whisper. She looks at the plate in her hand. "I need to get back to Harlem, but can we talk later?"

Sage gives Sukie a soft smile. "Definitely." And Sukie disappears down the hallway. Sage searches the room until her blue eyes land on my bloodshot ones. "Ash." She shuffles her feet against the floor, wearing the pants she wore yesterday paired with one of my black cotton shirts she slept in. Her bed hair halos her face. She stops and stands in front of me. Her eyes go to the empty bottle in my hand, and her forehead creases. "Are you drunk?"

"Yeah, babe."

Sage crosses her arms over her chest. "Why?"

"Why are you always busting my balls?" The room spins, and the sun filtering through the windows makes my eyes burn more.

"What's going on, Ash?"

"I can't do this anymore." I hear my words slur.

"Do what?" Sage sounds genuinely confused by my behavior.

"Us!" I boom, my voice echoing through the rafters. "You." I point to her. "Me." I jab myself in the chest with my fist. "It's too much—you're too much. Since you've come into my life, I can't think straight."

I watch Sage's blue eyes turn into pools of unshed tears, and I feel the moment both our hearts shatter. She holds it all in. My woman is strong, and I'm about to feel the full force of her pain. Good. I prepare myself. I deserve it.

"Are you serious right now?" Her breathing speeds up. "After all we've gone through to get here." Her bottom lip trembles, and her voice wobbles. "You telling me that's it; you're done?" Sage wipes her eyes. "You made me believe you cared. I'm yours, and you are mine, remember?" Her voice is much lower than before, and the hurt in it makes what I need to do harder.

"I belong to no one," I lie, the words leaving a bitter taste in my mouth.

"You're a liar, Ash. You're a liar and a coward." Sage doesn't hide her emotions from me. Tears flow in unbroken streams down her face.

"We done here?" I make my voice sound detached and uninterested. Sage stares at me for a moment longer. She stands before me broken, and I'm to blame. *It's for her own good,* I keep telling myself, using all the strength of my soul not to jump off this sofa and take it all back. But I can't. I won't. To keep her safe, I have to let her go, and I know no other way to get her to let go than make her hate me.

She could never hate me more than I loathe myself.

Not saying another word, Sage turns her back to me and runs out the front door, taking my heart with her. I stand, hurl the empty whiskey bottle I've had a death grip on across the room, and it shatters against the stone wall.

Mystic advances on me, getting right in my face. "The fuck, Salem?" He shoves me, and I stagger backward.

"Remember your place, brother." I ball my fists at my side. Right now, I'm not the person to be pushing around.

My attitude doesn't faze Mystic. "My place?" He's in my face again. "I'm your best motherfuckin' friend, asshole." Mystic points toward the door. "She's just been through hell, and you go and cut her loose."

"I don't need to justify jack shit to you," I growl.

"You fuckin' love her, brother. What the hell are you doing?"

I beat my fists against my chest. "My love for Sage almost got her killed."

"You need to go after her and make it right," Mystic urges.

"She's better off." I back away and notice the rest of my men watching the shit show called my life. "I had to let her go." I exit on those words, dragging my sorry ass back to my room, where I face plant into the pillow. It smells like Sage, and I breathe her scent in, trying to fill the void in my chest left behind by letting the woman I love go.

20
SAGE

These past two weeks have been a true testament to my sanity. It's not every day a girl is kidnapped, punched in the face twice, put into a concrete casket, rescued by her boyfriend, then not twenty-four hours later has said boyfriend completely and carelessly shatter her heart. I keep playing that scene at the clubhouse over and over again and still can't wrap my head around it. The biggest question I keep asking myself is *why*. How can a man, who loses his mind at the threat of you walking away from him and making you promise to never leave, do a complete one-eighty and tell you it's over? Not just that, but also the way he said it...with no emotion. And to top it all off, he did it all in front of his brothers. It was humiliating. I have experienced every breakup emotion stage there is. Shock, uncontrollable crying, and staying in bed for three days until your best friend reminds you that you are a bad bitch who doesn't allow men to have that much control over you. Then there's the anger stage that led me to leaving numerous voice messages and texting Ash at two o'clock in the morning, telling him he's a cowardly piece of shit. Five minutes after leaving that message, I called and left another telling him he's not a coward, and I don't really think he's a piece of shit. I also said I wouldn't bother him again. I meant to keep that promise. But now, as I stare down at the positive pregnancy test in my hand, I know I'm about to break it.

"This is bad, Juju. Really, really bad."

My best friend looks at me with pity. "Maybe it's a false positive because you've been on the pill since forever."

I shake my head. "I've taken three tests, Juniper, and my period is two weeks late."

I hadn't even realized my period was late with everything going on. It wasn't until this morning that I saw I was late when I opened my calendar to book a client. I freaked out, then went to the store and bought a test. When that came back positive, I assumed, like Juniper, that it was probably a false positive because I'm religious about taking my birth control. I bought two more tests to take, and both came back positive.

"What are you going to do? Do you want me to cancel our girls' night with Sukie?"

"No." I shake my head. "I need time to wrap my head around this news, and I'd like to do that with my friends nearby."

"Are you sure?" Juniper's worried gaze catches mine.

"I'm sure. I could use the distraction. And I need to build up the courage to confront Ash. I'll have to mentally prepare myself for the fact I'll likely be raising this baby on my own."

"So." Juniper treads carefully. "You for sure want to keep the baby?"

I don't even hesitate when I answer. "Yes. I may not be sure about a lot of things, but I want to keep this baby." It's the truth. The second those two lines appeared on the first test, there was no doubt in my mind.

"What about Salem?" Juniper asks.

"What about him?"

"What if he says he doesn't want to be a dad? What then?"

I shrug. "Like I said before, I'll raise this baby on my own. He can either be involved, or chooses to stay away. He's already made it clear where he and I stand, and I don't want him thinking I got pregnant on purpose to trap him."

"If that asshole even insinuates you trying to trap him, I will castrate him," Juniper spits.

"And that right there is why you're my best friend, Juju."

Juniper puts her arm around me. "Forever heifer." She squeezes. "Just so you know, you won't be alone. Your baby will have his or her Aunt Juju."

Later that night, Juniper and Sukie and I are seated on the floor around the coffee table, and I'm three slices into the pizza we ordered when I notice Sukie is quietly picking at her food. "What's up, Sukie?"

"Hmm?" She looks up from her plate.

I set my pizza down and wipe my hands on a napkin. "Something's going on with you. You're awfully quiet tonight."

"Nothing," she says.

Juniper and I eye each other. "Bullshit," Juniper calls her out, and Sukie's head snaps up.

"We're your friends, Sukie. And friends tell each other what's bothering them," I add.

"It's really no big deal." Sukie sighs. "Just been dealing with a lot at home. Mom has been sick, and my car died on me a couple days ago, so I've been driving my mom's old truck. The speedometer doesn't work, and it doesn't have any heat." She shrugs. "But hey, at least it's running." Sukie smiles, but I can tell it's forced.

I feel like a bad friend for not noticing before that Sukie has struggled.

"That sucks, babe. Is there anything we can do to help?" Juniper asks.

"No, no," Sukie rushes to say.

"Are you sure?" I ask again. "Did you find out what was wrong with your car?"

"Not yet. I had it towed to a shop, but the mechanic says he hasn't had a chance to look at it yet."

"Are you talking about Harrison's?" Juniper asks.

Sukie nods.

"I took my car in yesterday for a service, and the place was dead. The guy down there was able to get me in and out."

Sukie purses her lips but doesn't look all that shocked. "Yeah, well, I don't usually get the same customer service as everyone else."

"Are you shitting me?" I seethe.

"It's not worth getting upset over," Sukie huffs. "I'm used to people being shitty toward me."

"That's the thing, Sukie. You shouldn't have to get used to eating shit from the uppity assholes in this town."

Sukie notices me getting worked up. "Sage, seriously, it's okay. I plan on going down to Harrison's tomorrow to see about my car, and if he hasn't fixed it, I'll take it somewhere else."

Sensing the topic is making Sukie uncomfortable, I decide to drop it. It took weeks to get her to start opening up to Juniper and me, so I don't want to push it. We still don't know her story, just little tidbits here and there, but I am confident Sukie will trust us enough to tell us more if we don't pressure her.

We spend the rest of the night stuffing our faces with pizza and sticking to safer topics, which leads to a heated game of Who'd You Rather, where I choose Wolverine over Aquaman, and Juniper threatens to revoke my best friend card because how dare I not pick Aquaman.

. . .

I will admit that the few hours I goofed off with my friends went a long way in helping me forget about my broken heart. But now that I'm lying in bed alone, I have nothing but my wandering thoughts and the memories of Ash's arms around me keeping me up. When I close my eyes and think about him, it's like I can still smell his scent. And I can still hear his words whispered in my ear or the way he would hold the back of my neck when we kissed. I think that's what hurt the most when he said he was done with me. It was like he was saying all those things that mattered to me didn't matter to him. Because if they did, it would not have been so easy for him to walk away. I have to face the fact that I was and still am in love with a man who doesn't love me back. And now I'm carrying his baby.

Bringing my hands up to my lower belly, I close my eyes and finally let the tears I've been holding back since I saw those two blue lines on the test. I kept it together in front of Juniper and held my head high as I made a vow to stay strong for my baby. But now, I'm not feeling so strong. I'm feeling broken down and defeated. I don't know how long I lie crying, but soon I feel the bed dip and an arm curl around my waist.

"Shhh," Juniper whispers into my ear as she strokes my hair. "Let it out."

The sound of my sobbing fills the room, causing my body to shake.

"It's going to be okay," Juniper whispers.

I wake the following day to the sunlight peeking through the bedroom window, and I welcome its warmth as it beats down on my face. Peering over my shoulder, I find Juniper sound asleep beside me. Careful not to wake her, I slide out of bed and make my way across the hall to the bathroom. Once I'm finished with my business, I splash some cold water on my face then stare at my reflection in the mirror. Looking back at me is a pale face with red-rimmed eyes. Aside from a bit of yellowing along my cheekbone, the bruises on my face are mostly gone.

When I walk out of the bathroom, I peek in on Juniper to see her still passed out, so I decide now is a good time as any to call Ash. I don't want to put off telling him about the baby. If he's going to bow out of having a hand in raising this baby, that is something I want to know now so I can get used to the idea of being a single parent. Deep down, I know Ash is an honorable man, but children were not something we ever discussed.

After pacing the living room for several minutes, I take a deep breath, find Ash's number, and place the phone to my ear. It rings twice before going to voicemail. A sign he saw my call and sent it there. Pushing away from the sting of his rejection, I bring up our previous text thread and type out a new message.

Me: Can we talk?

I watch as the little bubble pops up then disappears. I wait two minutes before trying again.

Me: It's important. Please.

Two seconds later, it shows he read my text. I wait again for him to reply but nothing.

Me: I know you are seeing this. I wouldn't be texting if it wasn't necessary. I need to see you. There's something we have to talk about.

That little bubble pops up again, and this time he replies.

Ash: There's nothing to talk about. This shit with you calling and texting needs to stop.

That asshole. Looking at the time, I see it's almost noon. He'll be at the club. Looks like I'm just going to have to go down there. If he doesn't want to give me two minutes over the phone, then I'm going to force him to provide me with the two minutes I need, face to face.

Me: You can go fuck yourself. And since you won't talk to me on the phone, I will come to say what I need to your face.

I don't wait for him to reply. Marching over to the kitchen island, I snatch my purse and toss my phone inside. I don't bother changing from the same clothes I wore yesterday that I slept in. I locate my tennis shoes over by the front door and slip my feet inside. Then I quickly scribble a note to Juniper and leave it beside the coffee pot. She's probably going to kill me for going down to the club to confront Ash alone, but I'm getting this shit with him over with. Plus, his asshole behavior has amped me up and given me the courage I need to face him.

Storming into the club, it takes my eyes a moment to adjust the dim lighting. When they do, the first person I see is Mystic.

"Sage, what are you doing here, darlin'?" His voice is gentle.

"I came to talk to Ash."

"He know you were stoppin' by?"

"I didn't exactly ask permission, but I'm sure he's expecting me."

Mystic studies me for a beat as if he's deciding whether or not he's going to let me stay.

"Look, Mystic. I'm not here to start trouble or beg Ash to take me back. Despite how much I love him, I have more self-respect than that. I came because I really do have something important to talk about with him."

Mystic then does something that shocks the hell out of me. He kisses the top of my head, then walks away.

With Mystic out of my way, I carry on through the club and down the corridor that leads to his office. Once I reach the door, I don't bother knocking. Instead, I push open. Except I realize my mistake the second I enter the room, because sitting behind his desk is Ash, but what has all the air leaving my body is the sight of

Astrid on her knees between Salem's spread legs. Astrid at least has the decency to look somewhat apologetic, but it's the smirk on Ash's face that drives the stake entirely through my heart.

I turn on my heel with my flight mode kicking in and run. The second I push open the heavy door and a blast of cold air hits my face, my legs give out, and I proceed to lose the contents of my stomach in the parking lot.

"Sage." I vaguely hear Mystic's voice through the whooshing in my ears. Then I feel a pair of hands lifting me to my feet.

"What the hell is goin' on?"

I wipe my mouth with the back of my hand as I look up at Ash's best friend. "Tell him I heard his message loud and clear."

"What?" Mystic looks at me with an angry but confused expression. "What the fuck did he do?"

I ignore his question. "You can also tell him we don't need him." I turn and walk away.

21
SALEM

I watch the woman I love run, shattered by my actions for a second time. My gut churns, threatening to rid my body of the whiskey breakfast I had this morning.

Astrid rises from the floor between my knees. We did nothing, but I sure as shit made sure it appeared otherwise. It had to be done. I couldn't trust myself to stay true to my choice that Sage is better off without me. And one way to put the final nail in the coffin of us was making her believe I'd moved on.

"You're a dick, Salem." Astrid glares at me with contempt. "Don't you ever order me to do something so fucking cruel again. I like Sage." Astrid shakes her head. "You destroyed her just now," she seethes.

"Good." My voice gets stuck, trying to get past the massive lump in my throat. I reach for the bottle of booze nearby and put it to my lips. I throw my head back, letting the whiskey burn my already raw throat some more. Since cutting Sage loose and breaking hearts, I've been on a bender—a liquid diet of fuck my life.

"God. Men are so stupid." Astrid fixes herself while walking away but spins around and looks at me one more time. "How can you love someone that much and let them go?"

How can I not?

I don't say or do anything but stare back at Astrid. Her judging eyes burn a hole through my skull. "You are a fucking idiot, Salem." She shakes her head. "The safest place she could ever be is with you." Astrid storms off.

I lift the bottle to my lips again. What's done is done. Sage gave me no other choice once announcing she was going to the club.

I hear someone stomping up the stairs just before Mystic comes into view. "Brother." My tone is flat, and I go to take another drink only to have the bottle ripped from my grasp. "What the fuck?" I fly out of my chair, my blood pumping.

Mystic chucks the half-bottle of whiskey across the room, shattering it against the wall behind my head. "You're a stupid son of a bitch!" Mystic shouts, giving my chest a good shove.

A fight is just what I need, so I shove him back. "Know your fuckin' place, brother," I bite back, hoping like hell Mystic will throw the first punch, and he does. His fist cracks the right side of my jaw.

"My place?" Mystic keeps his fists in front of him, protecting his face. I shake off the hit and connect my fist with Mystic's mouth, knowing he'll counter with a punch of his own. His knuckles smash across the side of my head. I allow my best friend to throw a few more punches without fighting back. I absorb the pain because it gives me something to focus on besides the torment eating at my insides. Realizing he's giving me exactly what I want, Mystic stops.

I breathe heavily, scrub my palm over my face, and taste the copper of fresh blood as I lick my lips. "Go." I turn my back on Mystic, walk over to my desk, and pull open the drawer where I keep my weed stash.

"What the fuck did you do to her this time?" Mystic asks. "I didn't think two people could look more broken than you and her, but somehow, whatever you said or did managed to do just that."

I light the joint between my fingers and pull the smoke deep into my lung, holding it there until it burns and my head tingles.

"She walked in while Astrid was on her knees in front of me." I wheeze my confession as the smoke is expelled from my body.

"Fuckin' hell, man." Mystic sighs. "Why, Ash?"

I lift my head, looking at my best friend. I can feel my left eye beginning to swell. He already knows why so I remain silent.

"Would you like to know what she told me on her way out of your fuckin' life for the second time?" Mystic stares me down, waiting for my reply. I take another toke off the joint. Nothing he can say can make the pain I'm in worse. "She said to tell you 'we don't need him.'"

My eyelids feel heavy as the weed's effect takes hold. Did he say *we*?

"Did you hear what I said?" Mystic's growing more agitated at my silence as I process Sage's message.

I shake my head and blink my eyes, trying to clear the fog from my brain. We don't need you. Is she...? I look at Mystic, my eyes going wide. No. That's not what she meant by we. It can't be. Then all the mind-blowing moments we shared and all the unprotected sex we had smack me in the goddamn face like a freight train.

Mystic nods slowly. "Yeah, brother. I think Sage is pregnant."

It's a good thing the sofa is directly behind me because my body goes numb, and my ass sinks to the cushion. Sage said she needed to talk, that it was important. Shit. She was coming here to tell me she's having our baby.

The cushion beside me dips as Mystic takes a seat on the sofa. "It sinkin' in now?"

"She's havin' my kid." I breathe in deep.

"Yeah, man. Fuck, she didn't say that but—"

"I'm gonna be a dad, brother." I hang my head. "What the fuck am I to do now?" I stare at the scuffs on the toes of my boots.

"I don't know. That's somethin' you need to figure out."

"I have no clue how to be a father." I throw myself back into the sofa and stare up at the ceiling.

"The fuck you don't. Your father was a piece of shit, but you had my dad." Mystic stands and hovers over me. "He loved you like a son, and he showed you how a man takes care of his family. You're a Fallen Raven because he saw something in you. He saw a son. Chicago wasn't only my dad and role model. He was yours, too."

Mystic is right. Chicago was always there for me.

"Dad is the reason I'm so goddamn good at this father shit. No matter how rough life got, he showed up for us, and that's what I do for Lorelei daily. I love her, and I show up."

I jump from the sofa and sway a bit. Mystic grips my cut, steadying me. "I'll be back." I go to brush past him, but he stops me.

"Go where?"

"Get my woman back."

"I like your go-get-her spirit, brother, but you're in no condition to go beggin' for another chance. And judging by the state she left in, you're the last person she wants to see. Sober up. Get your head out of your ass and thoughts straight before crawlin' on hands and knees, brother."

I nod and run my hand through my hair. "I really fucked shit up."

Mystic huffs. "You sure as shit did."

"But I'm gonna fix it," I tell myself, scrubbing my palm down my face. I will fix Sage and me. Somehow, some way, I will right all the wrongs I have caused.

"Smartest fuckin' thing I've heard you say in a long time."

Mystic clamps his hand on my shoulder. "Sorry about your face."
He eyes me.

"Don't fuckin' apologize. My dumb ass deserved it."

"Damn right you did." Mystic smirks.

"Wouldn't want to do life without you, brother." I place my hand on his shoulder.

"In it together for life."

22
SAGE

My hands are shaking as I insert the key into the lock, opening the door to my apartment. Juniper is sitting at the kitchen island drinking coffee, and her eyes go straight to me, then she's off the stool. "Sage, what happened? Why are you crying?"

Instead of answering her questions, I walk straight to my bedroom. Juniper is at my back when I shove open the closet and pull out a suitcase.

"Sage, what the hell. Talk to me," she demands.

I fling the suitcase onto the bed and wipe my face with the back of my hand. "I have to get out of here. I'm going to my parents for a few days," I croak.

Juniper stills. "What did the son of a bitch do?"

I yank open the top drawer to the dresser, grab a handful of bras and underwear and throw them in the suitcase. "I'll tell you what he did. Ash made it clear I meant absolutely nothing to him. If it wasn't clear before, it is now." I stomp back into the closet and start snatching shirts from hangers.

"What did he say to you?" Juniper asks.

I stop what I'm doing and look at her. "Not say—do. His actions spoke loud and clear."

Juniper studies me for a moment, then she puts her hand over her mouth. I'm sure she can guess what went down at the club full of strippers.

"Tell me he didn't."

"He did. I walked in on him and Astrid." I go back to packing my clothes. "You should have seen his face, Juniper."

"What do you mean?"

"The asshole looked right through me. No emotions. He looked at me like I was nothing. Can you believe that? After everything we've been through and all that we shared." I shake my head. "I walk in on him with another woman, and he doesn't even have the decency to look remorseful of the fact the world could literally hear my heart breaking into a million pieces." A sob escapes past my lips, and I reach out and brace myself against the dresser to keep my knees from giving out. "God, Juju, I think he was glad I caught him."

"I'm going to castrate him," Juniper seethes. "Cut his balls off, then shove them up his cheating ass."

I look at my best friend and blink. "I appreciate the visuals."

"You don't think I'll do it? Because I will."

"Oh, I know you will. But maybe sit this one out, because I'm not keen on visiting my best friend in prison."

"Why don't you let me drive you? I don't think you should be driving when you're this upset," she suggests.

"No." I shake my head. "I could use the time to think. I need to be alone with my thoughts. I'm going to use this time to get myself together. I'll be back in a few days, a week tops."

"Are you sure? You know I'll come with you."

"I know you would, Juju and, I'm sure."

Juniper lets out a heavy sigh. "All right. You go and take care of you and bean." She touches my tummy. "And I'll hold the fort down here. But if you change your mind about needing me, you say the word, and I'm there."

"Thanks, Juju."

I'm packed and sitting in my car when I dial my father's number and put the phone to my ear.

"Shortcake!"

I burst out crying again at the sound of my dad's voice. Always so cheerful and always excited to hear from me. At this moment, I know the only place I want to be is home, because sometimes all this girl needs is her daddy.

"Hi, Dad." There is no mistake in the hitch in my voice that something is wrong.

"Sage, what's wrong, baby girl?"

"Are you okay with me coming home for a few days?"

"Of course. You never have to ask. But what's going on? Is it Juniper? Is she okay?"

"Juniper is fine. I've just had a rough week and need to get away," I semi-lie. I haven't told my parents about my breakup or being kidnapped.

"What's going on? Where is Ash?"

Hearing his name causes me to cry even harder. "Ash and I broke up, Dad. It's a long story."

"What did he do to my little girl? Do I need to drive to Salem and shove a socket wrench up his ass?"

"No! What is with you and Juniper wanting to shove stuff up Ash's ass? First, she threatened his balls, and now you're threatening a wrench."

"It's nice to know that Juju has my back when I'm not around to perform my fatherly duties."

I snort. "Lucky me."

Dad is quiet for a second before clearing his throat. "When are you heading out?"

"I'm in my car now. I'll drive until I get tired and find a hotel. I should be there by tomorrow night."

"Okay. I want you checking in with me, no matter the time."

"I will, Dad."

"Do you have your taser and pepper spray?"

I think back to the last time I used my pepper spray, and a shiver runs down my spine. I also never replaced it, but I do have my taser.

"Yeah, I have them."

"All right. I guess I'll see you tomorrow night."

"I love you, Dad. I'll check in later."

"Love you too, Shortcake."

Wanting snacks for the road, I stop at the gas station. Before getting out of my car, I dig my taser from my purse and put it in my back pocket. After the incident with the Demon Jokers, my father's voice inside my head is a little bit louder. Usually, when he reminds me about my safety, I roll my eyes, but now, I won't take any chances. It doesn't take long to load up on all my road trip junk food favorites, then I'm back on the road.

I'm just passing the Salem city limits sign when I spot a familiar truck stalled on the side of the road. Slowing to a stop beside the open driver-side door, I find Brandon.

"Hey, you stuck again?" I ask.

The frustrated look on his face is replaced by a smile. "Hey, Sage. Yeah, the damn thing stalled on me again, and I can't get my uncle on the phone to give me a jump."

"That sucks, but I can give you one if you want."

"If you don't mind, I'd appreciate it."

"Not a problem. Let me turn around and pull up in front of you."

Brandon jumps out of his truck, and I watch as he retrieves a pair of jumper cables from the back while I check to make sure the traffic is clear before making a U-turn in the road, then pull off to the shoulder, parking with my front bumper facing the hood of Brandon's truck.

Brandon is already at work hooking up the cables by the time I climb out of my car. "This is the second time you've saved my ass. Thanks again." Brandon smiles, making his dimple pop.

"I'm happy I happened to be driving by."

"Where are you heading anyway?" he asks.

"I'm going home to visit my parents for a few days."

Brandon hooks one cable end up to his battery, then eyes me from under the hood of his truck. His face goes soft. "I heard about you and Salem."

I shift from one foot to the other, not wanting to talk about Ash. If Brandon senses my unease about the topic, he ignores it. "You know," he adds as he walks around the front of the truck back to the driver's side, "I did try to warn you Salem was no good, and you should have listened."

I'm taken aback momentarily by Brandon's remark. "Ah, no offense, Brandon, but whatever happened with mine and Ash's relationship isn't any of your business."

"All I'm saying is you should have listened to me."

"Brandon, seriously, you are way out of line."

Something in Brandon's demeanor snaps. I see the moment all his good-guy pretenses vanish. The look he gets in his eyes is enough to send shivers down my spine. He notices the second I see it, too. Before I can back away, he reaches out and grabs my arm while his other hand reaches for something under the driver's seat of his truck. Then, I see a flash of metal before a pain explodes on the side of my head and the lights go out.

23
SALEM

It's been 24 hours since finding out Sage may be pregnant with our child. After literally getting some sense knocked into me, I spent the remainder of the day reflecting on my life. I even apologized to Astrid. I should have never asked her to get involved by helping me make Sage believe I got my dick wet with another woman.

Now, here I stand outside the salon, broken, sober, and most of all hopeful that she'll at least give me the chance to be a part of our child's life.

I've never been so fucking nervous as when I pull open the salon door and step inside. The place is empty of clients, and Sage is nowhere to be seen. "Be with you in a minute," Juniper calls from the back. She appears a few seconds later, her arms full of hair care products. The moment her eyes land on me, they turn ice cold. "You need to leave." Juniper storms past fast enough to create a breeze.

"Where's Sage?" I turn my head, following her movement.

Juniper starts unloading her arms, placing shampoo bottles on the glass shelves hung on the wall. "I don't think that's any of your business." She slams a bottle down a little too hard, causing the glass to rattle.

"I need to talk to her," I grind out.

Juniper whips her head around and glares. "Haven't you tormented her enough, Salem?" She moves toward me and jabs her finger into my chest. "You broke her heart, asshole. She was nothing but good to you, loving you for who you are, and you chose to throw it all away. You, Salem, not her. I'm the one who held her all night and dried her tears." Juniper takes a breath and walks away.

"Is she upstairs?"

"She's gone."

My stomach hits the floor. "Gone where?" I start to panic. Juniper walks into the back again, completely ignoring me. "Shit," I mutter, and Juniper strolls back out with more products in hand.

"You're wasting your time." She gives me a resentful scowl.

"Juniper, please. Where is she?" I resort to begging, and it's an unnatural feeling I suspect I'll become familiar with from now on.

Juniper's face softens a bit. "Jesus. She is going to murder me." She sighs. "Sage left last night to visit her parents." Juniper pauses, studying me for a second. "It destroyed her catching you with another woman."

I blow out a breath. "It didn't happen."

Juniper scrunches her face. "Don't give me that bullshit line." She folds her arms over her chest. "Sage didn't hallucinate Astrid on her knees between your legs."

"It was all a lie—a bullshit act to drive Sage away. I knew she was on her way, so I set the scene to appear as if Astrid and I had done something." I rub the back of my neck, not really knowing why I feel the need to confess anything to Juniper.

Juniper stares at me, shaking her head. "She was going to tell you she's pregnant, and instead, she gets her soul crushed by a fucking lie." Juniper tosses her arms above her head. "Unfuckingbelieveable." Then she slaps her palm over her mouth, and her eyes widen. "Shit." Her curse is muffled.

"Don't worry. You didn't spill the beans. I put shit together, and that's why I'm here," I say, and Juniper drops her hand.

A phone rings before more is said, and Juniper walks across the salon to a workstation. "Hey, Mr. Briggs." I watch Juniper's face fall. "No, she told me she would call once she got there." Juniper's eyes find mine. "Sage never check in," she tells me and grabs the counter beside her.

I'm at Juniper's side before she lowers herself into the salon chair. I take the phone from her hand. "Charles."

"Ash?" He sounds surprised, which leads me to think he knows Sage and I are no longer together.

"Talk to me."

"She hasn't made it here, son. Didn't check in, either. I haven't heard from my daughter since she called to say she was hitting the road." His voice sounds grim. My mind starts thinking the worst. What if she was involved in an accident and hurt, or worse. "Her mother and I are worried sick."

"I'll find her. Stay by the phone. If, by chance, she arrives, call." My voice sounds clipped. There's an uneasy silence that settles over the phone line, and I know Charles is conjuring up worse case scenarios, too.

"Ash." I hear the thick emotions Charles is attempting to keep at bay. "Find my daughter."

"Yes, sir," I say, and the line goes dead.

I pass the phone to Juniper, whose unblinking, concerned eyes look at me for answers, and I have none. She drops her attention to the phone in her hand, swipes the screen, pulls up Sage's number, and puts the phone on speaker. The call goes straight to voicemail. Thinking maybe she'll communicate with me, I dig the cell from my pocket and call her as well. My results are the same.

"What do we do?" Juniper's voice wobbles, trying to keep her shit together.

"Someone should be here in case she doubles back home, so stay put."

Juniper nods. "She's fine. She just needs time to regroup," she whispers to herself, trying to ease her mind but clearly it's not working as her hard-shelled exterior begins to crack. She closes her eyes. "Please be alright."

I'm wasting precious time just standing here. I keep my phone in my hand. "Juniper," I call out, but she doesn't respond. "Juniper." I raise my voice, and her eyes fly open. "You hear from Sage, you contact me immediately, got it?"

Juniper nods, and I turn on my heels, heading for the door. "What do you plan to do?"

"Get my men and find my woman," I say without looking back. Once outside, I have my phone at my ear, putting a call in to Mystic as I swing my leg over the bike seat.

"How'd it go?" is Mystic's greeting.

"It didn't. Sage is missing," I say, and it feels like something keeps clawing at my insides, because I can't stop thinking the worst.

"What do you mean missing?"

"Sage packed some shit and left town more than 24 hours ago, heading home, but her father reported that he hasn't heard from her since," I explain.

"Shit," Mystic hisses. "Think maybe she's resting up in a hotel between here and there?"

I run a hand through my hair. "I don't know, brother. She isn't answering her phone for no one. If it was only me tryin' to contact her, I'd understand, but her father and Juniper aren't having luck, either." I breathe deep a few times, trying to rid myself of the uneasy feeling pulling at my insides.

"Give me something to do." Mystic offers his help.

"Get in touch with the others and have them at the clubhouse. I'm headin' there now," I order and shove my phone away.

I roll up to the clubhouse and bring my bike to a stop beside Mystic. I glance at my men, all alert and ready to help. Harlem, who is sitting on the stone steps of the church, stands. His face tightens. He's still recovering from his injuries, and his body isn't healing as fast as he's trying to push it. He shouldn't be riding today, but by the determined look in his eyes as he makes his way to his bike, there isn't a damn thing I could say to make him stay behind. Seated on his ride, he eyes me, and I nod, knowing he needs to do this. "There are miles of road between here and Nebraska, along with several hotels we need to search," I say, and the others mount their bikes. Nothing more needs to be said. I throw my hand in the air, and engines rumble.

Most days, I welcome the air on my face, the sun on my back, and the sound of bike tires humming against the asphalt. This ride is different. Even with my brothers riding beside me, I feel isolated and can't shake this bad feeling manifesting.

Up ahead, the Salem city limit sign comes into view, along with a truck with the hood raised. We ease our bikes off the road, and I head straight for the vehicle. Inside I find a man's jacket sitting on the passenger seat. Nothing about any of this is correct. "Something isn't right here." I duck out of the truck.

"Whoever the owner is was having issues." Baja reaches down and lifts a pair of jumper cables off the ground.

"Prez," Juneau shouts, and I turn to see my brother walking back from the tree line several yards from the road. The sun reflects an object in his hand. Juneau hands me a cellphone— Sage's phone. My chest tightens with panic. I flip through more than two dozen missed calls from her dad, along with the ones from Juniper and me earlier, as well as numerous text messages from both her parents. Harlem strides around to the truck's driver's side, his eyes fixed on the ground.

"Prez." Harlem continues to stare downward.

I round the front of the truck and look down at what has his attention—drops of blood. My stomach sinks. I open the driver's door and start rummaging through the cab of the truck, searching for a vehicle title, insurance car, anything with a name. Through the back window, I catch the others digging through loads of shit in the bed of the truck. I come across a folded piece of paper lying under the jacket. It's a check stub from Billy's hardware with Brandon Murphy's name on it.

"Prez," Juneau shouts. "You need to take a look at this."

I fist the paper in my hand and fly out of the vehicle. At the bed, I look over the side and peer into a metal trunk the men have busted open. Inside are women's blood-spattered clothing, a couple of handguns, a stack of notebooks, and photo albums.

"Don't touch nothin'," Laredo orders as he digs a pair of black leather gloves from his coat pocket. Laredo reaches into the truck and lifts a piece of clothing out, studies it, then places it back inside. He moves the handguns lying on the stack of notebooks, then flips through the pages. "Holy shit."

"What?" I ask as he skims through another, becoming highly focused. "It's him," Laredo murmurs.

"You need to give me somethin', brother. I'm on the edge of losin' my shit," I say through clenched teeth.

"The owner of this truck is the serial killer." He closes the notebook. "Those are journals, with detailed written accounts of the crimes." Laredo's words have all the air leaving my lungs, and I can't breathe. My brother turns to me. "And Sage checks off every box to be his next victim. The women murdered have distinct physical features in common: dark hair, blue eyes, fuller figures."

I finally come back to my senses enough and remember the

check stub held tight in my fist. I shove the wadded paper into Laredo's hand. "The killer has a name." Rage begins to decorate my insides as I watch Laredo flatten the paper. His eyes meet mine again.

"Brandon Murphy," he announces.

"You mean the fucker who's had a hard-on for Sage since day one? Billy's nephew?" Juneau asks.

"Shit," I hear Mystic hiss behind my back.

"Bikes!" I roar. Doubling back, my men and I head back to town. The motherfucker has my woman, and she has already been missing for too long. I speed down the highway, racing against my worst enemy: time.

It's not long before we're busting through the doors at the hardware store. Billy, Brandon's uncle, pulls his eyes from the computer screen. "Salem?" His eyes cut around me to my men. "What's going on?" He voices concern at our presence. His attention lands back on me.

"Where's Brandon?"

Billy's forehead creases. "Probably in his cabin by now."

"You're certain?"

"Yeah. He was heading up that way for a few days." Billy steps out from behind the counter. "What do you men want with my nephew?"

I don't answer him. "You got the address?"

"Of course."

"Write it down," I bark, causing the old man to flinch. Billy has always been respectful of the club, and if he continues doing so, we won't have any problems. Billy finds a sheet of paper and a pen, then jots down the information I asked for and he passes it to me.

"Is he in some kind of trouble?" Billy asks, sounding more disappointed than concerned.

Again, I don't give him the answers he's looking for, but I do level a look at him that has him putting additional space between us. "Keep your mouth shut. Don't go callin' your nephew, either. If I find out you have, I'll pay you another visit."

Billy swallows hard, his eyes roaming the faces of my brothers before coming to rest on me again, and nods. "Understood."

"Good," I say, then walk out of the store.

Death's presence follows me out the door.

I welcome him like an old friend, allowing his shadow to consume me in darkness.

I become one with the killer inside.

I'm out for blood, and hell's coming with me.

24
SAGE

My eyelids flutter, blinking away the brain fog I'm currently experiencing. Unfamiliar surroundings come into focus. Where the hell am I? Alarm immediately sets in. I bolt upright but quickly realize my mistake when the pounding in my head makes my breath catch. I wince. There's a throbbing tightness at the back of my skull. I reach back to touch the spot, and my fingers brush over a tender lump.

I push myself up into a seated position, look around the small living room, and take in the matching recliner, coffee table, and the large screen TV mounted above the fireplace.

"I'm glad you're finally awake."

The voice comes from behind me, and I jump to my feet, turning toward the person speaking. Brandon?

It's then my memories flood my mind. Catching Ash with another woman, rushing home to pack, the conversation with my dad, stopping at the gas station, helping Brandon.

"Brandon, what's going on?" I take a hesitant step backward, and my body tenses.

"You know, it's always the same with you all." He ignores my question. "Always playing the same game, desperate for attention."

"Brandon—"

"Is it so hard to be straight with men without adding in your games?" he cuts me off.

I'm confused. "What games? Brandon, I don't know what you're talking about. Tell me, what's going on? Why did you hit me, and why am I here?"

"You're here because it's what you want."

My stomach drops. "No," I say, shaking my head. "I want to leave." I take a step toward the door. He shakes his head at me then stands. My eyes dart down to the piece of rope wound around his fist and the tattered end dangling at his side. A dozen scenarios start running through my mind, all of them unpleasant. This Brandon speaking to me now is not the same man I met when I first moved to Salem. He isn't the easy-going guy next door with a crooked smile and cute dimples. He isn't the good friend he's portrayed himself to be. No, the man in front of me is someone entirely different. His eyes reveal someone with no soul. How did I not see this before?

"Brandon." I place my hands out in front of me. "Please."

He cocks his head to the side. "I misjudged you, Sage. I thought you were going to be different from all the rest." He shakes his head in disappointment. "I should have known. You're all the same."

Why does he keep saying that? "Who? Who's all the same?"

His eyes narrow. "All the women before you." His lip twitches. "A good guy comes along, shows you some interest, then you decide to play hard to get. But you don't do that for the bad boys, do you?" He scoffs in disgust. "Oh no, the bad guys come along, treat you like whores, and, just like that, you spread your legs for them." He snaps his fingers. "While good guys like me get caught up in your games, using us but not giving in return."

He's not making any sense. Who are these women he's talking about? "Brandon, I don't know what you're talking about, but I'm sure if you just calm down, we can—"

"Don't you dare fucking patronize me." Brandon's voice rises, and his face turns red. The chill in the air goes from cold to arctic. "I saw the way you would look at me, and I knew you were interested. But you had to play the game. Then that fucking criminal came along, and you decided to add him into the mix. You ran around town dragging both of us by the short hairs. Because that's what sluts like you do, isn't it, Sage?"

I try to calm my rapid pulse and take a different approach to this situation growing ever more like it's straight out of a horror movie. "I'm sorry. It wasn't ever my intention to lead you on or hurt you."

Brandon lets out a menacing cackle. "You hurt me?" Taking another step in my direction, he shakes his head. "You could never hurt me. Whores like you don't have the power to hurt me. But I, however, do have the power to teach you a lesson."

"Brandon," I try again.

"Tsk-tsk. Here's where you're going to want to shut up. We're about to play a game, and I'm about to explain the rules. You don't want to miss them."

I swallow. "What game?"

Brandon smiles, and it sends a chill down my spine. "It's your favorite game...chase." His fist clenches and unclenches around the rope in his hand, and as a predator would, he starts stalking toward me.

I back away only to trip over a pair of boots sitting next to the fireplace. I lose my footing but quickly recover. "Brandon, please," I plead.

He ignores me and continues. "There are only two rules in this game."

I circle the living room as he inches closer and closer to me.

"Please stop," I try again.

"Rule number one, I give you a sixty-second head start."

"Brandon," I say with more urgency. "You don't have to do this."

He continues. "Rule number two."

I cut him off. "Please, Brandon." My voice shakes. And for as long as I live, I will never forget the cold dead look pointed at me when he utters his final rule.

His eyes flare. "Run."

The front door is five feet to my right, and I don't hesitate to bolt out. The second my back is turned, he counts, starting at sixty, and I'm out the door by the time he spits number fifty-nine.

Night has fallen, and the moon is shining bright in the sky, lighting my way. I don't know which way I should run. Brandon brought me to a cabin in the middle of nowhere, surrounded by trees. I see a narrow dirt road ahead of me but decide the logical choice is to hide amongst the trees. He no doubt knows the lay of the land like the back of his hand. I don't feel confident in my chances either way.

"Fifty-five! Fifty-four! Fifty-three!" Brandon bellows.

I pick up speed, moving my legs as fast as they will carry me. Twigs and leaves crunch beneath my shoes. With every step I take, his voice trailing behind me echoes. I dodge hanging branches and weave through the trees, all while ignoring the burning in my lungs. I don't know how many seconds have passed when I realize I no longer hear Brandon's voice. I stop in my tracks and throw my body against a tree. My chest heaves as I breathe in the cold air. Aside from the sounds of my heaving breathing and croaking frogs, I hear nothing. My past and future flash through my mind like a movie reel. The last vision I see is Ash's face. I briefly close my eyes and imagine him holding our baby. The very child growing inside of me. Then I envision my parents. I think of how my father just hours ago called me Shortcake. If I had known it might be the last time I heard his voice, I would have told him he is the best father a girl could ever hope for.

No matter how much time you have on earth, it will never be enough with those you love.

My eyes snap open when I cease to hear the frogs croaking. A prickly sensation washes over me. Brandon is close, and I can feel it.

25
SALEM

We abandon our bikes, leaving them under a dilapidated lean-to shed made from rusty tin roof panels located on an overgrown field directly across from Brandon's property.

Weapons drawn, my men and I keep to the side of the dirt road while trekking toward a small cabin in the distance. Night has fallen, shrouding everything in darkness, with only moments of light from the moon hanging high in the sky breaking through the clouds continuing to roll in. As we get nearer the cabin, I spot Sage's car parked out front.

The pounding in my head intensifies as an extra rush of adrenaline kicks in, then suddenly I stop in my tracks when I hear a low-pitched whistle. I hold my breath to avoid making a sound, trying to listen for the noise again. There it is, faint, but I definitely hear what sounds like someone whistling. I turn, looking at my brothers. "Tell me I'm not the only one who hears that."

"I hear it," Harlem grunts.

The sound happens again. "Come out, come out, wherever you are." A man's voice soon follows the whistling. The hairs on the back of my neck stand on end, and my blood runs cold. It's Brandon.

"That way." I keep my voice low, pointing to where a path cuts through the trees beyond the cabin on the left.

"Sage," Brandon bellows, his voice carrying through the trees.

We move past the cabin without making ourselves known. It won't be so easy once we enter the woods. A twig snaps beneath my foot as I step beyond the tree line, continuing to make my way in the direction Brandon's voice is coming from. A large fallen pine tree lies across the dark hiking trail, and we end up climbing over instead of going around to avoid giving ourselves away. To the side of the trail, a set of glowing yellow eyes, probably a raccoon, watches as we pass by the thicket it's hiding in.

As the seconds tick by, more clouds blanket the stars and block out the moon, making the woods around us darker. My thoughts never waver from Sage. She's out there, all alone, in the middle of nowhere. If I wasn't such a fool, she wouldn't have left town in the first place.

The sudden hoot of an owl from high atop the trees makes us jumpy. "Shit," Mystic hisses.

We're all on edge, and the slightest sound has us ready to pull the trigger.

"I know you're close, Sage," Brandon says, and he sounds close. I stop moving, and so do my men. Dread settles in my gut, thinking the bastard could find her before I do. "I smell your perfume."

Not saying a word, I signal my brothers to split up, and we each head in a different direction. The tall trees loom over me, their branches swaying with the wind. I step foot off the hiking trail, and the leaves covering the forest floor crunch beneath my boots. With my weapon raised, I keep trudging forward, needing to find Sage before it's too late.

The air around me thickens, and an ominous silence engulfs the forest. My skin tingles, and my senses heighten even more. I breathe deeper and listen with greater intensity. My vision sharpens as I become more tuned in with my surroundings.

I'm not alone.

Then, slowly, I turn, never expecting to feel an abrasive material wrap around my neck. "Well, well. Look who decided to join the fun," Brandon hisses in my ear. He jumps on my back like a spider monkey and pulls the rope tight against my throat. I stumble, losing my grip on my gun in the struggle.

My fingers grasp at the rope Brandon has constricted around my neck, and I back-pedal until we're slamming against the trunk of a tree. The force of the impact causes Brandon to loosen his hold, and the rope slackens enough to slip my hand between it and my neck. I throw my head back, and it connects with the son of a bitch's face, then I repeat the process. His hold on me doesn't waver. The bastard has some fight in him. With my free hand, I reach behind my head, fisting as much of his scalp and hair as I can, lurch forward, and fling Brandon off my back. The piece of shit hits the ground in front of me with a heavy thud. With the rope no longer around my neck, I take a full breath. Brandon rolls to his knees. I search the ground, looking for my weapon, but it's pitch black, making it impossible to find.

I allow the motherfucker to get on his feet.

I don't need my gun.

I'll kill him with my bare hands.

Brandon squares off with me. "You're not so tough without bullets or your men," Brandon sneers, and though it's dark as hell, we can make out each other's movements. "You and me, we're a lot alike, Salem." He pauses. Not a sound can be heard but our heavy breathing.

The clouds drift apart, and the moon's glow breaks through

the bare tree branches, shining a dim light around us. Brandon takes a step closer. That's when I catch the gleam of a blade in his right hand just before he rushes at me. I stand my ground and wrap my hand around his neck the moment he's within reach. I feel his blade sink into the flesh at my side. Pain radiates across my skin, but I absorb it, letting it feed the monster inside me. I squeeze my hand tighter around the bastard's throat.

I wrap my hand over Brandon's, where he's holding the handle of the knife still embedded in my body, and walk forward, slamming his back against a tree. The force of the impact jars the blade, causing it to dig deeper into my side. The pain only causes me to inflict more onto Brandon. His eyes bulge as my hand crushes his windpipe.

Spittle flies from his lips as the son of a bitch struggles to breathe.

My other hand gripped tight around his and the handle of the knife, I rip the blade from my body. Brandon uses what strength he has, trying to overpower me. I twist his wrist, bringing the knife into the space between our bodies. All the muscles engaged in his arm strain, attempting to force the weapon away while his other hand still tries to pry my hand from around his scrawny neck.

I stare into his fear-filled eyes. Brandon knows he's about to die. "We are nothing alike." I thrust the blade into his lower abdomen, and his eyes widen. "I'm worse," I growl, then pull upward, gutting the son of a bitch from navel to chest bone.

His entire body spasms as I listen to the blood flowing from a gaping hole in his gut, and blood splatters against my boots and the dead leaves on the ground. I hold the fucker in place while he gurgles, spitting out his last bit of life. Only when his eyes are void, do I release my hold around his neck, dropping him at my feet.

I step back, staring at his corpse and breathing heavily.

An intense fire burns across my midsection where the bastard stabbed me, but I don't have time to think about it. I need to find Sage.

A twig snapping has me whipping around, ready to fucking fight again. Harlem steps from the shadows amongst the trees. "Were you here the entire time?" I ask, and Harlem slowly nods. I go to move and grab at my side. Adrenaline no longer masks my pain. Harlem extends his hand, and he's holding my gun. "Thanks, brother." I take it and place the weapon inside my holster. "Let's go find my woman."

A few yards now separate Harlem and me from a dead man when we hear Mystic calling out, "I have her." This is followed by a beam of light cutting through the darkness like a lighthouse beacon, giving us their location. Another rush of adrenaline pulses through my veins, and I break into a sprint, weaving through trees and dodging branches on my way to Sage.

We come upon them beside a creek bank. There's Sage, wrapped in Mystic's jacket, her lips blue and body wet, shivering from the cold. "Found her hiding beneath that fallen tree over there, at the water's edge."

I take my coat off, kneel and blanket her body. "Baby."

Sage's teeth chatter as she turns her face toward me, and her pale blue eyes lock on mine. "Ash," she whispers, tears streaking down her cheeks. "I'm so cold."

"She's probably suffering from hypothermia. We need to get her body temperature up," Juneau states, and I respond by scooping her into my arms, grunting through the pain at my side, and holding her close, letting her soak up the heat of my body. I look at Mystic since he has a flashlight. "Get us the fuck out of here."

It feels like an eternity before the hiking trail comes into view, leading us back toward the cabin. I head straight for Sage's car. "Someone drive, and we'll get the other bikes later." I open the back door and slide Sage and myself into the backseat, keeping her tucked close to me. Harlem places his large frame behind the steering wheel.

"No keys," he says, then proceeds to hotwire the motherfucker. The car starts, and Harlem cranks the heat to full blast.

Baja, Laredo, and Juneau jog down the dirt road as Harlem pulls away from the cabin. "Brandon," Sage says, her body shivering against me. "He wanted to..." she doesn't finish.

"The motherfucker can't hurt anyone anymore. You're safe, baby." I hold her a little tighter. The rest of the ride back to the clubhouse is filled with silence. I pull the phone from my pocket, knowing her loved ones need to hear she is safe.

"Ash," Charles answers on the first ring. "Please tell me you have my baby girl."

"I have her," I say and hear him release a sigh of relief, followed by relaying the news to Sage's mom. "Do me a favor and let Juniper know," I add.

"I can do that. Her mother and I are on our way to her now. We'll be there as fast as this old truck will drive." There is a brief silence before Charles adds, "And, Ash...thank you."

I did my job. But I don't tell him that. "See you soon." Then I end the call. The pain at my side intensifies as my body relaxes, having my woman close. She has always had that effect on me. I press my lips to Sage's forehead and whisper against her skin, "I love you." The silence hanging after my confession, I won't lie, fucking hurts. My pain is nothing compared to what Sage has gone through or what I've done to push her away.

An hour later, we arrive at the clubhouse. To my surprise, Sukie and Juniper are there waiting for our arrival. They rush toward us, laying eyes on their friend as I get out of the car. "What the hell happened to her?" Juniper asks, on my heels as I carry Sage inside.

"Brandon" is the only explanation I give. "Stay here," I bark, stopping her and Sukie in their tracks. To my surprise, they listen.

I head straight for my room. Once inside, I set her exhausted, cold, wet body on the edge of the bed, walk into the bathroom, turn on warm water, and begin filling the tub. I stroll back out, and Sage's eyes follow me.

"You're bleeding again," she says, still shivering, but not as bad as before.

"Let's get you warmed up." I lift her into my arms again.

"I think my legs still work, Ash."

Back in the bathroom, I put her on her feet. Her eyes stay locked on my face as she allows me to remove her wet clothes. I help Sage step over the edge of the tub. Her legs shake as she lowers into the warm water. She tucks her knees to her chest, her gaze still fixed on me as I reach for a rag, soak it with the warm water, and begin washing her down, rinsing the dirt from her arms. I wring the cloth out, then wipe her face, where fresh tears break free, rolling down her face.

"Ash," she whispers. "I'm pregnant."

"I know." I continue caring for Sage.

"I'm keeping it," she adds.

"Good. I want the baby." I lift my eyes to hers. "I want you, too."

Sage stares at me for a few seconds, blinking the tears away. She takes a shuddered breath. "Tonight changes nothing. You broke me, Ash. And I'm not sure I can ever look past all the words you said or the things you've done to hurt me." Sage shakes her head. "I'm not sure I can forgive you, either." Her words are followed by another moment of silence before continuing. "But I want our baby's father in his or her life, even if we aren't together."

I take what she can give me right now and hold on tight to the hope she might find her way back to me. I need to show up and prove my worth. "You'll always be mine, Sage. Together or not, I'll spend the rest of my life taking care of you and our child, or die tryin'," I vow.

26

EPILOGUE
SAGE

"Excuse me."

I look over my shoulder to the young woman who just walked into the salon. "Can I help you?"

The woman holds up a white paper bag. "I have a delivery for Sage," she tells me.

I set down my shears. "I'll be right back," I say to the lady sitting in my chair.

"No problem." She smiles at me through the mirror.

I begin to make my way to the woman holding the bag. I already know what's in there, and the delicious smell makes my tummy rumble. "I'm Sage."

She hands the bag over. I go to pull a few bills out of my pocket to tip her, but she declines. "The tip has been taken care of. Have a nice day."

"Oh, thanks. You too." I don't have to look in the bag to know what's inside from the smell that wafts through the air. This morning I woke up with a monster craving for lobster rolls and told Juniper I was thinking about getting some for lunch.

My best friend thinks she's slick, but she's not. For months whenever I've voiced anything I'm craving, said food suddenly appears by either a delivery person or one of the guys from the club. Yesterday it was Baja with a jar of peanut butter and a whole watermelon. The day before, it was pizza and cheesecake. Hell, even a night last week, Mystic showed up to our apartment at one o'clock in the morning because I'd woken up with a sudden need for mint chocolate chip ice cream and French fries. Apparently, my tearing the kitchen apart, looking for something sweet and salty to satisfy my craving, had woken Juniper from slumber. But it was months ago that I caught on to what my best friend was doing. She was feeding information back to Ash.

I cut my eyes over at Juniper, and it's clear she's trying really hard to pretend she doesn't see the daggers I'm tossing her way. The first couple of months after the Brandon incident, Juniper was all about my Ash freeze out. But then my best friend went from team Sage to team Ash in a blink of an eye.

I will admit, he did a damn fine job at winning her over. Ash has been better than impressive. If I'd had any doubts before that he was up for the job of being a dad, they were demolished the moment he showed up at my first doctor's appointment. Ash and I may not be together anymore, but I have no intention of denying him his role as this baby's father. Which is why I texted him about that appointment in the first place. I told him when and where and that the choice was his. I also learned he is not the kind of dad who sits in the waiting room. He was right there by my side through the entire examination. I was in complete and utter shock when he asked my doctor at least a dozen questions about pregnancy and the health of our baby and me. He wanted to know all the do's and don'ts, what foods were not safe to eat, what foods might be the most beneficial, and what my limitations were. Honestly, he'd thought of questions I didn't know to ask.

He even won over my parents. I know because my father let it slip one day that he and Ash talk on the phone regularly. I called to give him and my mom an update on the pregnancy after my thirty-week checkup, but he said Ash had already told him how big the baby had gotten and seemed excited about the last ultrasound. It's safe to say my parents are also on team Ash.

It's not as though Juniper and my family are making me feel guilty that I haven't given in to him. They never would. I don't really believe in making a man grovel. We're all human, and we make mistakes. Forgiveness is subjective. It shouldn't carry shame. There is also no time limit on when forgiveness is given. I do, however, draw the line at deliberately punishing someone for their mistakes. Did Ash fuck up? Yes, no doubt. Even though he didn't really cheat and only made it appear that way on purpose, he still hurt me deeply. But what good is it for me to nag, bitch and demand he jump through hoops to prove he's sorry? What does it say about me as a person? That I'm going to deliberately hurt you for every mistake you make? If a person is genuinely sorry for the hurt they've caused, they will do whatever it takes to prove their remorse. It's their responsibility, not yours. If that person chooses not to do anything, well then, you let them go. Simple as that. Ash choosing to be present and supportive throughout my pregnancy has always been his choice. Do I believe it's for me? Yes. Do I think that's his sole reason?

Absolutely not. Ash is doing what a good father does, and he's going to bat for his child yet to be born by taking care of me. Fatherhood doesn't start at birth.

I'm not delusional. I know Ash wants me back. He's been vocal on the subject since Brandon kidnapped me, but he is respecting that I'm not ready.

Ash broke my heart in a way I have never experienced and shattered my trust in him. For months my head and my heart have been in constant battle with one another. But if I'm going to be honest with myself, my heart won the war. Now I just need to find the courage to tell the man I love that I'm ready. The thought alone terrifies me.

Later in the afternoon, I'm just finishing up Betty's hair when a young woman walks in. She's a pretty little thing with a petite frame and long blonde hair pulled back in a braid. And despite it being a hot summer day, she's wearing a baby-blue long sleeve cardigan.

"Hi, how are you?" I smile.

The girl looks at me, then to Juniper, then back to me. "Hello. Do you take walk-ins?" she asks.

"Of course we do." I usher her over. "Have a seat here." I pat the chair Betty just vacated. I look over my shoulder to Juniper. "You mind taking care of Betty and getting her set up for six weeks from today?"

"Sure." Juniper takes care of Betty while I turn my attention back to the woman now sitting in my chair.

"So." I spin the chair and look at her through the mirror. "What do you want?" I smile at her in the mirror. "I'm Sage, by the way."

"Aya," she says softly. She bites her bottom lip. "I'm... I'm not really sure. It's been a while since I've done anything with it."

I wave my hand at her. "That's okay. How about I take a look at what we've got. May I?" I hold up her long braid, and she nods, giving me permission. Removing the elastic, I release the braid, revealing what I know are luscious curls.

"Girl, I would kill for all these curls you were hiding."

Aya's cheeks turn red. "Thank you."

After running my fingers through her locks and inspecting what I have to work with, I immediately know what I want to do. "Do you want my thoughts?" I ask.

Aya nods.

"Your hair is gorgeous, so I suggest a little enhancement to bring out what is already naturally beautiful. I'd start by trimming the ends, maybe three inches. Then I'd add in a few layers to bring out the fullness of those curls and then top it off with some highlights for a sun-kissed look."

Aya appears thoughtful then says, "Let's do it."

"Yeah?" I start to get excited.

She nods. "Yeah."

"Perfect!" I clap my hands. "Let's get you shampooed."

After I get Aya shampooed and begin cutting, I ask, "So, have you always lived in Salem?"

Aya shakes her head. "No, I grew up in Boston. I moved to Salem about a month ago."

"Oh. Do you live here on your own or with family?"

Aya looks hesitant to answer but does anyway. "It's just me. My family is still back in Boston."

I meet her gaze in the mirror and smile. "I get that. I'm from Nebraska. My best friend and I moved here last year and opened up this place. Spreading our wings and all." Then I rub my belly. "I might have spread a little too far," I joke, making Aya laugh.

"When are you due?" she asks.

"In a week," I say, making her eyes bug out.

"Really? Wow."

With each minute that ticks by, Aya relaxes, and after witnessing her tense up when I asked about where she is from and her family, I decided to keep the conversations light and steer clear of anything personal. Being a stylist, you become an expert at reading the room and people. The end goal is for the client to feel comfortable while in your chair and happy enough with the end result to come back. Honestly, your stylist is like a best friend and therapist, rolled into one.

I'm almost finished with Aya's hair nearly two hours later when a familiar rumble catches my attention, and I turn to see Ash pull up in front of the salon. The sight of him still gives me butterflies.

"Hey," I say when he walks in. "You're early."

"I was around and thought I'd stop by and see if you were finished."

Yesterday, Ash texted and asked if he could take me to dinner. He said he wanted to talk. I was taken aback by his request. For months, Ash has respected my boundaries and has been giving me space. Though he hasn't stopped showing he cares, he's never asked me out. Last night I couldn't sleep. All I kept thinking about was, this is it; he's done waiting, and he's going to tell me he's moved on. Then I started wondering if he was seeing another woman. Before now, that thought hadn't crossed my mind. I'd be a fool to think a man like Ash would pine over me forever.

I blink. "Oh, well...sure."

When I feel Aya tense under my hand resting on her shoulder, I look down to see her giving Ash a surprised look, but when she notices me watching, her eyes dart away. I turn back to Ash. "I'm going to need about fifteen minutes."

"No problem, baby. I'll wait." Ash sits down on the sofa.

I go back to working on Aya's hair but can't help noticing her tense behavior has gotten worse.

"You okay, Aya?" I ask.

She jumps at the sound of my voice and nods. "Yeah...I'm fine."

Over on the sofa, I see Ash pick up the TV remote, and a second later, the local news fills the room.

"This just in. The body of Judge Jack Westgrove was found a few miles from his home in Boston in a rural, wooded area. We spoke to authorities who described the body as unrecognizable, but they were able to identify his remains using dental records. Upon further investigation, police found incriminating documents in Judge Westgrove's home office that led authorities to believe he was the suspect of numerous unsolved rape cases in the Boston area dating back as far as 2012. The chief of police made a statement saying he will be looking into the cases himself but gave no further details."

The news cuts to a commercial, and I notice how Aya's body has gone completely still, her eyes glued to the TV.

"Aya, are you sure you're okay?"

Aya snaps out of the daze she's in. Her body relaxes, and a calm settles over her. I feel like something monumental just happened, but I'm clueless about what.

Aya looks up at me and blinks several times before she answers, "I am now."

I smile. "Good, because I'm done." I spin the chair back toward the mirror, so Aya can get a look.

She gasps and touches her curls, and with the softest voice, she says, "Thank you."

Only she's not looking at me. Her eyes are on Ash.

Thirty minutes later, Ash pulls up in front of his place. I unbuckle my seatbelt. "I thought you were taking me to dinner."

Salem cuts the engine. "I cooked," he grunts.

I stare at him. "You cooked?"

He shrugs. "Tonight, I want all of your attention, and that's not going to be possible in a crowded restaurant."

"Oh...okay."

"Stay put," he orders.

Before I have a chance to protest, he's out of the car and pulling open my door. When I take Ash's offered hand, he murmurs, "I got you, baby."

My breath catches in my throat when the word baby leaves his mouth. And when I peer up at him, I can see in his eyes he knows how powerful his effect is on me, and his pupils dilate. When he brushes the pad of his thumb along my jawline, I lick my lips and close my eyes in anticipation for a kiss that never comes. Instead,

I'm knocked out of my daze when he takes a step back. Not wanting him to see how hurt I am by the sting of his rejection, I fix my face and straighten my back. When I try jerking my hand out of his, he doesn't let me.

"Calm, baby" is all he says.

Ash leads me into the house, and I'm assaulted by the smell of garlic bread. "Hmm, smells good."

"It fuckin' should. I spent almost all damn day on that sauce," he grumbles.

"Sauce?" I lick my lips and rub my belly

Ash leads me to the dining room. "Spaghetti and meatballs with garlic bread."

My mouth waters at the thought of spaghetti. "I didn't know you could cook like that?"

Ash laughs. "I can't. I tried to get Ophelia to do it for me, but when she heard the dinner was for you, she said she would teach me, but I had to do it myself. She's been bustin' my balls all fuckin' day makin' sure I got the sauce just right."

I stop and stare up at Ash. "You learned how to make home-made spaghetti and meatballs for me?"

Ash grips the back of my neck. "I'd do anything for you, Sage."

Oh my god!

I go to say something, but I'm stopped short when Ash hooks his arm around my waist, pulling my body flush against his. Leaning down, he rests his forehead against mine. "I'm sorry, baby. I'm so fuckin' sorry."

"Ash," I murmur.

"I need you, Sage. I need you so bad I can't fuckin' breathe."

The air in my lungs gets caught in my throat.

"It's killin' me not having you close every second of the day. Not touching you. To not smell you. To not hold you in my arms at night. To not touch your belly every time you feel our baby move." He squeezes me. "Please find your way back to me."

I clutch the front of Ash's shirt. "I'm right here."

His eyes snap open. "What?"

I lick my lips. "I miss you too. Every day. I love you, Ash. I'm so in love with you." I start to cry. "I'm sorry it's taken me so long to get back home. I was just so scared after the way you hurt me."

"Baby." Regret flashes in his eyes.

"I forgive you, Ash. I forgave you a long time ago. I don't want to hurt anymore. I want you."

"Fuck, baby." Ash's mouth crashes down on mine, stealing my breath. "Stay with me tonight."

"Yes." I run my fingers through his hair and moan when his palm skims over the top of my sensitive nipple. One thing that has been agony is how horny pregnancy has made me. Which will explain why I'm currently trying to climb Ash like a tree.

"Ash," I pant.

"What do you need, baby?"

"You. Please, I need you."

Ash doesn't have to be told twice. A squeal escapes past my lips when he hooks one arm around my back and the other behind my knees, scooping me up. "What are you doing?" I laugh.

"Taking you to bed, so I can fuck you proper."

Salem

"Congratulations, brother." Mystic stands beside me as I hold my baby daughter in my arms. Ashlyn Crawford was born at 2:20 in the morning after putting her momma through twenty-two hours of labor. I'd never seen a more fantastic sight than watching the woman I love bring our daughter into this world.

I look over at Sage, asleep in the hospital bed, and *she has never looked more beautiful.*

Mystic claps me on the back. "You know you're fucked, right?"

I look down at my daughter, knowing instantly Mystic speaks the truth. "Yeah, brother."

My best friend chuckles. "Welcome to the club."

FALLEN RAVENS MC